LOVIN' YOU CRAZY

LOVE & LIES IN PARADISE-BOOK 2

NORA LEDUC

ILLUSTRATED BY
PATTI ROBERTS

Created with Vellum

MURDER SUSPECT THOMASINA (TOMMIE) MURPHY GAMBLES ON HER CHILDHOOD FRIEND, AN UNPROVEN, SMART PI, TO CLEAR HER NAME AND BURY HER SECRETS.

Tommie Murphy is shocked to discover her dinner host shot dead in his elegant Florida home. As the police examine her past relationship with a jailed convict, she becomes the prime suspect in the homicide. While Tommie pushes fast-forward on changing her impetuous lifestyle, a death threat left on her car warns that the killer has plans for her, too. Desperate, she turns to her former next-door neighbor, PI Jace Jackson. Yet, if she wants his help, she'll have to break the promise she made to herself, never trust a man.

Jace knows he's in trouble the moment Tommie, his long-time crush, suddenly shows up. She's looking for something, and he always has difficulty denying her requests. When she proposes hiring him, he refuses. After all, he investigates cheating spouses and insurance frauds. However, the challenge of her case and Tommie's need for protection persuade him to finally accept. As days pass, he worries she's hiding evidence. Soon, he discovers the truth that nothing is what it seems, especially the woman he secretly loves.

Spoiler Alert This story contains revelations about "who done it" in Trail of Secrets-Love & Lies in Paradise -Book 1.

To my: Family, Critique Partners, and Reader Friends, you are the best. Thanks.

CHAPTER ONE

Somebody was following her. A shiver of warning ran up the back of Tommie Murphy's neck. In her rearview mirror, the beam of headlights mimicked her actions as she increased and decreased her car's speed. Add the fact that she was lost in the small city of Sebastian, Florida, and, well . . . she wasn't having a good evening.

Her stomach grumbled and ached with nerves. She dragged in a large breath and inhaled the lavender air freshener she'd hung on the rearview mirror. It was supposed to possess a calming effect. The scent wasn't working well. She should hit an intersection soon and could figure out her location and lose her shadow.

Besides, a vehicle behind her in the middle of nowhere didn't mean anything sinister. She'd spent too much time worrying about Roy Davis, and she was on edge. Every day, she regretted that she'd trusted the ex-police chief. His kind, fatherly act had encouraged her to believe in him. Mistake. She'd gotten too close to him and suffered for it. Roy had suffered too. He was in prison, and his friends were hanging low. She was safe.

And I'm alive. Others weren't as lucky. Once she had enough money, she would move away where nobody knew her past. Now the darkness wrapped around her, offering little comfort. Clouds shrouded the moon and stars in the sky. The headlights revealed oaks, palms, and bushes lining the way.

Lights from an approaching car caught her attention. She tightened her grip on the smooth steering wheel and concentrated on driving until the other driver disappeared in the blackness.

Stay focused. Charming Arturo at dinner is my number-one priority. Once I find my way to his house.

She'd worn the deep blue dress that she'd bought from a secondhand shop. The original price tag was attached when she found it. She kept it in the closet for special occasions. She'd included a necklace her host, Arturo Alvaro, would recognize. By most standards, she'd overdressed, but not for what she had in mind.

Tommie slowed her maroon, decade-old clunker. She'd saved a part of her pay from her former job at the Aloha Surf Stop to buy her used hatchback because her surfboards and gear fit inside. Instead, she should have purchased a car with a functioning GPS system.

Hold it. Her phone had one! Why hadn't she thought of that before? She stretched her arm around the two-tone yellow and indigo surfboard between the front seats—as far as the shoulder harness allowed. Her fingers scraped against her cell and knocked it to the floor next to the door. *Thud.*

Great. She straightened, exhaling a resigned huff. *Spot a clearing and pull over to get her cell.*

As the vehicle tailed her, she was reminded that she wasn't alone. Muttering, she rounded a curve. On the side of the road, a well-lit store and fuel pumps beckoned to her. Civilization. She veered into the lot and stopped. Tommie tensed. Where was her shadow? Seconds ticked to a minute. A pickup truck lumbered past.

She could have sworn it had been a car trailing her, but what could she tell in the dark? Maybe the driver had turned around for some reason. She massaged the knot in the back of her neck.

In the large, storefront window, a clerk lingered by a register. Relief swept over her. With luck, the market employee would be able to direct her. She squared her shoulders. She wouldn't let her imagination ruin her plan for Arturo Alvaro. He was in for a big surprise.

I hope you enjoy our get-together, Arturo. I will.

CHAPTER TWO

"Wherefore art thou hiding, Romeo?" Arturo Alvaro whispered, rummaging through a bookshelf. "I need you." Tonight required all his powers of persuasion and romance to make Thomasina Murphy feel at home.

"Ah, there's the Bard's work." He pulled his copy of *Romeo and Juliet* from the wall-sized bookcase in his study. The Shakespearean story would help set the stage.

A thrill of success rippled through him as he wiped away the perspiration on his brow. The mid-November day had been unseasonably warm, even for Florida. The humidity had invaded his 3,000-square-foot house, despite the whir of central air. He'd adjust his thermostat setting. First, he had to finish his preparations for his guest. Everything must be perfect.

He plopped down in his wooden, slatted-back chair at his oversized, mahogany desk. His mind wandered to Thomasina, or Tommie, as she preferred to be called. She was young—almost twenty-four—and bordering on broke. During the last two weeks, she'd provided him with entertainment and camaraderie, something he'd been missing lately with his recent special lady. Tommie could brighten his life while he sought a more suitable and profitable relationship.

Why should she object? From his observations, she was spirited but alone. He'd supply her with the companionship she lacked. He would relish showing her how his world worked. This dinner would be their beginning. And who knew how long he'd stay in Sebastian? Maybe longer than he'd thought.

He sprayed the spicy white orchid scent on the novel's cover. The fragrance escaped into the air. The yellow glow of the bulb spilled over worn pages onto the desktop as he thumbed to Act 2, Scene 2—the balcony. He'd leave the page open for her to find. She'd enjoy his little joke. She liked teasing and calling him Romeo, since he'd given her a modified version of his romantic past.

He laid the tome next to his laptop, playing his most beloved song from *Madama Butterfly*. He'd seen the opera performed twice. Where else could you get such a fine drama containing sex, betrayal, and death? But the tale's tone wasn't right for his intimate dinner. He'd choose different music.

Ten minutes until she arrived. She was usually prompt. He brought up his playlist.

Across the floor, his ninety-pound, coal-black dog, Picasso, lay hidden by the shadows. He lifted his snout and growled. "What is it, boy?" Was his guest here? Arturo tapped the keyboard's mute button and tensed. Dead silence.

The pooch approached him. His ears pricked forward. His stare fastened on the French doors that led to the lanai and pool.

"Picasso, nobody is there." Last night, the dog had whined and barked while constantly running along the perimeter of the front lawn. Nothing had appeared. He'd eaten several treats before he calmed down. Perhaps that was his game—to get tidbits. Arturo lowered the sound, and the song resumed softly.

His pet pawed at the cuff of his dark trousers.

"Do you need to go out?" With a snap, Arturo could attach the leash to the canine's red harness. He'd bought him an expensive vest with pockets to carry doggie bags, biscuits, and water bottles.

The chair creaked as he eased his two hundred pounds from his seat. He paused to listen to his favorite part of the opera. The melody from the dramatic scene, where Butterfly finally accepted the truth that her husband had abandoned her, played in the background.

The dog sniffed the air, his nose twitching. Outside, an unearthly howl broke across the murkiness. The fur on his pet's spine stood up.

Dread rolled in the pit of Arturo's gut. He prayed the crying animal would wander out of range.

Another scream cracked the quiet, as though the creature was being tortured. The eerie screech shot a cannonball of fright through him. He'd never heard such a mournful bay. Was a hunter stalking injured prey in the darkness? Was it caught in a trap? Any beast could hide in the palm fans surrounding the screen cage to spy on him. His heart pounded. He snapped off the lamp and stared into the gloom, searching for animal or human prowlers.

Picasso scurried by him and ducked under the desk. His long tail was bent downward. His body shook with alarm.

Sweat bathed Arturo's skin. He pressed pause on his laptop and listened past the thunder of blood rushing through his skull. Was something or someone in his backyard? No, the shriek hadn't been that close, had it? He squinted toward the terrace, praying he'd find zilch. Vaguely, he could determine the outline of the lanai chairs. A fence of boxwood blocked a full view of the woods beyond.

His collection of mismatched clocks on the far wall filled his thoughts with *tick-tick-tick.* Perspiration dripped from his chin.

A blur of motion at the edge of his veranda grabbed his attention.

Grab the antique pistol. Hurry.

In the dim light provided by the French doors, he sorted through pens, pencils, and markers in the desk drawer.

There. In the back. He grabbed the firearm's handle. The click of the screen latch echoed in his ears.

The music kicked on, muffling the sound of movement. Madama Butterfly's cry of anguish poured from the speaker.

One of the glass entries swung open into the study. The shadow slithered inside.

He gasped. Stumbling against his chair, he raised the handgun.

"Arturo?" a woman called.

He recognized the voice and the shape of the small female. He swallowed hard. His shock cleared enough for him to drop his weapon to his side. "Gloria? Why are you here? Why did you use the rear entrance?" Relieved, he loosened his shirt's top button.

She paused in the doorway. "You mentioned getting a quote on the surfboard. I came for the estimate and to pick it up. One of my clients has a son who's interested."

Under the desktop, Picasso inched forward to whimper at Arturo.

"Come out. Nothing will harm you." He snapped on the lamp while still clutching his gun.

The dog crawled out and fled to the hallway.

"Why were you holding a gun in the dark?" Gloria retreated a step. "At least put on the desk light if you plan to shoot at the shadows. And I always park by the pool, but as I got out of my car, I heard a hair-raising noise from the reserve. It scared me. I saw you and ran in. Didn't you hear the . . . scream?" Her last word burst from her mouth. "What was it?"

"I'm not sure. Perhaps it was an unhappy animal on the preserve."

She gestured at the door. "You should lock up."

"Why? I'm safe in my home. I mean, who would rob me? My house contains old, cheap stuff. My community is secure. We have cameras at the main gates."

"Save the ancient-junk tale for the tax audit. I'm familiar with those antiques that you pass off as worthless when you need to and priceless when you don't." She tugged on the lanai curtain cord. "It's stuck." She abandoned the rope and yanked on the patio drapery. "You should shut these and buy a better—"

A muted ping whizzed into the room.

She dropped with a thud in front of the glass. Motionless. The drape hung down over part of her body.

"Gloria? Are you all right?" He froze in place, refusing to believe what his brain was telling him.

A trespasser in black, wearing a ski mask, glided out of the gloom through the open door. The intruder pointed a weapon at him.

Chills sped up his spine. "Wh-what do you want?" He barely could breathe.

"Justice," the interloper rasped, facing him.

Was this a crazy person? *Shoot.* Arturo raised his pistol and pulled the trigger. The soft click echoed in his head. *Huh? No bullets?*

The invader fired at him.

Pain exploded in Arturo's chest. He fell backward against the chair, and it spun away. He collapsed onto the floor. The pad of hurried footfalls told him the shooter was coming. For him. *Run!* Panicked, he tried to rise and failed. A fiery agony paralyzed him. He gasped for air.

A masked figure bent over him, eyes peering out of the slits. "I know what you did. You went behind my back. Cheat. This is your only chance. You have five seconds to start confessing to everything you've done and beg for mercy."

The eyes. He knew them, didn't he? "My emergency fall button . . ." He wet his lips, trying to catch his breath. "Too late . . . for you. Police. Ambulance. En route."

"Liar," his attacker spat.

"The band . . . on my wrist." Arturo lifted his forearm with effort. "Not a step tracker. My transponder."

A phone in the house began to ring.

"My medical alert device. They're calling. My landline." His heart was on fire.

"NO. NO. NO." The figure threw out a gloved fist and stepped forward. Cold metal dug into Arturo's forehead. "I'll leave you here. Your next guest will enjoy my surprise."

Arturo pulled in a gasp and whispered, "Parting is such sweet sorrow."

CHAPTER THREE

The sign for Manatee Lake Estates pointed down the side street. Tommie took the turn. Finally, she was close to Arturo Alvaro's gated community. *Note to self, if you're in a hurry, don't try unfamiliar back roads in the dark. Yes, and I won't imagine people are following me because they drive the same way I do.*

According to the clock on the dashboard, she was seven minutes late. That was nothing. It had felt like an hour. The tension of the trip had drained from her. Soon, she'd be eating dinner with Arturo. She wasn't naïve. He and she both had their own ideas of how their meet would go. Despite their differences, she was eager to assess the man's house, his inventory. How much was the thief worth? She wasn't greedy. She wanted only the amount he'd stolen returned.

Tommie's thoughts drifted to their first meeting. She'd found Arturo's ads and business address online. A day later, she'd entered his antique booth at the co-op.

"I'm browsing," she'd replied when he asked if he could help her.

He was short. His shock of white hair stood out, and his strong, mesmerizing voice drew her in. She'd rated his sixty-plus looks an eight out of ten.

She'd sifted through a basket of jewelry, hunting for a good deal.

He'd talked up a gold necklace with blue sparkling glass gems. "This is an excellent reproduction. I had included a similar piece, but it was grabbed by another customer, an old flame."

"I don't need matching earrings or a bracelet." She waved away the thought.

"A wise decision. You shouldn't distract an admirer from the true beauty." He winked at her before gesturing at the chain in her hand. "Your trinket is a copy of a past design that was created to sparkle in the romance of candlelight. Now it's yours to treasure."

When she'd bought the necklace, he'd smiled, and his handsomeness rating had shot to a ten. Tommie didn't doubt he was a born salesman, especially around the ladies. The man could hawk Florida swampland. She'd signed up for notices of future sales and said goodbye.

He'd contacted her that evening and informed her of a special he was running. For the next three days, he'd sent several emails about deals and the weather. Casual stuff. Quickly, they'd moved to texting each other about their days. He'd related funny tales about his dating adventures and ended the messages with a confession of loneliness and how her cheery spirits brightened his day. Zoom chats followed.

She'd told him her surfing stories and how she'd spent a summer working at the local surf shop. There, she'd sold and memorized the stock of high-quality surfboards while dreaming of owning her own store and teaching the sport. Before ending the calls, she expressed how much she looked forward to hearing from him again.

When he learned of her retail experience, he'd asked her for a favor. His cousin Gloria needed an estimate on a longboard she wanted to sell. Her former husband, Rex, had left it behind. She assumed he'd dug it out of storage to impress one of his "bimbettes."

Perfect. Tommie had an excuse to push their relationship to a different level. She'd agreed to assess the surfboard for free, and to sweeten the deal, she'd suggested meeting somewhere. She was positive he wouldn't reject a causal almost-date. They'd met at a neighborhood coffee shop where they'd chatted in person, and he'd passed along the board for her to check out.

Arturo was hard to dislike. He was a flirt and had kept her smiling. He'd mentioned he wasn't the type to commit for the long haul. Excellent. She'd no romantic interest in a senior-aged man, and she didn't need anyone else in her life.

She forced the memories from her mind. The community gates and a metal key stand popped into sight. She pulled up to the estates' keypad to punch in the code. She took in her surroundings while lowering the window. Palms, oaks, and white pines camouflaged the homes. Insects, concealed in the bushes, peeped and chirped. The sweet scent of the bordering hibiscus plants floated toward her.

She rolled her shoulders to release the stress. The damp air invaded the jalopy. The humidity had set loose a few stray curls from the clip that held her hair. Darn.

Eager to go, she shoved at the strands before punching in the digits. Sitting in the open, she felt like a target. Her heartbeat increased with each soft click of the keys on the pad. Finished. During her wait for the wrought-iron gate to roll back, she checked her messages. Zero there. Arturo wasn't counting the seconds until she arrived. And nothing from her mom. The pull on her neck dulled.

Tommie had spent her life trying to parent her mother and

rescue her from her addictions and men. Her mom had always bounced from man to man. Falling in love, she'd called it. That emotion had sure caused her to do insane things.

Why get seriously involved? Little good came of it, Tommie told herself. And she'd managed to survive her childhood and teen years despite her mother, thanks to the kindness of her neighbor, Gigi, and her grandson, Jace Jackson.

The mechanical grind of the metal barrier broke her reverie. The gate swung wide. She touched the gas. Her rattletrap auto crept into the land of expensive houses where she didn't belong.

The street and sidewalk were empty. People should be busy eating inside at this hour. The sparse, black lampposts' light guided her. She puttered by a large rectangular structure with a lit pool. The building must be the Manatee Lake Estates Clubhouse and the location of resident get-togethers.

Jace would be welcome in this community. He was the most upstanding person she'd ever known. She'd often wondered if she'd been a popular kid, would she have been one of those girls he asked out? Not necessarily the cheerleader type, but the brainy got-it-all-together sort. Class president, school newspaper editor, or all-around girl-next-door was his kind.

But it was no use moping over her lack of a traditional boyfriend or family. Her life had taken her down different paths from Jace. As for her mom, she wasn't a capable adult. Tommie had accepted the truth long ago. And before she rode out of the city for a fresh start, she'd vowed that she'd pull her mother out of only one more disaster.

The lights grew farther apart. She blinked and readjusted to the dimness. On her right, she cruised by sizable ranches with three-car garages clustered on the edge of the man-made lake. A fountain in the center bubbled with water. Towering royal palm trees and a barbed-wire fence lined the boundary of the road on her left. She'd grown up near here in Star Pointe Crossings and

Vero Beach. Nearby was the preserve with its waterways, native plants, and wild animals.

Her car hit a dip. She steadied the surfboard that thumped softly between the front seats and extended into the car's rear end. Arturo's cousin Gloria hoped to get a high assessment. Too bad it was an ordinary, used longboard, suitable for beginners, but without a big resale value.

Tommie tightened her hands on the wheel and forced herself to focus on driving. At the curve, she spotted his drive. Almost there. She wet her dry lips and pulled up to the wrought-iron entrance. Arturo had explained he'd moved six months ago from Melbourne, twenty miles north of Sebastian. He'd wished to be nearer to his cousins. He'd bought the former home of a builder because it had many extras, including another set of gates and a call box.

Now his entry was open. *Super*. She passed through. One side of the drive pitched downward. Below was the river with the alligators. She *hated* gators. She shivered at the thought of the scaly bodies floating like logs and their small, beady, red eyes glowing in the darkness. The creatures' powerful jaws struck quickly, painfully, and clamped around their prey, allowing no escape—dragging a shrieking quarry underwater to death.

Her heart skipped a beat. She shoved her foot down on the gas while swiping at the perspiration on her forehead. The temperature was roasting. Her AC clanged noisily.

The scrape of branches against the car's sides warned vegetation had closed in around her and to slow down. The creepy feeling of being watched returned. She shifted uneasily in her seat.

In a second, the foliage opened up. Spotlights on the lawn illuminated the two-story house with a four-pillar porch and a double front entryway. The drive was composed of brick pavers. She drove in and cut the engine. Maybe Arturo would appear and greet her. When no one stirred, she pushed down on the handle and hit the doorframe with her shoulder twice before the catch released. She swung out of her car.

A loud, frightened scream burst through the air.

Tommie halted. What was that? She darted glimpses around the yard and into the trees and bushes beyond. *Stay calm.* What the heck was happening beyond in the darkness? She closed her mouth to stop her teeth from chattering.

Think logically. A panther? She'd heard November was the animal's mating season. The female's answering call resembled a woman's cry. Yeah, that explained everything.

She scanned the tall palms and shrubs surrounding the home. Nothing glared back at her. But not spotting a puma didn't mean it wasn't out there. Should she run? Would the big cat's instinct kick in and chase her like she was his dessert? She inched forward. Her shoulders tightened as the wail stabbed the air again. It sounded a few yards away.

She should have driven between the flower beds right up to the entry. Arturo wouldn't complain if she created tracks in the grass. Better than getting attacked. She picked up her pace. Sweat ran down her chin. A wind blew but provided no respite. The walkway seemed to stretch into miles. Finally, she reached the entrance.

She punched the bell. Muffled chimes played a refrain from a Broadway tune on the other side of the door, decorated with a metal Welcome sign. Clasping and unclasping her hands, she stared behind her. All was clear.

Oh, she'd left the board in the car. She'd get it later. The distance to her hatchback appeared farther than ever.

A scratching sound came from inside.

Huh? What was that? "Arturo?"

A bark and a whine identified who was inside. A dog. She released a breath and relaxed with relief. She yanked on the black iron knob. The door flew open. A furry pony-sized animal wearing a red vest or harness ran past her.

"Picasso?" Arturo had mentioned she'd meet his pet at his house.

The dog circled the lawn, crying, and darted back into the home.

"Some people react that way to me." She shrugged and stepped into the lit hall.

The wide, herringbone pattern of the oak-planked floor drew her eye to the hallway. Golden-framed oil paintings covered the walls. They must be part of Arturo's antique collection. He'd admitted everything in his house was for sale.

"Hello," she yelled. "It's me, Tommie. I'm here." She shut the door and took a couple of steps. Had she arrived on the wrong date? "I'm starving. I hope you are. I brought Gloria's surfboard. It's out in the car."

She paused again. Soft classical music was playing. He'd had her listen to one of his favorite songs during an online get-together. He'd explained opera was his first love, and he wanted to share it with her.

She hadn't had the heart to tell him the wailing drove her to wish for earplugs.

The whimper of the dog at the other end of the foyer redirected her musings. He paced by an open doorway three yards away. His tail hung between his legs.

"Are you okay?" A prickle of warning shot through her. She whistled to the dog. "Come."

Picasso stiffened.

That wasn't good. "Arturo! Please, answer me." She hadn't locked up. Any four-or two-legged beast could enter. Maybe she should leave. As she turned, she spotted the foil-wrapped chocolates. The sweets trailed down the corridor and curved into the room by Picasso.

She smiled. Aha, Arturo was teasing her. Yesterday, he'd joked about a path of rose petals leading her to him. She'd told him she'd rather have candy.

"I get it, Romeo," she said loudly. "Cute." He might not think the nickname was so funny after she flung her accusations at him.

She followed the goodies to the dog and stopped on the threshold of a chamber to her right. The space was poorly lit by a lamp on a huge wooden desktop. The chair was pushed against the bookshelves. Nobody was there.

A sad melody floated to her. "Arturo?" She squinted into the shadows. Where was he?

Metal artwork and a grouping of clocks covered a wall. A sultry breeze blew through the open glass door behind the desk. She bet it led to the lanai and the pool he'd boasted about. No signs of anyone. This was odd and a little creepy. *Don't be a drama queen.*

Something furry brushed her. Tommie gasped.

Picasso scurried past her, turned, and barked.

She flinched and struggled to stay calm. "It's all right. You're fine. I don't like the music either. It's eerie."

Picasso paced and stared at the other side of the furniture.

She took a step forward, although she sensed she should run away. "Arturo? I'm leaving unless you talk to me." She gripped the elbows of her folded arms to control the shakes running through her.

Had he fallen? Was that why the animal was upset? She inched to the dog until she could touch his soft, shaggy fur.

She bent to pat the pet and spotted a man lying on the floor. "Arturo?" He was dressed in dark clothing. Her throat tightened as she crouched beside him.

The man's legs were angled under the desk. His stare fastened to the ceiling. His mouth gaped open.

"Arturo?" What had happened? Had he had a heart attack? Could he answer? Was he . . . dead?

The blackish mark on his forehead snagged her attention. Tommie peered closer. He'd been shot! She gagged. She was getting out of here. As she wobbled on her feet, wooziness attacked her. She paused and inhaled deep breaths.

By the lanai entrance, Picasso growled and lowered his snout, staring at a bulge at the bottom of the curtain. What was that? High-heeled sandals poked out at one end. Strange. What was at the opposite end? A woman's head!

Another lifeless person? Tommie scrubbed at her tears with the back of her hand. How? Who?

The dog howled and stood, trembling and whimpering.

Could more bodies be on the lanai? Please, no. she was going to be sick. *Think. Call 911?*

Not the police. Anyone but them. She and the cops didn't have a good relationship. Since she'd hesitated to help imprison their homicidal ex-chief, Roy Davis, they'd delved into her background and dug up every smear and disgrace to persuade her to testify. No, they couldn't find her with these two possibly murdered people.

Picasso eyeballed the yard and resumed growling and barking.

An inhuman scream interrupted Tommie's thought. This time, it was louder and at the boundary of the tree line. Was the creature on the property? Worse, what if the shooter was outside or lurking in the house?

Her gut warned there was nothing she could do for Arturo or his visitor. *Contact emergency from the car.*

That was what she'd do. Nausea pushed upward to her mouth. She managed to get to the main entry. The dog followed, yapping and snapping at her heels.

"Get away." She waved at him, but he continued to tail her.

Prickles of fear raced up her spine. She forced herself to walk quickly from the dwelling to her old car while she prayed not to be ill. She yanked the door open. The dog leaped into the driver's seat Now the monster canine was going with her.

"Down." She jabbed a finger at the ground.

In the distance, she heard the wails of an ambulance and a cruiser. Shivers of warning shot up her spine.

Se*nd them an anonymous message. Later.*

The dog whimpered and begged with his sad brown eyes.

"Fine, Picasso. But I drive."

He bounded onto the passenger side.

Tommie dove inside and jammed the key in the ignition. The motor roared to life. She drove over the lawn and flowers. The dog sat, panting, crying, and drooling. They were almost to Arturo's gate. Concentrating on her goal, she floored it around the bend.

Out of the darkness, someone jumped into her path. What the heck? She hit the brakes, and her seat belt dug into her. Picasso lurched forward before regaining his balance.

Tommie stared out at the figure caught in her headlights. A person dressed in black shielded their eyes from the glare of the lights with one hand and clutched something in the other. Was it a gun?

The glimmer of a strobe broke through the trees and foliage. Sirens screamed. The stranger escaped into the wilderness in the opposite direction of the approaching police.

Now was her chance. She gunned her car and barreled toward the exit. She was going to make it.

A cruiser shot into the driveway. She slammed to a stop and barely missed a head-on collision with the squad car.

Trapped.

CHAPTER FOUR

Lying on her lumpy mattress at the Yellow Flamingo Inn, Tommie stared at a water stain on the ceiling. The building was quiet in the early morning, which allowed her mind to wander. How did she end up in these horrid situations? Mentally, she examined her mistakes, determined not to repeat them.

First, there had been Police Chief Roy Davis. Roy had pressured her into planting illegal drugs in his son's car to get him arrested. Then his son, Lucas—also a member of the police force, would be too occupied with his own problems to discover his father was the killer everyone was hunting for. She'd failed in upholding her part of the plan, but the worst wasn't over. She struck her lowest point when Roy had bragged to her about killing the local woman.

Tommie rubbed her aching head, but she still recalled the day. That was when she'd fled Florida. Thank goodness, Roy had been captured and jailed, and she'd returned from her hideout in the Northeast.

Finally, after numerous delays, she'd testified against him. And she'd spent a lot of time searching her conscience. She'd committed a lot of wrongs throughout her years. She'd also recently realized the men she went out with were like the men her mom dated.

The truth hurt. And that was when she'd vowed to change her life. She'd become a better person, make wiser choices. She started her amends list. Soon, she'd look in the mirror and see a strong individual.

Picasso snored loudly, and she snapped her attention to him at the foot of the pullout sofa bed. He was sound asleep. Exhausted, she rested her wrist on her throbbing forehead. She prayed the haunting memories would stop, and she'd enjoy an hour or two of stress-free slumber.

She breathed shallowly and stirred under the sheet. The fragrance of orchids floated in her studio, reminding her of Arturo's house. The scent nauseated her. Wait, she didn't have any fresh flowers. She peeked across the room. She'd piled yesterday's clothes on a kitchen chair. The aroma must be coming from her outfit. She'd stuff the garments in the laundry.

The dog whimpered when Tommie got up and tossed her dress and undergarments into the bathroom hamper. "It's okay, boy." She lay down again and tugged the covers to her chin.

Picasso made his way up the bed and snuggled next to her. The softness of his fur calmed her until her thoughts darted to the shootings. She'd learned from the medics that they'd arrived because of Arturo's health alert. The accompanying volunteer policeman had ordered her to go back to the house to await the Sebastian patrol officer and other reinforcements.

"You were smart to stay in my car, Picasso, while I was stuck inside with the cops."

The dog burrowed closer.

Yup, she wished she could have hidden in her hatchback. One of the officers had discovered the deceased female's wallet in a car parked near the lanai. He'd identified the dead woman as Gloria Alvaro, Arturo's cousin. Tommie had stood there praying that no other bodies would turn up. None had, but Detective Grey—a man she feared and avoided like COVID—had shown up.

Grey had escorted her home from her hideaway to testify against Davis. When he'd spotted her at the scene of the Alvaro murders, his eyes had lit up, and she knew he'd branded her a suspect.

Picasso hopped off the bed and shifted her attention to the present. In the midmorning sunlight, she rolled onto her side. Maybe she should hire a lawyer. Getting an attorney wouldn't be cheap. Her part-time server job at the Whale's Spout Restaurant barely kept her afloat. She could investigate legal assistance, but those lawyers were often young, inexperienced, or too overworked and not too available.

She'd maneuver on her own.

The voice in her mind warned, *Dangerous.*

Too bad, her mom hadn't saved a little of her inheritance from Aunt Sissy. Tommie should have known her mom wouldn't come through on her offer to help her relocate. If good intentions were riches, her mom would be a millionaire.

Tommie shouldn't be surprised the $50,000 legacy had vanished either. Her mother would have spent the cash on one of her favorite vices: men, drinking, or a handout. Her mom was a pushover for a hard-luck story. Once the truth dawned that she'd been used, she'd grumble and curse, but she never changed.

And Tommie didn't relish explaining to her sometimes unreasonable parent that her daughter was a person of interest in the latest local slayings.

Picasso flopped down by the door, interrupting her mental

replay of her troubles. Okay, she was done wallowing in her problems. She'd slipped up, but she wouldn't blow it again.

She pursed her lips and considered her next action. The surfboard was sitting in her car. Aha, a new idea struck her.

Today, she'd return Gloria's board and Arturo's dog. He'd frequently spoken of his cousins Gloria and Thalia. They were the only family he had left. She wished he had told her more about himself. Her online searches of his name had uncovered that he had been accused of money scams. The investigations had been dropped or settled outside of court. Was there a connection between Arturo's unproven crimes and his death?

The dog's claws clicked on the tiled floor as he wandered toward her. She sat up and petted his furry body by her bed. His floppy ears flattened, blending into his wavy fur. His head sank downward and tugged at her heart.

Poor guy. "This must be quite a step down from your former place." Yup, her suite was basically a one-room. She skimmed a glance over the studio, hoping to find a positive. A wobbly pine table, the worn, green pullout sofa, two mismatched chairs, and an old box-style TV on the chipped dresser completed the contents. Nope, her rental wasn't a five-star.

The dog whined.

"Don't worry, Picasso. I'll bring you to your aunt Thalia. You'll love her. I hope." Arturo had seemed ambivalent about Thalia. He'd said that she'd been briefly married and divorced many years ago. From that time on, she'd given everything to her work. Would she want a pet?

The dog wagged his tail.

Tommie rolled out of bed. Quickly, she showered and dressed in a blue T-shirt, a pair of gray shorts, and her flip-flops. Finished, she Googled Thalia's business for directions.

She outfitted the dog in his red vest. She fed him a biscuit and attached a belt instead of a leash. Oops, he needed one final touch. She finger-combed his hair. Perfect.

Nobody lingered in the lobby as she tiptoed through with Picasso. The desk clerk had suggested she keep her pet out of sight.

His exact words had been, "If no one complains, the dog can stay. It's kind of a don't ask, don't tell policy."

She was pretty sure the manager wouldn't allow creatures bigger than a snail. She would follow her own rule—don't rock the boat.

They walked outside into the sunshine. Picasso did his thing on the grass by the curb. The two of them crossed the lot to her car. She tugged the door open, and the dog jumped inside. The late hours had been cool, so she'd left the board in the vehicle. They were set.

Thalia's salon sat kitty-corner to a drugstore on the busy intersection of Roseland Road and US Route 1. Traffic was steady.

While Tommie's car idled at a stoplight, she remembered Arturo whispering in her ear. *I'll bring you on my yacht. We'll sail out into the blue ocean and watch the dolphins play in the surf. I'll teach you how to fish in the deep sea. Later, we'll toast the sunset, and we'll tell each other our secrets.*

Poor Arturo. Good or bad, he was gone forever and had taken his skeletons in the closet with him. Tears trickled down her cheeks. She brushed at them. She couldn't go into a salon looking a mess.

When the light hadn't changed, she texted her mom that she'd catch up with her soon. Tommie hit send as the green clicked on the signal. Shoving her phone away, she drove onward.

She still had a problem—no lawyer. A brainstorm struck her. Jace! He was a PI. And they'd known each other since they were kids. He might agree to a payment plan.

A flash of relief flowed over her. He must have heard she was involved in the Davis case. That was bad. Her connection to the homicidal ex-chief had made her an infamous celebrity. The defense attorney had tried to discredit her on the stand. He'd attempted to portray her as a foolish, young girl in love with Davis. When he hadn't been interested in her, she'd been angry and vowed to get even by telling lies about him in court.

Did Jace think the lawyer's false statement about her was true? He was an upstanding, well-respected guy who treated others fairly. How long had he been an investigator with his own business, Jackson Investigations? Three or four years? He was exactly who she needed. Someone who could track down Arturo's murderer or eliminate her from the list of suspects.

Her phone buzzed. Must be her mother finally catching up with her. Tommie pulled to the shoulder. By this time, Mom probably had learned about the Alvaro deaths.

Detective Grey's name appeared on her screen. *Not him.* A faint feeling washed over her. Every viewer of crime shows knew the person who found the body usually was considered a suspect. She would ignore Grey today, but she couldn't avoid him forever. Obviously, his call meant he didn't believe she was guiltless. What should she do?

Jace. She'd text him. Her decision eased her frayed nerves. Wait, she'd ask him in person. She imagined his lean build striding toward her, his intense scrutiny focused on her, stealing her breath.

And tell him the entire story?

She pictured his condemning stare when she confessed to a dinner date with a man who could have qualified for an AARP membership. Jace Jackson was kind of old-fashioned and smart. He'd guess she was up to something shady and refuse to help her. She'd have to limit her explanation to innocent, major points.

Hmm. There was another way to get him to consent. She could use her secret weapon, Gigi, aka Grandmother Gabby Jackson. It was thanks to her that Tommie had had any sort of normal childhood. Gigi and Jace had been her anchors in the world.

She U-turned at the next street.

CHAPTER FIVE

The Pelican Diner was filled almost to capacity during the brunch hours. Jace Jackson waited at a table for his order. Around him, friends and family clustered together, talking and relaxing.

Jace was too busy to indulge in those luxuries. He was working. Tapping his fingertips on the paper placemat decorated with local companies and trades, he allowed himself to drift for a few seconds. Maybe he should consider listing an ad for Jackson Investigations. The business had earned a reputation as dependable and solid thanks to his grandfather. Pop had built it and willed it to Jace when he died.

He'd inherited many of Pop's contacts in useful positions and quickly learned that people liked to confide secrets others didn't know. They'd assisted him on a case or two.

A server rushing by snapped his focus back to the rectangular dining room. He'd scoped it out once, but a second glimpse wouldn't hurt. Partitions separated the cashier and waiting space from the eating section. A rear exit led to a patio, where no one sat on this breezy day. In two months, the snowbirds would arrive in full force. The restaurant's reasonably priced homemade food and location on the edge of the municipal golf course attracted both the vacationing sunseekers and the townies.

On his red cushioned seat, he could easily observe all the patrons. He ignored the wall of windows overlooking the golfers' practice range. Through the panes of glass, bored, lonely, or intrigued diners could watch the colorful parachutes at the nearby skydiving center. The jumpers sailed over the links men, who paid them little attention.

Jace fixated on the customer settled in the far-end corner. Dressed in a white knit shirt and tan shorts, the man blended in with the hungry regulars. Streaks of gray in his thinning brown hair hinted he'd met middle age, and it was winning. His server, a blond, curvaceous female in her late twenties, bent forward, pointing at the menu in his hands.

Standing next to him, her posture suggested more than a casual cuisine recommendation. She leaned into him. Her raised arm rested lightly on his shoulder while she indicated an item. The man smiled up at her as though the grub he was considering was much tastier than anything he'd ever put in his mouth.

Jace angled his phone to click a snapshot, hoping the staff and customers would think the window of skydivers was his subject. The photo was exactly what his client needed to hurry along her divorce. Jace had been trying for two weeks to obtain documentation that the man and the woman had had contact with each other. Finally, he'd discovered a connection. These two were risking everything, for what? People became irrational when lust took over. In his job, he'd seen plenty of men and women risk it all for so-called love and get zero in return.

Jace had worked on numerous cheating spouse cases and had lots of evidence that a long-term commitment wasn't the right option for most, including himself. He glanced at the couple.

He'd soon wrap up this investigation. Satisfaction rushed through him.

Yeah, too bad he had no one to share his good news with. His last girlfriend had left six months ago. She'd grown weary of the unpredictability of his business, his life. Since then, he'd taken a break from dating and relationships. He wasn't the everlasting romantic type. Working nine to five and joining a wife and kids in the evenings and on weekends—he didn't see any of that happening.

His parents wished he'd settle into a regular routine and traditional career. They rarely discussed his occupation, except to ask why he didn't get something steady, or better. He would attempt to describe the deep fulfillment he got when he finished his investigations, but that hadn't impressed his mother and father, both college professors.

When he was a kid, they'd drag him along on vacations to distant lands. At age ten, Gigi and Pop had offered to let him stay at their house while his mom and dad traveled. The arrangement had continued for years. He still had his room there. Now, his folks were retired and on a cross-country trip. They weren't around to judge Jace. He seldom heard from them, which was normal.

"Get a decent shot?"

Jace snapped his head up to discover the dark-haired, slim, young woman pulling out a chair at his table. Automatically, he fell into professional mode and wondered two things. Where had Tommie Murphy come from, and what did she want?

They'd grown up together. She'd been a fixture at his grandmother's home when Mrs. Yvette Miller, her second husband, and her daughter, Tommie, lived next door. Even after his neighbors had moved to Main Street, Tommie had ridden her bike three miles to Gigi's to hang out.

Now, she plopped down across from him, wearing faded gray

shorts and a T-shirt that hung loosely on her. She looked ready for a day of lounging in the sand. How had she happened to find him?

It didn't matter. *Send her on her way, fast.*

Her lips turned upward. Her blue eyes sparked in a playful, inviting way. He wished he could shove his chair beside hers. Not smart. He pushed an extra inch away.

"Those skydivers are amazing, aren't they?" She nodded to the window and raised her dark brows.

"Not as good as the golfers on the driving range." He set his phone on the tabletop and allowed his thoughts to skip to her latest problems.

He and everyone else in Sebastian had learned of her legal troubles from the news. They'd run a big, splashy story and picture about "Davis's Surfer Girlfriend, Thomasina Murphy." In the photo, she'd appeared lost and scared. The caption had read, "Innocent victim or co-conspirator?" and mentioned she had allegedly conspired with the chief to plant illicit drugs on his son.

"Jace?"

"Hmm?" He stirred from his musings.

"I said, 'Too bad you were busy watching the blond server and her customer over there.'" She lifted her chin to the corner. "You missed the golfer in the straw hat throwing a mini-fit on the green." Her black, shoulder-length, curly hair bobbed up and down as she moved in her seat.

He'd never seen her in anything but a short cut. She looked . . . pretty. And grown-up. She must be about twenty-four now.

She beamed a smile at him that should have put him at ease. It did the opposite. Instinct warned him she hadn't stumbled across him by accident. And truthfully, he was more annoyed than amused since she'd identified his true quarry, the middle-aged man and the waitress.

"Heard you were in Sebastian." He stiffened in his chair to build up an invisible wall around him. He couldn't pinpoint when or how these feelings of attraction had taken hold. It seemed like he'd had them forever. All he knew was that if she touched him, the hairs on the back of his neck rose skyward, and his blood ran faster. "Meeting someone?"

"It's just me. I guess you found out I was home." She searched his features for something she didn't seem to find. Disappointment, or maybe sadness, crossed her face but vanished quickly.

A twinge of sympathy twisted through him. Tommie was a kind but impulsive person. Traits possibly formed from sharing a life with her addicted mom, who would go out of her way to support anyone except herself and her daughter.

While growing up, Tommie and Jace had shared their successes and moments of disappointment. Both had longed for a big, close family who'd cheer for them at school events and post pictures of their holidays at the local hangouts on social media.

He hadn't seen her in a while. Maybe he should act friendlier. No, that would be risky. He'd always been careful to hide his reaction to her. Getting involved with her emotionally would be like living with a series of constant emergency alerts.

He was four years older than his once-nosy tag-along neighbor. As a child, she'd been determined to keep up with the bigger kids. He recalled she'd often attempted to wheedle her way into the boys' pickup baseball games. At sixteen, she'd crashed a beer party and been brought home by the cops. Another time, she'd filched a gnome out of a cranky old man's garden because he'd bawled out a little kid for chasing a ball into his yard. She'd almost ended up in court for stolen goods. Only producing the ornament and an apology saved her.

"Everyone knows about me and the chief since I testified at his trial."

Her statement tore him away from his reflections.

She twisted her lips before adding, "I try to avoid talking about Roy Davis. I wish I'd never met him. My biggest mistake was trusting the man. I won't do that again. And I was *not* his girlfriend. He was too old. I thought he was the fatherly, protective type who'd help me. The defense tried to portray me as the woman he dumped and who was getting even with him in court. Many believed the lie."

A lot of residents considered a neighbor's dog barking as criminal activity. Tommie hooking up with a coldhearted killer was unforgivable to most and fed the gossip.

"That part of your life is done. How are you now?" He should get to the point and end the stalling.

"Trying to do better. And I have something important to say." She pulled her phone out of her shorts pocket. Her belt was cinched in the tightest hole, emphasizing her thinness.

He sat in silence while she scrolled.

"Here it is." She held up her screen to read. "I apologize for borrowing your favorite baseball bat when you were thirteen. Yes, I should have asked permission to take it."

"What?" he sputtered in disbelief.

She raised her index finger for him to listen and give her a chance to finish. "I had no excuse for taking what wasn't mine. I know you searched everywhere except for the garbage. So, I hid it there when I snuck it back. And I'm sorry about the Halloween I took the pumpkin off your step. I carved it to prove I could handle a knife after you informed me I was too young to use one."

"You did that?" He sat up straight in his chair. "I blamed the boy at the end of the block. I'm glad I didn't accuse him."

"The little guy?" She wrinkled her nose. "He wasn't artistic or imaginative. My creation was unique."

"The jack-o'-lantern had one eye. The expression was ugly."

She frowned at him. "You won a first-place ribbon in the neighborhood contest."

"Because I constructed a paper pirate hat and strung an eye patch on it for the judges."

"Right." Her chin sank downward. "I was wrong. And for all the times I joked about those big black glasses before you got contacts. The fact you wouldn't speak to me for a week after I pointed out you looked like an owl when you wore them—"

"Stop." This wasn't fun or entertaining. He shoved at his hair. "I appreciate the honesty, but enough. I absolve you of all past offenses." He waved a hand over her before she could spiel off other wrongs.

She lowered her phone. "I'm working on doing better. I've been reading self-improvement books and created an apology list of individuals I've hurt by my actions." She set her cell on the tabletop. "And I got a job at the Whale's Spout and a room at the Yellow Flamingo Inn."

"I'm glad to hear it. If you don't mind, I'll offer a bit of advice." He had to tread lightly. "Try reciting your regrets in a single sentence. 'If I offended you, I apologize.' It does wonders. Bringing up unpleasant memories can cause grief or anger. People rarely react positively if they're in an emotional state."

"Maybe." She shrugged in her old, typical manner, as though she was shaking off an opinion she disliked. "Thank you for listening." She folded her hands together and sat forward in her chair. "I stopped at your grandmother's this morning."

"My Gigi?" The abrupt change in conversation threw him off.

"Yes."

Why was he surprised? Unlike most folks, Gigi entertained in the early or late hours, especially for Tommie. His grandmother had taken the girl under her wing and never let go.

"Was it a pleasant meeting?" He would pretend he and Tommie were having a friendly chat. Instead, he was trying to build up his resolve to turn her down. He sensed she was about to make a request that any wise man would reject.

"Of course." The corner of her eyes crinkled, and a slight smile curved her lips.

He was struck again by how good-looking she was. How had he forgotten? *Hold on. Don't give in.* Her world was always in turmoil.

"Here you go." The server was at his side, setting his plate before him with a *thud*. The aroma from the eggs, bacon, fries, and maple pancakes spiraled up to him. Heavenly.

"Something for you, hon?" The fiftyish woman stared at Tommie.

"No. I'm set."

The waitress rushed to another customer.

He picked up his silverware and caught Tommie watching as he speared a bite. "I guess you had breakfast with my grandmother?"

"I did. I was wondering if you planned to eat all that meal. I don't need leftovers." She gestured to herself. "I have a dog and forgot to get him a can of food. If you could spare a leftover from a doggie bag . . ." She raised her brows and paused.

"You got a pet? Nice." At least he'd found out why she'd sought him out. Free eats. Cinnamon rolls probably hadn't filled up an animal or Tommie. He signaled to the waitress, who hurried over to him.

He pointed to his dish. "I'd like a second Hungry Man. And she'll pick it up at the register to go. Put it on my bill."

"I'll pay you back." Tommie said as the wait staff left.

"Sure." Now eager to end this unusual conversation, he put

down his fork. Her order better cook fast. Being around Tommie, he'd learned to expect the unexpected.

She dropped her gaze to the tablecloth.

He felt a stab of guilt and disappointment. Maybe it was the memory of her carefree attitude, her willingness to try anything once, or her odd sense of humor that intrigued him. Most likely, it was her kind heart that she usually hid that had him longing for her to stay longer. Either way, he wanted her to fix those blue eyes on him, as opposed to staring down at her hands, as she was doing.

"Your grandmother suggested you'd help me. With some legal issues." She locked her blue eyes on him.

The fact that Gigi had volunteered his services wasn't a surprise. Both his grandparents, Pop and Gigi, had always thought their grandson would conquer the world.

"Will you?" Tommie asked.

"Don't you have an attorney? I read his name in the paper." How had she gotten herself involved with the lethal chief?

"I'm done with the whole profession." She waved a hand in the air. "The one I had for the trial did nothing except to gift me a huge payment-due notice. I don't have a great-paying job, but I've managed to pay him off in installments. When I move, I'll get something with a living wage."

What was Tommie mixed up in? Didn't matter, he couldn't say yes to her. "You should lie low if you did nothing wrong."

She sank deeper into her seat.

Was he being too harsh? Regret surged through him. "I doubt I'm the guy for you. I'm a private investigator."

Stray tears trickled down her face.

Were those for real? He was a fool when he had to deal with a crying woman. He suppressed a groan of surrender. "Tell me what's happened." He'd kick himself later.

"The police found me at the home of a double homicide."

He felt his jaw drop. "Arturo and Gloria Alvaro?"

"You heard?" She wiped the heel of her palm over her cheeks.

"The newsflash has been everywhere about the 'untimely' deaths. Everyone knows that's code for suspicious or worse."

"I arrived *after* the shootings."

"They were shot!" A sudden coldness hit his core.

He imagined his grandfather sitting up in his grave, protesting. *That's not our type of case. Too risky and messy.*

Tommie winced and grabbed Jace's water glass, gulping a mouthful.

He studied her reaction while tamping down his shock.

She set the drink down. "Did you meet Arturo?"

"I saw his television ad about assessing home valuables. His spiel was, 'Give me a room full of your old junk, and I'll turn it into a load of money in a trunk.' I wouldn't have predicted his life would come to a violent end. He seemed pleasant, convincing, and relatable—a natural salesman."

"I didn't see his advertisements." She fiddled with her placemat. "While I was there, I overheard a uniform tell Grey he'd found lists of Arturo's collections and the dates of sales, in his desk drawer. The poor guy got the job of matching up the contents in the home with the inventory pages."

"Interesting. They'll probably check out his customers and if anything of value was missing. How did you and Arturo get involved?" He couldn't picture them together. What was she not saying?

"We weren't. I bought a piece of jewelry from him. We talked online and met in person for coffee about a surfboard for me to price when I'd told him I'd worked at a surf shop. He invited me to dinner at his place since I was stopping by to return the board. When I got to his house, he and his cousin were dead inside." The color fled her cheeks, and her shoulders caved inward.

He straightened in his chair, prepared to say no. "I can send you referrals for reputable lawyers. I'm not trained to deal with that level of criminality." He supported himself by tracking cheating spouses, digging up dirt during custody battles, and revealing insurance frauds, not investigating murders.

She wet her lips and stood. "I understand." She looked down at her phone and tapped on it before continuing. "You've let your hair grow longer. I like it. The color always makes me think of the beach." She forced a faint smile and left.

He felt an ache in his chest. Was it sympathy or the tug of attraction he'd locked up, escaping again? He brushed at the strands falling over his forehead. When was the last time he'd gone to a barber? He'd skipped two or three cuts. He'd go to a barbershop, pronto.

His cell dinged. Probably his grandmother checking to see if he'd met with Tommie. Was she aware the girl's problems included two shootings? Knowing Gigi, it wouldn't matter. She believed in the best of everyone. Remorse nipped him. He glanced down to read the email, but the one he found on his screen wasn't from Gigi.

It was from Tommie. She had his newest number? Gigi must have given it to her. Across the room, Tommie was hurrying away, dodging patrons, and wait staff. Her arms were crossed in front of her, and her gaze was fastened downward, avoiding eye contact.

On his phone, the images of the blond, twentysomething server and her customer appeared. Their expressions of open lust were on full display as they stared at each other. Perfect for divorce court.

He scanned the dining room. Tommie had disappeared. When had she taken the photo? He must have been obvious when he snapped the pictures of the couple. So much for keeping things private. He pushed his chair away from the table and threw his money down.

Maybe he should offer to take her to lunch. She'd looked like she could use a big meal. Would that cure his nagging sense of failure, that he'd disappointed her? He darted into the hallway and out the door. Cool air rushed at him in the crowded parking lot.

How had she vanished so fast? What kind of car did she drive? He shot her a text. *Where RU?*

People passed by with a nod. The wind blew cigarette butts and fronds over the sidewalk.

His cell rang. It had to be Tommie. "Hey. Glad you called."

"Jace, that's lovely to hear."

"Gigi?"

CHAPTER
SIX

Tommie drove into the lot of Thalia's Tranquil Salon and Day Spa. From the car, she and Picasso watched vehicles whiz past or stop for the lights at the intersection. The temperature had plummeted to a cool fifty-eight degrees and was hovering there. Geesh, she should have worn mittens.

The two-tone yellow and teal surfboard was nestled between the seats. Should she write a simple note for an employee to give to Thalia? *Condolences on your tragic losses?*

That might make Thalia's pain worse. Two people killed. Tommie shuddered. The least she could do was offer a personal word of kindness before leaving the board and the dog. She unfastened her seat belt and studied her surroundings. No one had followed her. Trees were sparse around the lot. Not many spots for a person to hide and spy on her. Across the street in the shopping plaza, shoppers were pulling into the Bealls Outlet.

What about Grey? She hadn't read or answered his last text. He'd be popping up somewhere. She should keep an eye out for him and his tailing black SUV until she had a plan.

Hunger and nerves mixed and twinged in her stomach. She

shouldn't have left the breakfast Jace bought her at the diner. She imagined the taste of the pancakes' sweet maple syrup.

Think of something else. Jace cropped up in her memory. She recalled the scent of his clean soap blending with the restaurant's mouthwatering aromas. Too bad his striking, sea-green eyes had held so much disapproval when he'd fixed them on her. Yet, she'd had to fight the urge to turn and look at him when she'd fled the eatery.

Picasso's whine caught her attention. Was he hungry? How could she tell? She'd snuck him a couple of rolls at Gigi's house. Keeping him could be expensive. Her mother had always said they couldn't afford a pet. Was this the truth? Her mom often chose a story that fit her argument, not the most accurate.

Tommie glanced at her phone. Three minutes until the boutique opened. A few cars were parked behind the blue-gray concrete spa, probably the workers. She prayed Thalia wouldn't give her a chilly welcome. She thought back to what Arturo had told her about his cousins during one of their FaceTime meets when they'd both been sitting in their homes.

"Gloria and Thalia originally worked together at the Sebastian Barber and Beauty Stop on the opposite side of the city," he'd explained. "Gloria and her husband, Rex, ran the shop. Thalia was her second-in-command. The arrangement ended when Gloria divorced cheating Rex and discovered that he and her sister were secretly opening another salon business."

"That was a low blow." Tommie raised the screen of her phone to her chin.

"It would have been better if Thalia and Rex had become lovers, rather than Gloria's competitors." Arturo gave a knowing nod. "Rex was never a good partner."

"He doesn't sound like a catch," Tommie responded. "Why did she stay with him?"

"Rex was his own biggest fan and seemed to have brainwashed his wife. After eons of his wandering ways, they dissolved their union. Rumors circulated that he'd grown tired of being married to an older woman who loved only her job. I suspected he was responsible for spreading the gossip." Arturo shook his head. "It's true Rex was in his forties, and she was in her fifties, but that hadn't bothered him for nearly a decade of marriage."

"Many people have unconventional unions," Tommie said.

"They do," Arturo agreed. "There was a rumor Rex used money he'd secreted away in a hidden bank account for his new business with Thalia. It was his way of sticking it to his soon-to-be ex."

Tommie was intrigued by the whole betrayal tale. "What happened?" she asked, bringing her screen up to her nose.

"When Gloria learned of the scheme and her sister's part in it, she and Thalia engaged in a loud public quarrel in front of their clients. It was terrible. Rex had moved out and no longer worked with Gloria." Arturo splayed his hand over his chest. "The fight was the talk of the staff and customers for days."

"I bet." Tommie could imagine the argument.

"Afterward, it was hard to stay friendly with either of my cousins. I did my best. They'd always been jealous of each other."

A bright fire-red convertible turned into the salon's driveway and interrupted Tommie's daydreaming. The driver parked near the entrance. A man exited the sports car. His jaunty, look-at-me walk held her attention. He had a long, golden-brown ponytail and wore a flowered shirt, beige shorts, and sunglasses. Was this Rex, Gloria's former spouse?

He tossed a keychain in the air and caught it before strolling to the edge of the building, where Tommie spotted him disappearing through a door.

He hadn't acted sad. More cars pulled into the back lot. Looked like the employees would be unlocking the entry soon.

She peeked in the rearview mirror. Dark smudges above her cheekbones suggested she hadn't slept. Her hair was frizzing. No wonder Jace had ordered her food. He'd pitied her. She poked her fingers at the crimped strands and gave up.

The dog nudged her arm.

Maybe strolling inside holding a surfboard and leading a dog wouldn't be a good idea. First, she should make sure she could entrust them with a dependable person. "Stay here, Picasso."

The dog's tail thumped on his seat. Did he think she planned to buy him a second breakfast? She turned the engine key and lowered his window. Pocketing her fob, she slipped out of the vehicle. At the salon's entrance, she tugged on the nickel-plated knob. Locked.

She tried to peep through the door's glass pane. White lace curtains hid the inner happenings. Standing alone on the stoop, she felt that uncomfortable sensation of somebody peering at her.

You'll regret crossing me. The warning from Davis echoed in her mind.

Uneasy, she took in the rushing traffic and walkway. No signs of people hiking or biking past. In the lot, Picasso was hanging out of the car, sniffing the air.

"I'm imagining things," she muttered. Unease gripped her despite her attempt to keep her cool. Whirling around, she spotted a doorbell. She pressed the button.

She shifted from foot to foot. "C'mon. Let me in."

The thud of steps in the building alerted her that someone was answering. She retreated a few feet to put a dignified distance between herself and whoever unlocked the entryway.

The door swung wide. The man in the flowered shirt stared at her. Lines bracketed his mouth. "Ma'am," he said in a husky voice. "We're not opening until two p.m. today. Family emergency and staff meeting. I was about to hang a sign, and the news was posted on our website. One of our employees is contacting our guests about their appointments. My apologies if you missed the text."

Up close, he was handsome in a rough kind of way and extremely tan. His intense, brown-eyed gaze raked over her with a disapproving expression.

His obvious assessment of her elevated her discomfort level. Determined not to react openly, she raised her shoulders and spoke firmly. "I wish to speak to Thalia Alvaro. It's a private matter." Not exactly the whole story, her conscience prompted.

"Is this related to business?" he demanded in an arrogant tone. His cold gleam slid up and down her form while he licked his lips.

"Indirectly." She fought the urge to leave while her heart skipped a beat. "I'm Tommie Murphy. I was a friend of Arturo Alvaro. I have some of his belongings to pass along."

He nodded several times and seemed to be considering what to do while keeping his unnerving stare on her.

For a moment, she thought he'd tell her to go away. A part of her wished he would. Was he involved in Arturo's death? That question wasn't reassuring.

"Come in." He glanced at Picasso, who was sticking the top of his huge body out the window of her hatchback. The man's mouth slipped into a frown of censure before he stepped aside for her to enter.

He led her at a quick pace through a hall. A thick, wine-colored carpet dulled the noise of her flip-flops. The scent of sweet flowers from the pastel bouquet on a side table filled the air. Spa brochures were spread across the tabletop. Curious, she wandered over to the pamphlets.

The odor of tobacco hit her. She whirled to discover the Hawaiian shirt man crowded up to her shoulder.

"Oh!" Her hand went to her chest.

"We just printed those out." He waved at the flyers, ignoring her reaction. "Take a couple to share. Arturo came up with the idea originally for Gloria's store, but she was too cheap to spend the money." A muscle twitched in his cheek when he brought up his ex. "Thalia agreed to publish her own. Arturo insisted his name be included, since he'd proposed the handout. That was Arturo, always looking for the spotlight."

What had Gloria seen in this man?

He gestured to the mural-size picture on the wall. "Find the lady with the oversized, black glasses. She's easy to spot. Arturo is standing next to her. He photobombed us. He should have known better, but that was one of his traits. Doing things he shouldn't."

"Yeah." How many people had Arturo done the wrong thing to?

"Wait here. I'll speak to Ms. Alvaro." Mr. Hawaiian Shirt spun on his heel and trod off.

She wiped her perspiring brow. If she was lucky, Thalia would appear alone. She moved to the blown-up photo of the ribbon-cutting in front of the building. A short, silver-haired woman held a giant pair of scissors in the center. She had to be Thalia. On her right was the ponytailed man.

Dressed in a light blue suit topped off by an ivory Panama-style hat, he looked suited for a Caribbean cruise. His wide smile exposed perfect white teeth. His palm engulfed Thalia's on the handle of the shears. Yup. He was Gloria's ex, Rex.

Everyone was beaming. Must be nice to have such a huge gathering of loving friends and family. A sadness settled near her heart and spread upward. But was one a killer?

"Can I help you?"

Tommie turned to a petite female with pewter-colored hair walking up to her.

Her high heels thudded on the hallway carpet and added

about two inches to her five feet. A ton of makeup covered her fiftysomething face. The abundance of powder gave her a mask-like appearance.

Tommie's hands dampened. Too bad, the AC wasn't aimed at her. "You're Thalia Alvaro?"

"I'm Ms. Alvaro." A cross dangled from a chain above the V-neck of her gray blouse. Her mid-knee, black skirt swished as she strode to a stop.

No sign of Rex. Phew, though, Ms. Thalia Alvaro's stern manner wasn't welcoming. She'd explain. "I'm Tommie Murphy." She pointed at herself. "I knew your cousin Arturo."

"We're dealing with emergencies this morning. Nothing else. If you wish to give condolences, save the sympathies for the service." Her clipped tone carried no hint of sorrow.

The abrupt dismissal threw Tommie off for a second. "Uh, it's not about sympathy, although his death was tragic," she blurted, trying to recover from her blunder. "You've suffered two intimate losses."

"It was soul-wrenching. Fortunately, my coworker Rex was working with me when I heard the news. He was helpful." Thalia laced her fingers together at her waist and raised a thin, penciled eyebrow over an olive-green eye. "What brought you to me?"

The woman's brusqueness wasn't encouraging. But she'd undergone two major fatalities. "It's about some of Gloria and Arturo's belongings."

"You want to buy their leftovers, and you're worried you'll have competition. So, you raced over to beat the other buyers. They are not for sale."

Thalia didn't understand. "I have Gloria's longboard. She hoped to sell it."

"What? Ha. My sister thought she'd profit on anything within her reach." Thalia waved her hand in the air. "Bah, she disliked the salt water and the sandy beaches as much as I do.

You are mistaken if you think I'm interested in the long or short piece of wood. Go find someone else."

Their conversation really wasn't going as Tommie had hoped. "No. No." She should revert to her usual straightforward way of talking. "I'm a surfer, and Arturo loaned me Gloria's surfboard to evaluate and price. I wanted to pass it on to a family member."

"Let me explain. My sister possessed poor business sense. Your story reminds me of the time she insisted the French twist would be in style again and encouraged our clients to get the fashion."

Huh? "The twist? The dance?" Ice cream?

"It was a popular hairstyle that never came back." Thalia dropped her hands to her sides and fisted them. "I'm not getting involved in Gloria's silly scheme. Do whatever you wish with the slab of lumber." She scowled.

Tommie bit her tongue when she was tempted to clarify the longboard was composed of fiberboard. This hadn't been a great idea. She inched toward the doorway. "Their deaths have been a shock. I apologize for bothering you."

"One moment." Thalia's tone softened. "Do you know who hurt Arturo? Or Gloria?"

"I don't." The woman suddenly seemed to possess a bit of heart. "I'm here to return their belongings."

"Try Alfredo Russo. He might want the board to sell." Thalia's lips twitched tight.

"Alfredo?" Where had she heard that name?

"He rents a booth at the big indoor flea market in Melbourne and sells once a month at the church bazaar on Route 1. He collects odd lots and discards on consignment. He'll take a surfboard, I'm sure."

"I remember now, Arturo's ex-partner." Arturo had warned her Alfredo was a cheat.

"I can tell by your expression you're aware Arturo accused Alfredo of stealing from him, but Arturo wasn't a saint himself. And nothing was ever proven against Alfredo."

The former associate sounded like a possible suspect in the murders. "Why did Arturo work with him?"

"He felt sorry for him. Alfredo was shuttled from relative to relative when he was a child, and his dad abandoned him and his mother. Arturo spent years in foster homes when his divorced mother gave him up for adoption."

Was that an excuse for Arturo to behave badly? Tommie wondered. "Arturo mentioned that your sister and Alfredo knew each other well."

"For a brief time, after her marriage broke up, she went out with him. They weren't a match, too different." The tense lines around Thalia's mouth eased. "Arturo loved everyone, but if he could persuade a buyer to pay a bigger price than an object was worth, he would." She gawked at Tommie. "How did you and he meet?"

"I was a customer at the Artisan Co-op."

"Now I understand. You're an acquaintance, not a good friend, who was left holding possessions you bought from Arturo. You think I'll give you your money back." Her lower lip pouted out in distaste.

"It's true we met briefly, but I'm trying to give things back to you. For free."

"You look familiar." Thalia scrutinized her. "What's your name again?"

She should go before Thalia recalled the Davis murder case. "Can you tell me who would like Arturo's dog?"

"I forgot he had that unkempt creature. Take him to the pound. Arturo got him there shortly before he died. The animal—"

"Pardon me." The man in the flowered shirt stepped forward.

"What is it, Rex?" Thalia asked.

Tommie took in Gloria's ex-husband's lean, muscled body. He could have snuck into Arturo's house, overpowered him, and killed him and Gloria. Tommie increased the space between them.

He sent her a cool glance while he talked to Thalia. "Detective Grey phoned. He's on his way to speak with us."

The detective was coming here. Tommie couldn't believe her luck. Finding her at the salon would raise his suspicions. If he caught her, he'd continue to cross-examine her about the murders. She gripped her hands together. "I won't intrude any longer." Perspiration formed on her palms. She trotted to the exit. In one tug, she flung the door wide. Sunlight temporarily blinded her after the hallway's dim light. She blinked and barreled across the blacktop.

Picasso whined in happiness when she hopped into the driver's seat. She drove to the street. A line of traffic drove past her as she watched for her chance to merge. A break in the queue arrived when an SUV slowed to turn into the lot.

As she merged into the stream of vehicles, Tommie shot a look at the hulk of a man behind the wheel of the SUV. *Grey.*

He did a double take as they passed each other.

Would he follow her? If he caught her, he'd pepper her with questions about the victims and their deaths. She shoved down on the gas.

CHAPTER SEVEN

The breeze through the open car window blew Tommie's hair in her face. She pushed at the strands while running a red stoplight at Roseland Street. Drivers honked. A man swore at her, but it was better than Grey catching her.

Picasso stuck his snout out of his window, pointing it upward. In her rearview mirror, Tommie glimpsed a Prius behind her. Her fear lessened. No self-respecting law enforcement member would drive a slow-speed hybrid. In a car chase, they'd be left in the dust. She spent the next ten minutes aimlessly driving side roads and monitoring her whereabouts. No signs of the detective or any officer.

Find a quiet place. And think.

On automatic pilot, she drove toward the sea, her sanctuary. She knew what to do now. She wasn't dressed for the ocean, but she carried spare clothing in her trunk and stopped to change at a public bathhouse. To hide her vehicle from view, she pulled beside a large truck in the lot and hurried inside.

Quickly, she put on her suit and ran back to Picasso. A little way down the road, she turned into Turtle Beach. The unpaved area was empty. Sparse trees lined the perimeter and would partially hide the sight of her car from the busy traffic.

Picasso jumped out when she opened his door. She grabbed a worn moss-colored blanket from the rear.

The surfboard sat in its spot between the seats. A lot had happened in twenty-four hours. Today, Arturo and Gloria were gone. Life had changed in a blink.

The dog's wet nose nudged her hand.

"We're going to enjoy a small dose of sanity." She stuffed her pocketbook under the seat. Next, she removed the longboard from the car and rested it on the ground. She wrapped her keys and phone in the throw and put it on top of the board. With care, she positioned the bottom of the surfboard on top of her head and balanced her load.

Picasso raised one ear and stared.

"I agree. I look strange. Let's go."

He lifted his leg and watered an oleander shrub on the edge of the gravel.

"C'mon, boy." A sign at the beginning of the path listed No Lifeguard and The Rules. Number one: No dogs allowed. Nobody followed that instruction. Tommie took the trail that cut through the dunes. She inhaled the tangy air. The dog sniffed and pawed at the bushes lining the access. At the end of the way, she halted. The white coast stretched forever. Light blue water swept the coastline and disappeared into the horizon. No signs of another person or ship.

The now-constant throb in her shoulders eased. The whir of traffic had completely faded. The breeze danced across her skin and disappeared. She was safe.

Picasso sprinted around her in excited circles. Waves rolled in. Their familiar white noise called to her. Mesmerized, she walked to the sea. The tide raced toward her flip-flops simply to slide away before reaching her. She chose a smooth spot on the beach and lowered the board to the ground. Seizing the throw, she spread it out, set her phone on top, and kicked off her sandals.

Anticipation rippled over her. She ventured into the Atlantic with her longboard, searching for the perfect wave. All she needed was one. She paddled farther out and stopped. Waiting. The continuous swaying motion of the sea soothed her worries. She scanned the azure vastness stretching as far as she could see.

There it was. Her wave. Eager, she set to paddling once more. She met the swell and positioned herself, facing the seashore. The back of her board rose, and her arms and feet automatically shifted her balance as she stood for her ride. She took off.

The spray salted her lips and showered her as she hovered on a gigantic, powerful surge. Joy rushed through her. She was cruising on top of the world.

She tipped her head upward and shouted, "I'm rockin' it."

Picasso barked at her and pranced in front of the breaking tide.

Tommie laughed. The board glided along. If only the surf were endless. Instead, the breaker's lip feathered. Her trip ended two yards from where she began. She wiped and blinked the salt from her eyes. Gathering her longboard, she waded to land.

She plopped down on her blanket. Nearby, Picasso chased a flock of seagulls who flew off, crying in protest. With the sand between her toes, she released a breath of contentment. Her thoughts wandered to Jace. What was he doing today? He was probably with his girlfriend.

He was a steady guy. His easy manner. The way he greeted each day with calm and certainty. It was never a question of right and wrong for him. And the simple love he had for his grandmother and parents fascinated her. *I wish I had such relatives.*

The thought reminded her again, she hadn't heard from her

mother. That was odd. She scooped up her phone and pressed her mom's number. She must have learned about the shootings by now. It would be easier to launch into the topics of Arturo and Gloria.

Her call went to voicemail. Strange. Tommie disconnected. The sun ducked behind gray clouds, leaving her chilled. She rubbed her arms.

Picasso stared at the footpath and growled. Tommie's neck prickled. Someone was on the path. Was it Grey? Her pulse jumped. The fur on the dog's spine stood up. He barked twice and sidled up to her. Goose bumps popped up on her skin. She scooped up her cell phone to punch in 911.

The sound of a whistle shot across the rustle of waves and the fears roaring in her mind. Yeah, whoever it was, she wasn't up to socializing. She snatched up her footwear.

A small white dog appeared. A man followed the animal. He wore a baseball cap, sunglasses, and an olive vest. He carried fishing gear in his hand.

It was a public spot, and her private moment had ended. Scooping up her belongings, she trekked to the parking lot with Picasso. They reached the gravel area. She grabbed her dry clothes from her hatchback and yanked them on over her damp suit as a dark SUV cruised in front of her.

Detective Grey. Was the man everywhere? She seized Picasso by his harness.

Grey's door opened. The burly man climbed out. "Tommie. Getting a tan? You don't seem too broken up over the Alvaro deaths." He strode to her with a fast gait. "I want to talk to you."

"Did you follow me?" She raised her voice in a challenge to cover her nerves.

"I'm an investigator. Remember? You mentioned this beach was one of your favorites during our last time together. I'm making sure you don't take a permanent vacation until we arrest the scum who committed the double homicide."

"I don't know anything." She scowled.

He stopped a foot from her, scratching his cheek. "Maybe not, but a few things have been bothering me. You claimed Arturo and you were nearly strangers. But you were found alone at his home for what looked like an intimate dinner. Why did the co-op vendors report seeing you talking to him at his booth shortly before he died? Why had he told his co-workers you texted one another frequently?"

Silence was the best answer while she panicked. Finally, she mumbled, "I'm not speaking to you."

He glared at her. "The phone records will provide proof of how often you contacted each other. My men are getting them now."

She bit off her protest. What if their messages were misinterpreted? And would their FaceTime calls be turned over too?

"It seems," he continued, "everyone at Gloria's salon suspected you two were involved. They referred to you as Arturo's surfer girlfriend."

Don't talk and incriminate yourself. "I'm late for another appointment."

His jaw worked as he tightened it. She understood what that meant. He was about to pressure her to make time. He crowded up to her, blocking her escape into her car.

CHAPTER EIGHT

Jace disconnected Gigi's latest call and hopped into his navy sports utility. He was doing his best to push his grandmother's last plea from his mind. *Who will help Tommie if you don't?*

He'd tried to avoid the answer, but he'd finally agreed with her. Although he wasn't convinced he should take Tommie's case, he could make sure she was all right.

Gigi had suggested he check the Turtle Beach waterfront for the girl. Tommie frequently hung out by her favorite spot to think. So Jace drove toward the ocean. He passed his preferred Mexican eatery at the gas station and didn't feel a twinge of compulsion to pull in.

Instead, he wrestled with the sinking sensation that he'd abandoned Tommie to drown in the legal system. There'd also been something vulnerable in her expression when he'd told her he'd known she was around, and he'd done nothing to seek her out. She'd covered quickly, but he'd seen the shadow of hurt cross her face.

She spent most of her life getting herself out of trouble to fall into worse. During her involvement with the sociopath Chief Davis, she'd hit rock bottom. She'd run away and hidden from the police. Now, she'd been discovered at the scene of two murders.

He wished he didn't have such clear memories of her—the little kid who looked at him like he could do anything and attempted to follow along wherever he went. He still heard her pleading to join him and his friends when they played ball.

"Let me go too. I can play with the boys. My name is Tommie."

"Thomasina," Jace had corrected.

"I've been practicing. I can pitch. I'll strike those guys out."

"Not today," he'd tossed over his shoulder and left her behind.

The memory faded, but not the truth. It didn't matter how he'd discouraged her. She'd tagged after him. He had no doubts she'd had a preteen crush on him.

And since he hadn't grown dumber while reaching the near end of his twenties, he recognized that in her moments of stress, she'd fallen back on him for support. Still, Gigi had a point. Who else could Tommie count on? Her mother jumped from one scrape to the next. Her father was nowhere to be found. No siblings. A significant other? Probably no one responsible. She'd shown poor taste when it came to men in the past, especially in her teenage years. They'd all been short-lived relationships, and in his opinion, none of them had been good enough for her.

Too bad, understanding why she'd sought him out didn't solve her legal problems. That's another reason he had to talk to her. He'd offer to loan her money, buy her food, anything except spend days wrapped up in her crazy life.

Steady traffic surrounded him. He cut over to the Wabasso Bridge. A gathering of people fished or rested in the narrow river park lining both sides of the road. On the walkway, bikers cruised by him, pedaling in the opposite direction. At the peak, he admired the view of the stately homes edging the shoreline of the intracoastal waterway. The buildings' soft colors and tall palms always seemed inviting.

He turned onto A1A in Vero Beach. High walls and expensive, gated communities flowed into each other and closed off sight of the sea from the street. Palms lined the double lanes. Adults and children strolled or biked on the sidewalks, in sharp contrast to the vehicles zipping by.

Where exactly was the public shore access? If his distant memory served him, Tommie had often surfed and sunned there. Unlike many of his friends, he wasn't a fan of sitting in the sand and perspiring. Being partially submerged in salt water didn't do much for him, either. Give him a good book and an air-conditioned room, and he was in R & R heaven.

Jace drove by the resorts and slowed. Parking should show up on his left. Blink, and he'd miss it. Out of the corner of his eye, he spied the sign. Yup, he'd driven by it. He did a U-turn at the light. In seconds, he went into the lot, partly camouflaged by trees and bushes. A black Dodge SUV blocked his approach. Had the driver broken down? He'd started around the vehicle when he spotted Tommie. She stood by a shaggy mini-horse near her car. A brawny man in a slate-colored shirt and dark pants crowded up to her. Jace was six feet, and this guy beat him by four or five inches.

Jace cut his engine. What was going on? He jumped out. "Tommie?"

She looked up. Her tight features eased with recognition and relief. The giant turned and pinned a disapproving frown on Jace. Tommie dodged past the distracted guy. The pony-size animal galloped at her heels.

She ran to him. He pressed the unlock button on his keychain.

She grabbed the passenger handle and yanked the door wide. The canine leaped inside first. She dove in next. He climbed behind the wheel.

Despite the huge furball on her lap, she managed to buckle her seat belt. "I owe you big-time, Jackson, for finding me. Let's go. Quick." She hit the lock knob. "Who's the gorilla man?" He gestured at the colossus attempting to shoot death rays at them with his eyeballs.

"Someone I'm not interested in speaking to." She lowered her window and yelled, "You took my statement. I have nothing else to say to the cops."

Police? "Are you under arrest?" In a flash, he'd become involved in her problems.

"He's a homicide detective and wanted to continue cross-examining me about the murders. He and a sergeant interviewed me at Arturo's house. That's enough."

Jace hesitated. The husky man looked as though he'd spit nails into them and pound the spikes in with a hammer. He wasn't leaving Tommie here. Decision made. "He'll have to find other friends. We're not staying." A new warning slipped into his mind as he hit the gas. "The man's not a boyfriend or on your apology list, is he?" Jace shot to the edge of the street.

"Ew. No. Grey should apologize to me. He's been asking me questions that only whoever shot the Alvaros could answer."

Jace slammed on the brakes, saw an opening in traffic, and floored the pedal.

Tommie draped an arm around the dog. "Wow, Jackson. When did you learn to drive like you're in a TV car chase? Impressive."

"Let's pray we're never in one. Where did you get the pony-sized canine?" He kept an eye on his mirror for the disgruntled lawman. How badly was she snarled up in the killings?

She raised her chin at the animal. "This is Picasso." Her tight mouth softened. "Say hello, boy."

The dog stretched over and slurped a wet tongue over Jace's cheek.

Mutt slobber. He brushed off the swill while scowling. "Has he had his shots?"

"Does he look ill?" She studied her pet. "It might have been the peanut butter sandwich he ate for supper. He gulped it down in two seconds. His manners could stand improvement. Are you okay, boy?"

The dog let out a loud bark.

Jace winced. "Is he testing my hearing?" He wasn't into pets.

"Don't be silly. He was talking to me. You're not used to animals. Don't worry. He'll love you. He's super friendly."

"I promise not to lose sleep if he doesn't." He raked a gaze over his shoulder. The dark SUV wasn't in sight. "Will your giant come after us? I assume the SUV was his?" Jace checked his rearview mirror. "By any chance, did he have a warrant on him?"

"I'm not a fugitive, I hope. Besides, we didn't get too far in our conversation."

"You hope?" Was that the best she had?

"I'm not wanted by the cops, Jackson." She frowned at him.

"It looked like you were in a standoff."

"He did go out of his way to track me down." She peered out the windows. "No signs of him. To be safe, you should detour off the main road."

"What did you say was the name of the big hulk?" A bad feeling seeped through Jace while he searched for a secondary route. Gigi might have been right to encourage him to offer his help.

"Detective Grey. He's the one who found me in New Hampshire after Roy Davis was taken into custody. That was a while ago. I was living at North Beach up there. He brought me back to Florida to be a witness at the trial."

"Who'd guess that you'd hightail it to a beachside to hang low?"

"Yeah, obvious choice." Her shoulders slumped.

"I'm not a big expert on that kind of law. You should get a lawyer and have him deal with the guy. He's serious business." And now probably angry with Jace.

Her lower lip pouted out. "I'll stay off Grey's radar, and he's not a friend."

The conversation wasn't going too smoothly. She was stubborn at the worst of times. He turned onto a side street, hoping it went where he thought. "Did you omit something from our talk earlier? That detective wasn't out for a stroll along the water. Tommie, if I work for you, I need an explanation of what's happening. I can't be left in the dark."

"So, you've changed your mind?"

"Give me your whole story, not pieces. Let's start with Grey."

"What do you want to know?"

Picasso moaned and scrunched up on Tommie's lap and over the middle cup holder. The dog's rear end hung dangerously near Jace's leg.

He'd have to ignore the animal while he determined how deeply she was involved in these shootings. He slanted her a look out of the corner of his eye. Was he committing a crime now, driving her away from the detective?

"Remember, I had nothing to do with the Alvaro murders. I arrived after they were shot." She blinked twice. "Hey, I nearly hit someone running across Arturo's drive when I tried to bolt before the police showed up."

"You were fleeing the scene?" She was unbelievable.

"I planned to call 911 as soon as I escaped from the house. I was worried their attacker was hiding inside. Anyway, I believed the person I almost hit was a security guard, but I've changed my mind. I'm guessing it was the murderer. I think." She massaged her temple. "I'm not sure."

He clamped down on his excitement until he got the whole story. "Can you provide a description?"

"I can't provide much. He or she wore dark clothes and ran into the preserve. Hopefully to a car and not to the river, unless he or she wanted to risk meeting gators in the water. I hate, hate gators."

"Understood. No alligators, stuffed or alive. Nothing else?" He rubbed his chin, keeping his gaze on the road.

"My main goal was to get the heck out of Manatee Lake Estates. I didn't think about much else after finding two dead people. I told the cops about the figure jumping out of the woods and disappearing."

Sounded like she'd nearly hit the shooter. "Who knew you'd be at the Alvaro residence besides your host?"

She opened her mouth and shut it. "You suppose I was set up?"

"Who?" he persisted.

"No one that I know of."

Was she concealing an important fact?

She touched his arm to get his attention. Her worry lines deepened. "I wasn't involved in the deaths. Do you believe me?"

He felt his resolve slip. No, he wouldn't weaken. "You need a lawyer."

"Or you can find the gunman or woman and clear me. You found a missing runaway girl a year ago. And you track deadbeats who don't pay their alimony. Now you can catch a deadbeat killer."

"Tommie."

"Please, Jace. I only have one name, and I can't have it associated with committing murder. Detective Grey must realize I'm innocent and arrest the real scum." She paused for a second. "I want to be able to meet people without having them eye me with suspicion."

She had always pretended that mean comments didn't bother her when they did. "Tommie, tell me what Grey said back there."

She twisted her hands. "He asked why I was trying to run away the night of the Alvaro shootings."

"And the answer was?"

"After Roy Davis, the police and I don't have a good relationship. It was kind of instinct too. I heard the sirens and took off."

"Okay. What else?"

"He told me vendors at the co-op reported me talking to Arturo at his booth shortly before he died and that Arturo mentioned we had texted. Big deal. I shopped at their store, and doesn't everyone text? Why is that important?"

"Depends on the content of the conversations and messages, Tommie."

"Nothing threatening was in them. Jace, you can solve the Alvaro homicides." She lifted her chin. Confidence erased the tense lines around her mouth.

The admiration and assurance on her face made him forget every vow he'd sworn about staying away from her. He wished he could pull over, take her hand, and promise to do anything she wanted if she kept eyeing him that way.

Wait. He was losing it, his common sense warned. She wasn't a kid, and he wasn't locating a lost toy for her. Her plan meant catching a person who held no regard for human life. Her scheme was unsound. "Homicide is a category I'm not an expert in. The authorities use their own trained men to investigate."

"I have faith in you."

Her words stirred his longing to prove his parents wrong about his career choice. He imagined the pride in his mother's and father's eyes as he relayed how he'd solved the Alvaro mystery. They'd congratulate him on a faultless job. Something he couldn't recall them ever doing.

He was weakening by the millisecond. "I could check out the persons of interest for you if we can agree to an understanding." How long would she keep her word? She had an act-first, think-later nature. Well, he'd try. "I'll research Arturo's and Gloria's backgrounds and the people surrounding them. In return, you will go straight to work or home. No wandering around in the open, hanging out at beaches, or visiting others for breakfast or any meals."

"Even a ninety-year-old recluse gets bingo." She folded her arms over her chest. "What happens to my amends?"

What if the shooter was on her apology list, and she upset him? All he needed was a ticked-off gunman/woman on their tails.

"How many names have you written down?"

She pursed her lips upward. "My previous boss at the Ocean Shore Grill is one. He hired me, and I disappeared without a word. A few of the servers who had to cover my shifts are on it. My former landlord deserves my regrets for similar reasons. I guess you can understand why my name circulated through the business community as a bad hire. I'm lucky to have gotten a job."

"Why are you doing the amends thing again?" Was she a member of AA or another group?

"I'm improving myself. I can't change my past. Instead, I can show I'm sorry and have changed my ways."

"You're fine as you are, and your apologies are on hold."

She considered him for a second. "What's your rate?"

He was sure nothing she could afford. "One hundred a day, but for you, half price." That was a deal.

"If you accept a delayed monthly payment, we're good." She bit her lip and clasped her hands tightly together.

"We are."

"I've been getting strange phone calls."

"Huh?" He shoved away his surprise. "Tell me the caller's exact words."

"No one spoke."

Her mind was in overdrive. "Those are robocalls."

"No, there's dead air followed by a live human being breathing on the other end. I bet it was Davis trying to freak me out."

"It could be the connection," he said. "Computers call the numbers, multiples at once. Sometimes the telemarketer has to catch up to the automation, and I bet a few lose their breath and concentration."

"So, no chance it was Davis?"

She didn't sound convinced. And it was possible he was calling. She might be right in her assumption. "The law does sweeps in prisons and jails. I admit they have discovered illegal contraband such as banned cell phones in their buildings."

"He's clever. They probably haven't found his. Anyway, whatever the calls are or were, I won't answer them."

"You will join the rest of us in the world of communication. And keep in mind he has restricted use of a phone. Anything else?"

"There were the drive-bys. I thought someone was tailing me yesterday evening, but I was nervous when I got lost and might have imagined it. Though, for the past two weeks, somebody has shadowed me on my way to work. The vehicle stayed three or four car lengths behind and headed in the opposite direction at the Route 1 intersection. The engine or the tailpipe jingles. I hear it coming as I cross the lot to my car in the morning." She hugged her arms tightly to her chest. "I'm on the breakfast shift, and the sun hasn't risen when I leave. The lights in the parking lot are dim. It's spooky."

"The driver could be on his or her way to their job or home. What time?"

"Six fifteen. The motorist acts like he's looking for me. Whoever is driving slows down and creeps by. One day, I waited inside the lobby to see if it went by."

"And?"

"The creep-mobile drove by the inn, turned around, and came back." She shifted toward him, causing Picasso to groan again on her lap. "That's when I was certain I was the target. I've changed my routine and gone out earlier or later, and I haven't heard or seen the car."

In his sleep, Picasso wriggled.

She could be on to something. "Can you provide the model or color of the vehicle?"

She squinted as though searching in the dark. "Blue, I guess. I'm not positive." She heaved a sigh. "I'll do better."

The sadness in her announcement prompted him to reassure her. "This is Florida. I bet it's a senior citizen who has poor eyesight and takes it easy. It could have been a coincidence that you caught them turning around when you glanced out." Or a misunderstanding on Tommie's part. "Any electronic surveillance at the inn?"

"They use the old fake-the-criminal-out trick by hanging cameras in sight. None work. You don't think I should worry?"

"Try to keep your schedule mixed. Park near the building."

She was staring out the front window, probably frustrated.

"Call the police to ask for a step-up in your neighborhood patrol."

"I don't really have a reason or proof of harm to request one, do I?"

"It's worth the try. How long have you owned the dog?" he asked, seeking a harmless topic.

She looked out at her side mirror. "A few hours."

"A stray off the street?" She hadn't stolen him, had she? How well did he know her now?

"Funny, Jackson. He's an orphan—Arturo's dog. I offered him to Thalia. She stated that I should take him to the pound." Tommie grimaced. "Apparently, she's not an animal lover."

He searched his mind for a quick answer. "Maybe Thalia was overwhelmed."

"She told me everyone loved Arturo, but he always attempted to get the highest price, even on worthless items." She patted the sleeping beast. "Now that you and I are a team, we—"

"Hold on. I never said we'd become partners. I investigate. You stay safe." Keeping her from getting hurt was his priority.

"Listen. I have a simple plan for my drive-bys. You can hide in your car near the inn's parking lot and tail my morning pervert to their home or work. Great idea, huh?"

Sounded like a scene from a TV script. "Thomasina, we're in Florida. As I explained, lots of drivers go below the speed limit and drive vehicles that cling or clang. They're older and have slowed down to enjoy life. I can't follow the entire group."

Her brows snapped together. "It's a jingle. I guarantee the driver isn't an innocent retiree."

He wasn't sure if he should believe her or not. This might be where he should start investigating. He could disprove her theory and reassure her at the same time.

The dog whimpered in his sleep and dug his back feet into Jace's hip. He shifted in his seat. The creature was too big. He should sit in the rear.

"Where are we?" Tommie pressed up to the glass. "Hey, there's the Black Alibi bar. Lucas Davis used to be their bartender."

Lucas was the ex-police chief's son, whom she'd tried to involve in a drug scheme, Jace remembered. The story had come out when she testified. An alarm rang loudly in his head. "If Lucas is on your list, forget him. He doesn't need any apologies. The man is doing fine." Better than most people with a father in prison for murder.

"I wish I could forget the problems I caused him." She ran a hand down the dog's furry spine. "Was Lucas your friend?"

"He's older. We share a couple of high school connections."

She remained quiet for two beats before asking, "Are we lost?"

"I have a GPS." He'd no idea where they were. Around them, unkempt yards and houses with plywood covering their windows lined the streets. He turned on his navigational system. The area wasn't the best. And how in the name of sanity would he keep her out of harm's way while he did his job? "You should understand, since I'm one person, I work differently than your local law enforcement. I'll immediately focus on the prime suspects instead of going through all the acquaintances."

"That's practical. Do I sign a contract?"

He almost laughed. "I'll take your word, but I have two conditions. You let me run the investigation, and you must always be open and inform me of every detail of the case. No secrets. If you have a copy of the statement you gave to the police, send it to me."

"I have it on my cell." She grabbed her phone from her pocket and sent him her account of last evening. "Done. I can't thank you enough. You'll find out who did these horrible shootings."

The look of confidence in her beautiful blue eyes convinced him more than any argument could that working for her was the right thing. He wanted to wrap an arm around her. Thread his fingers through—

Stop. What have I gotten myself into? At an intersection, he inhaled a slow, deep breath and steered toward Main Street. No problem. He'd set the boundaries. He was in control and could handle a little attraction or minor flirtation.

Besides, Tommie believed in him wholeheartedly, and he didn't intend to fail her. No matter how much time it took, he would solve the murders. He tossed a peek at her. She stared out the window.

What was she thinking? Was she planning her next step? A bad premonition ate at him. He'd opened himself up to loads of worries. Though, he had one lucky moment. The detective had vanished by the time he drove her back to the beach for her car.

CHAPTER NINE

The next morning, Tommie paused by her car sitting in the Yellow Flamingo's small, softly lit parking lot. The sun was slowly rising in the sky. Armed with her phone's camera, she was set for her drive-by. She tossed her apron inside and slammed the door. As her vehicle sat near the road, she had a clear view of the sparse traffic at dawn. Around her, bugs chirped. Headlights cruising in her direction caught her attention. Unease snaked down her spine.

Don't overreact. Likely, Jace's prediction was true. An elderly person in no hurry was at the wheel. *Yeah, no problem.* The familiar *jingle-jingle* of the car drifted toward her.

Her maybe-stalker was coming. *Get set.* She scurried to her car's trunk and crouched down beside it. She tapped on the camera app. With a steady hand, she lifted her phone in the air and aimed it toward her mark. Her heartbeat picked up and thundered in her ears.

The automobile reduced speed.

Was the driver searching for her? She tried to slow her rapid breathing. *Don't flake out.* She'd get the picture, and it would be of an old geezer on his way to an early-bird breakfast. No big deal.

Was she in a good position? No. This spot wouldn't work for a closeup. She edged to the rear bumper and moved in front of it. A breeze rustled the palms. She clutched her device in her clammy hands. Her finger poised to tap the screen. She focused on the oncoming car's *ping, ping*. Her heart thumped and thumped. Was the dinging car moving slower than usual?

"C'mon." She needed to capture a decent photo. Impatience pushed her to the curb. Almost here. She stepped into the street.

Any second. She tensed.

The jingling car was there.

Now. She held her cell higher.

An auto with tinted windows swerved toward her. The headlights flashed to high and blinded her. She raised her arm upward to block the beam. Instinct warned her to flee. She stayed rooted to the ground. Sweat burned her eyes. Blindly, she clicked random shots.

A horn blasted and drowned out the jingling.

The vehicle veered back into its lane and passed her by inches.

Tommie stood, shaking, her teeth chattering.

Another car cut into the lot and stopped a few feet from her.

CHAPTER TEN

Before Tommie could recover, Jace jumped out of the car, blocking her way.

Her racing adrenaline collided with relief and disbelief. "What are you doing here?"

"Me? Why were you standing in the street? That car almost ran you down."

She looked at the red taillights of her drive-by vanishing into the morning twilight. She swallowed twice. Her thoughts refused to cooperate. "You came because—"

"You mentioned your shift yesterday. I decided to offer you a ride. I never guessed you secretly had a wish to become roadkill." As he searched her features, the tightness in his face eased. "Are you okay?"

"I'm fine." She became aware she was lingering at the lot's edge, clutching her phone. She slid it into her pocket. Defense mode seemed like the way to go. "You could have sent me a text saying you were coming," she grumbled. "You nearly gave me a stroke when you swerved into the lot."

"Think of how I felt when I turned down your road and

discovered you in it." He rubbed the back of his neck. "You were trying to take a picture of the jingle car."

She wanted to argue, but in that instant, she was too relieved to have him there. "You know me too well." She gripped her hands together to hide their trembling. "I was certain a snapshot would give you the information you needed. Getting a photo of a moving target at dawn was harder than I thought."

"You put yourself in a perilous situation." He crossed his arms over his chest.

She didn't bother to remind him the driver had missed her. Although he did have a point, she wasn't in the mood to admit he was right. "Let's talk later. I need to get to my job."

He stepped up to her. "You scared me to death when I saw that car headed straight for you."

His quiet, caring gaze skimmed over her. A different knot of tension formed in her chest. He was a foot from her. She zeroed in on his mouth. Her heart emitted a soft thud.

He placed a hand on his hip. "Do you have anything else to say?"

Huh? He'd come to make sure she was safe, not lock lips. He might have a girlfriend. Off-balance, she gaped at the ground, uncertain for a split second how to answer. They weren't off to the best start today.

He lightly brushed away a stray strand of her hair on her cheek.

A little electric thrill swept through Tommie. What was that? Shocked, she stared at him, unable to look away.

"When do you get off your shift?" he murmured.

"After the lunch crowd," she mumbled, unsure what was happening. Adrenaline overflow, relief, and this attraction to him were all mixed up. Was she misunderstanding his intentions again?

"I'll treat you to a meal. We'll go to a spot you love."

Was this a bribe to get her to stop interfering? She studied him. His green eyes were glued to her with an intensity that set her nerve ends dancing. “Perfect.”

“When should I pick you up?”

He probably was saving the rest of the lectures for the restaurant, but he didn’t appear angry any longer. He was himself, tall, good-looking, and smart, and he smelled of fresh soap and just Jace. “I finish up at two.” Her heart did a small jig in her chest.

The squeak and squeal of a truck rumbling down the street pulled their attention to the road and back to each other.

His expression sobered. He stepped away.

The intimate second was over—if it was one. A twinge of disappointment silenced her.

He didn’t suffer the same problem. “From now on, I’ll drive you to and from work until we’re both certain it’s safe.”

“You think the driver was a stalker?” She’d liked it better when he’d doubted her suspicions about the passing car. “The jingle-mobile was going super slow before he or she realized I was using my camera.”

“I honestly don’t have the answer. Let’s discourage your morning admirer while we assess the situation.”

She wasn’t sure what that totally meant, but she wasn’t going to argue. “I’ll have to come home before we eat. The dog will need to go out.”

“I’ll take care of Picasso.” He spoke in his unruffled, direct way. “If you’ll loan me your room key, we’ll be set.”

“I have an extra that was for my mom. She never took it.” Tommie dug the key out of the purse she’d slung across her shoulder and passed the plastic card to him. How could she refuse food or a ride with Jace?

“I have to get my apron out of my front seat.” She hurried to grab it. Once she unlocked the car door, she leaned inside. Her phone poked into her thigh, reminding her to check out the snapshots she'd taken. *Please, let me have one clear shot.*

Tommie fished out her cell and tapped the photos app. There! She stared down at the blurs of black. She'd gotten zip. Well, she couldn't brag about her detective skills. She held back a groan of defeat. Disheartened, she scooped up her bib. For now, Jace was the investigator.

A steady rush of regulars made the hours fly at the Whale's Spout. Jace showed up on time for pickup. He refused to tell her the name of their destination, but she guessed it from the route along the shoreline and over the bridge into Micco. He was taking her to her favorite indoor/outdoor bar and grill. The gravel crunched under his tires as he pulled up to the restaurant.

"This is one of my preferred places to eat, Jace, and I haven't been here in forever. Nothing has changed."

The eatery was nestled in a marina. Tall tables sat next to the piers where fishermen and the locals docked to eat. A roof covered the open dining room and the bar facing the Sebastian River. Boaters and anglers could tie up and enjoy food and drinks before sailing off to parts unknown.

Jace chose a high table near a slip. The surrounding seats were empty. Nearby, an anchored sloop bobbed in the soothing rhythm of the lapping water. A tangerine-colored umbrella protected them from the sun while a gentle wind fluttered its flaps.

They sat beside each other on concrete stools. Did the rest of the customers think they were a couple? She peeked at him. His tan T-shirt stretched across his broad shoulders. Did he go to the gym, or was he blessed with a great body?

What was she thinking? She lowered her eyes and studied the menu. When they were younger, he'd been her best friend. Reliable, supportive, but she wasn't his type. They were too different.

The woman who fit the adult Jace would be a popular, respected member of the community. She'd hold a stressful, well-paying job, and easily juggle family and work responsibilities. They'd be equal partners as parents. None of those descriptions fit Tommie.

Didn't matter. She had enough to mull over without an imaginary, starry-eyed relationship. Besides, she didn't know if he was dating anyone. She frowned.

The delicious aromas of fries and onions cooking on the grill wafted through the air. Maybe she could keep the discussion casual for a while. She set her menu down. "Picasso was fine when you stopped in?"

"He did his thing outside and settled on the sofa to watch an episode of *Take My Cat, Please.*"

"Terrific. I knew he'd love you."

"Don't exaggerate. He's no problem. Up to now."

The waiter arrived with glasses of water and took their orders. Tommie sensed Jace was delaying until the server left to talk.

"Thomasina. I've been reviewing your statement to the police. A few things puzzled me." He grabbed a pen and a three-by-five flip notebook from his shorts pocket and laid them on the mat.

This was why he'd brought her to lunch. He was going to quiz her. She drank stalling sips of her drink, hoping to wash away the rising stress.

"Let's begin with Arturo Alvaro and the shootings."

Her breath tightened in her chest. Repeating her story was painful.

"I'm not sure if I have the complete picture. Did you see anyone or anything around Arturo's home when you drove up?"

Her glass thudded against the table as she put it down. She told him about the eerie cries she'd assumed were made by a panther and how she'd run to Arturo's house. As she spoke, she saw herself hurrying across the yard, terrified, and glancing over her shoulder for yellow, peering eyes between the trees.

"You reported that the door was unlocked, and you went in? Was the house tossed or look searched?"

"You are correct about how I entered. Apart from the lanai door being open, nothing else seemed out of place. The room I was in was not a mess." Chilled, she couldn't stop rubbing her arms until she rested her hands on either side of the silverware.

"You said the dog greeted you?"

"Right, I followed him through the hall to the study." Her head began to throb as she briefly described discovering the murder scene. "And when I ran out, Picasso tailed me and jumped in my car."

"And that's when the person ran into your path. When you stopped, and he or she disappeared into the woods."

"As I explained, I can't give you much description on that individual. I was totally in escape mode."

"Let's back up, Tommie. Did you research Arturo online before accepting his invite? He had at least two arrests, stemming from goods he sold. Both cases were settled between the parties. Did you know about these?"

Here was a question she'd dreaded. *Stick to the truth, most of it.* Her clammy hands stuck to the placemat. She rested them in her lap. "I read about him and the allegations. Before I could bring them up, Arturo confessed."

"What did he say?"

"Two elderly customers felt he had overcharged and lied about the age and worth of their purchases. Arturo explained to the buyers that some antiques can't be authenticated, and he had used his best judgment. He returned their money."

Jace tapped his pen on the notebook. "In your statement, you informed the police that Arturo had relayed to you that Gloria believed her ex-husband, Rex, bought a longboard years ago. He'd dug it out to show off to a young woman. Do you have her name?"

The pull on her neck eased. "I couldn't forget it. Arturo said it was Peaches Galore, and Rex wanted to impress her. He told me Gloria called her one of her ex's bimbettes."

"I'll check her out. Why did you like Arturo?"

Was he hinting at something? "We weren't dating."

He sat staring at her. He hadn't scrawled a word. "Arturo seemed genuine to you?"

She shifted her feet, unable to get comfortable. She repeated what she'd reported to the cops when they'd asked about their relationship. "Arturo was kind and friendly. He had a huge smile. He was happy and enthusiastic, and his interests were his yard-sale treasures and sailing his boat. Both sounded fun and different."

We'll sail out into the blue ocean and watch the dolphins play in the surf, Arturo murmured in her mind.

She shoved away the recollection. Was Jace going to nitpick her story forever?

"You stated Gloria wasn't expected for dinner."

"He didn't mention that she'd join us." A memory niggled at her. "The dining table where the sergeant and detective interviewed me was set for two, not three."

He raised a brow. "Maybe the shooter found her there and shot her because she was a witness. I'll keep that as a possibility."

"Poor Gloria." Tommie managed to swallow.

"If she made an unplanned stop, it was awful timing on her part." Jace leaned forward. "You haven't changed your opinion about the longboard's value?"

She shrugged. "I doubted Gloria would get much for it. I would have told her to get other estimates if she disliked mine.

Though I was, like, ninety-nine percent positive, it would resell for around two to three hundred. Someone might have felt that was a lot."

Jace clicked his pen while wrinkling his brow in thought. "Hmm. Sketch what you saw of the house."

"I'll do better." She grabbed her phone, glad to have his focus on her cell. "I discovered it posted on a real estate web page. The former Realtor didn't remove her listing." She scrolled to the site and pulled up the images. "Ta-da." She held up the screen to him.

Jace studied the photos of the drive, the garage, and the room layout. "The killer could have used the pool entrance because those locks are easier to break if needed. The preserve grew thick around the residence, providing less chance of being spotted."

Her water glass was empty. Her mouth was sandy-beach dry. She scanned the dining area for signs of their waiter. Jace flicked through the pictures of the home.

The quiet chewed on her nerves. "I can't believe anyone would kill for the surfboard. They could have bought it from Gloria."

"You have a point, Tommie." He returned her cell.

"I've been rethinking every conversation Arturo and I had before his death. I keep looking for clues or motives."

"Find any?" Jace nodded for her to continue.

"Arturo once had a business partner, Alfredo Russo. He sells at a local church yard sale and rents a booth at the farmers' flea market off I-95."

"The huge building and parking lot off the highway that's advertised on the cable channel ten times a day? Kind of tough to miss." He raised his palms in the air. "Go ahead."

"Well, Arturo alleged that Alfredo stole a painting from him. It was never proved. The accusation ended their partnership.

Gloria dated Alfredo briefly after her marriage dissolved. He's a suspect, right?"

"I'll need all the alibis." Jace paused as customers walked past them to seats at the bar.

Tommie continued the conversation. "Thalia said she was with Rex, Gloria's ex, at her salon on the night of the shootings. They'll cover for each other."

"Convenient. I'll try to learn who inherits or benefits from Gloria's or Arturo's deaths if it's not a bank or mortgage company."

"I'd guess Thalia." She imagined Thalia with her perfect silver hair, holding a weapon. Creepy. "You think it's as simple as following the money?"

"Usually, it is." He released a deep breath. "Capital is a huge motivator. Thalia could have followed Gloria to Arturo's and gotten rid of them both at the same time."

Tommie wrinkled her nose over the thought. "Except she looks like she'd become upset over a broken nail. I can't picture her sneaking around and firing a gun at her sister or cousin."

"Maybe Rex and Thalia planned the murders together to get rid of both of their problems. He did the actual deed."

"You've got it." She sat up straight. "Rex shot Gloria because she was their main competition, and he'd had enough of his ex. After shooting her, he killed Arturo, who had clearly sided with Gloria in the divorce."

Jace nodded. "It's possible he had been shadowing Gloria or somehow found out where she'd be that evening. Either way, he also stays high on our list."

Tommie's confidence grew. "Admit it, Jace. I get the facts. I could be a private investigator's assistant."

He sat back, his expression stern. "Thomasina, I'm the PI. I do the work. You've got plenty going on in your life."

She opened her mouth to protest and stopped. He was the

expert and had accepted her delayed payments. She shouldn't push it. Besides, he knew techniques she didn't. Her assurance dwindled. "That's true. I'm grateful you took my case."

The server arrived with their meals. The aroma of his fries drifted to her. Did they taste as good as they looked? Her salad appeared fresh and crispy. The waiter asked if he could get them anything else and left when Jace told him they had everything.

Another subject whirled in Tommie's brain. "Can I ask you something personal?"

"Should I brace myself?"

"Possibly." She plunged onward, not waiting for his answer. "Does your girlfriend mind you lunching with other women? Have I ever met her?"

He blinked and lifted the top of his bun and studied his meat.

"Her name was Alicia, and we broke up."

Hmm. Tommie imagined her in bright-colored dresses that matched her moods, typing up her notes in legalese with her French-manicured fingers flying over the keys. "Did she work for you?"

"No." He scooped up his burger. "She was a paralegal."

Encouraged by his answers, Tommie asked, "Did you go out for long?"

"Almost a year." He bit into his food.

They must have been serious. She shifted her feet restlessly under the table and tried not to ask. Finally, she surrendered to her curiosity. "What happened to her?"

"We got along when I had to take jobs out of the area. Oddly, she cheated with a friend of mine during a rough patch in the business while I hung around at home." Jace's mouth turned down.

Talking about her made him sad. He'd been involved with her. "She didn't deserve you," Tommie blurted, her irritation rising. "You're better off without her."

"It wasn't all her fault. Alicia needed more attention than I could give her." He looked over at a waitress, avoiding Tommie's stare. "The problem was I couldn't become what she wanted. The nine-to-five guy. That's never going to be me. The breakup was mutual. How's your social life?" He locked onto her gaze.

"No one since my last sweetheart went to prison, and yes, I'm being sarcastic about Roy Davis. Many have wrongly ID'd me as his girlfriend. I was not. I can't emphasize that enough." She folded and unfolded the corner of the placemat.

Their phones buzzed at the same time. They grabbed each of them from their pockets.

Tommie read her screen first. "Gigi sent me a message."

"Me too." He nodded. "She found something online that I should see right away."

"Isn't today her poker day?" Tommie tapped the link attachment.

"Gigi's friends should be at her house now. Maybe she learned a tidbit or two from them." He scrolled down his phone and read aloud, "A memorial for Arturo Alvaro and Gloria Alvaro will be held at the Reese Center tomorrow at seven p.m. All are invited to share memories of these loving people who left us too soon."

"The place is out by the fairgrounds." Tommie's interest perked up. "Did you tell Gigi you were working for me?"

Jace looked at his screen. "I might have mentioned I was helping you. Interesting, Alfred Russo is listed at the bottom of the announcement as holding the ceremony."

"Why would he host Arturo's service when they'd split over a stolen art piece?"

"Mr. Russo is probably trying to clean up his image. He could think that organizing a celebration of Arturo's life makes him appear less suspicious to the cops."

She laid her cell down. "I'm glad I own a decent black dress I can wear to pay my respects."

Jace drummed his fingers on the edge of the table. "We'll go together. I'll drive. We'll take in the crowd."

"I'm your cover." She'd be acting like an assistant or a partner. She could do that.

"We're respectful but otherwise quiet," he cautioned.

"Of course." A room full of suspects. The memorial could provide her a chance to prove she could assist Jace in solving the case.

CHAPTER ELEVEN

Tonight was Arturo's and Gloria's memorial. Tommie was looking forward to observing the mourners. Could she or Jace pinpoint the shooter by a guilty expression or speech? She'd find out soon. The quicker they made an arrest, the faster she could get on with her life.

The lampposts lighted Tommie's way when she dashed out to the inn's lot. Her purse strung over the shoulder of her black dress thumped against her side. The fine mist falling from the sky was better than a shower. If only the spray would wash away the clutter in her mind and remind her where she'd left her gold hair clip. It had to be in her car, which hadn't budged since Jace had begun driving her to work every day.

She trotted to her parking spot near the street. Something white was on the driver's window, anchored by the wiper. What was that? An ad? She stopped by her vehicle. The rain had plastered the eight-by-eleven sheet to the glass. Must be about a sale.

Barrette first. Cautiously, she peered inside—nobody was there. Nothing had changed. She unlocked the hatchback's door and slid into the seat. She ran her hand around the floor mats. Bingo, she discovered the metal accessory by her feet. She scooped up the clasp and straightened. The paper on her windshield was in her line of vision. She pressed up to the steering wheel and read the words blurred by the drizzle.

Tommie Murphy is coming down,
Coming down, coming down.
Tommie Murphy is coming down,
My dead lady.
Set yourself to watch all night,
Watch all night, watch all night,
Set yourself to watch all night,
My dead lady.
Suppose that you should fall asleep,
Fall asleep, fall asleep,
Suppose that you should fall asleep?
BANG! My dead lady.

She recoiled against the seat, blinking her eyes in shock. A small chill at the back of her neck turned to ice. Who would leave her such a sick rhyme? Did anyone else have a scary poem on the windshield? She checked the lot. Nobody had anything.

Jace's navy vehicle pulled into the inn.

She dashed out, slammed the door, and met him as he pocketed his keys in his black cargo pants.

She opened her mouth and allowed her fears to tumble out. "I found a threatening letter on my car's window. Come look." She whirled around.

Jace tagged at her heels to her auto. She pointed to the soggy sheet.

He laid a hand on her arm. "When did you discover it?"

"A minute ago." She shoved at her hair several times and repeated the last verse for him.

"Hey, you're okay." He gave her elbow a reassuring squeeze.

His lips tightened, and he glanced at her wet note. "I bet the paper will dissolve if I touch it. Someone must have put it there hours ago. Has the inn replaced the nonworking cameras?"

"Still no recordings." Tears threatened to run down her cheeks. She couldn't blubber. Jace wouldn't think much of a woman who cried over a silly rhyme. She fished out her phone and ducked inside her front seat. She snapped a shot of the message before bowing out.

"My turn." He switched places with her and read the ditty.

She wished he'd hurry. Maybe the poem's author was watching now. Fear flooded through her and transformed the warm evening into a cold one. She scanned the inn's windows, but nothing peered out at her.

He straightened. "I'll drive you to the station to report the threat."

What was the point? "We can't get fingerprints, can we?"

"I'd guess it would be a miracle, but I'd feel better."

"Forget it. We're going to the memorial." First, she was getting rid of the disgusting piece of garbage. She scooted her fingers under the wet parchment, lifting it. The sheet came off in sections. Her heart hammered, but she could do this.

He retrieved an empty plastic shopping bag from his auto and held the sack while she shook the clingy blobs into it. "I recommend you give the warning to the police. It might help later if somebody is arrested for stalking you." He knotted the top of the bag.

"I'll consider it." If only she could bleach her hands.

"I'll talk to the desk clerk. Send me the photo of the note and I'll show him. He'll want proof. Have you seen anyone hanging out in the lobby, on your floor, or near the inn?"

"No one." She attached the photo and hit send. "The lovely letter is in your box."

"Perfect. Are you sure you want to go and listen to them

speak about Arturo and Gloria? I promise to report everything I learn. You can stay here and rest."

"That's silly. Whoever left this might attend the Alvaro gathering. I'm walking into the ceremony like nothing happened. Let's see who keeps staring at me, hoping they'll frighten me." She raised her shoulders and her chin, daring him to contradict her.

"Remember, Tommie. You're a mourner and, in many ways, a victim. You don't need to storm the building. And I'm the investigator."

"I'll just observe our suspects." *Hang on to the anger,* she told herself. The emotion kept her determined and less afraid.

"I'll store the soggy paper in my car in case you change your mind about turning it over to the police. Now, let me do my job."

"And I'll scrub my hands." All she wanted was to find the lowlife who was trying to scare her to death. If she was lucky, that person would be at the memorial, pretending to mourn. She'd show them she couldn't be scared away.

At the entryway to the inn, she paused. "Don't take long, Jace." *There's a killer to catch.*

CHAPTER TWELVE

Humidity surged around Jace and Tommie as they entered the Reese Center for the memorial. Ceiling fans and air conditioners whirred and hummed in the domed, steel building, about half the size of a hockey rink. Cool air rolled off Jace's arms in his short-sleeved, white shirt. Tommie walked with a firm step, projecting a confidence he doubted she felt.

She led the way to the metal chairs, which were set up in rows. The seats stretched from the front to the back doors. Their footsteps thumped on the concrete floor. Blown-up pictures of Arturo and Gloria rested on easels set up on the makeshift platform. Despite the fact they'd arrived seventeen minutes late, the ceremony hadn't begun.

Before they'd left the inn, Jace had checked in with the clerk and had shown him the poem. The clerk responded that it was sad, but a lot of people had a warped sense of humor. Not much help there. He did offer to try to look out at Tommie's car more often. Jace had turned to the few residents willing to talk. All had claimed they'd not seen or heard of anyone lingering in the lot.

He'd encouraged them to be on guard and report anything suspicious.

Inside, Jace gestured to the rear seats. They provided the best view of all the guests, and yet, far enough away that they could speak to each other without being overheard. He needed a break in the investigation. Here, he hoped to learn something. Sometimes in moments of raw emotions or overconfidence, a mourner had revealed a secret. However, a shrewd, coldhearted criminal could often mislead others.

"Not many attendees," she noted once they'd settled. "The bereaved clustered up near the risers."

He glanced at his watch. "Apparently, Alfredo Russo isn't worried about promptness."

Five women in the third row sniffled and blew their noses in between whispering to one another. A couple of them turned to peek at Tommie and Jace. "Gloria's Beauty Cuts" was embroidered on their chambray shirts. Tommie whispered to him, "There's Thalia in the first row."

Jace fixed his gaze on Gloria's sister. She sat ramrod straight except to toss a scowl over her shoulder at two crying women. A posse of ladies sat beside Ms. Alvaro. They had to be her support group and were mimicking Thalia's stance.

"She's holding up," he said, failing to find a word to define her.

"She seems angry her sister's friends are grieving."

"She's definitely not weeping." He'd label her behavior as different.

A petite blonde in her twenties swayed down the walkway, grabbing his attention. She carried a tissue pressed to her mouth. Her outfit, a slinky, sparkly, black dress and super-high heels, seemed appropriate for an evening of dining and dancing, not mourning. Over her garb, she sported an open jean jacket with sparkles.

"Who do you think she is?" Tommie edged forward in her seat, studying the passing woman.

"She's Peaches Galore. During my computer searches, I found the employees' pictures on Thalia's salon's website. She appears to be with Gloria's ex-husband."

Tommie nudged him. "Ah, she's the one Rex wanted to impress with the longboard."

Jace focused on the man trailing Peaches. He had a ponytail and was dressed in a gray, flowered-print shirt and slate-colored shorts.

The pair continued past the grievers and climbed to the platform. He paused at the edge. Peaches strolled onward. Her shoes clicked against the floor as she traipsed to the blown-up image of Arturo set on an easel. She stared at the picture, displaying a perfect view of the rainbow on the back of her jacket. She positioned her palm on the frame, leaned in, and kissed his lips. Jace straightened in his chair. How close had Peaches and Arturo been?

"Is that normal at a tribute?" Tommie asked, her eyes wide.

"Maybe she does that at all the memorials."

"If she does, it must be hard on surviving spouses and significant others." Tommie wrinkled her nose.

The willowy female had grabbed the scrutiny of the room. "She has a unique sense of style for the occasion." Despite wearing too much eye makeup for his taste, she was attractive.

Peaches passed Gloria's blown-up image. She hesitated and wheeled around on her heel. She reached out and briefly touched Gloria's cheek.

"Ouch." Jace winced. "Her pause by Gloria looked like an afterthought."

Tommie nudged him, breaking his fixation on the blonde. "Did you learn anything important about Peaches in your computer searches?"

"Nothing remarkable shows up in her history—no record of marriages or troubles with the law. Parents reside in Ocala. On social media, she posted about evenings at expensive restaurants or gifts she received from her revolving male friends. Most of them looked like they were at the retirement age. She relocated here three months ago, after hopping around the state. Salons and spas seemed to be her source of employment. She lives in a cheap apartment and drives an inexpensive car. She shared pictures of Arturo and herself on his sailboat or out to dinner at five-star establishments. I'd say she gravitates to seniors who don't mind spending their hard-earned savings on her."

"You're probably too young for her," Tommie added with a wink.

"I'm sure I am. Arturo fit the dating profile of her men. Online, she wrote he was sweet to her. According to her social account, at the time of the shooting, she was cruising the mall. Something tells me Ms. Galore is high-maintenance. Nothing in her public comments hinted if Arturo dumped or cheated on her." He watched her and Rex leaving the risers. "She's definitely worth a deeper look."

"Maybe." Tommie sounded unconvinced. "If she's guilty, I hope the police arrest her quickly before Grey hauls me in for a cross-examination. I wish the crime was solved yesterday."

Up front, Thalia was staring at her ex-partner gliding by her with a young woman. At the last second, Rex nodded to her.

Peaches and Rex seemed cozy, Jace observed. Were either of them the shooter? Had he or she left the message on Tommie's windshield?

"Arturo would have preferred a fancier establishment," Tommie interjected. "There aren't any flowers on the stage. I should have sent a bouquet. This was too rushed."

"Exactly." Jace raised his chin and indicated three middle-aged ladies marching down the main aisle. The trio wore different-colored blouses. Each woman's hair matched the shade of her shirt. The threesome walked to the third row from Tommie and Jace where a brown-haired, thin lady wearing overly large black glasses sat. Two of the women accidentally knocked the chairs together. *Clank, clank* echoed in the complex as they scooted past the first seats.

"Seems to be mostly Thalia's and Gloria's employees. I recognize them from their work pictures," Jace commented. "Staff are usually a great source for gossip." Which one was talking the most and a likely informant? He'd keep an eye on them.

An average-height man, near forty, approached the podium, drawing Jace's attention to the front of the room. The gentleman had sparse, graying hair and his mustache spiraled up into handlebars at the ends. He tapped on the microphone. *Thwack, thwack* thumped from the speakers on the walls.

He bent toward the mic. "Good day and thank you for joining us. I'm Alfredo Russo. Arturo and I were business partners for several years. We were two independent and stubborn men, who didn't always agree on how things should run. We learned to settle our differences over mugs of beer and worked cooperatively. But life threw us a curve. Sales went down. We agreed to go our separate ways and live peacefully apart."

Was the man telling them he didn't hold a grudge and hadn't killed his old partner? How truthful was he? Jace had doubts.

"I can't help but think if we'd still been working together, Arturo would have been with me and the other flea market vendors ordering supper at the Barn Grill. Instead, he was in his home with a shooter."

Jace shifted to Tommie. "Guess he's announcing his alibi."

"Today," Alfredo continued, "I wish to honor Arturo and his cousin Gloria, who he loved like a sister." Alfredo gestured at their pictures. "It's no secret Arturo could charm any female and a few males too. He was also a smart and talented antique dealer."

The women in the rainbow blouses exchanged nods.

"He taught me a lot, especially in the field of—" Alfredo squinted as though facing a loss for words. "Let's call it customer relationships." He hesitated and let his statement sink in for a few seconds. "The family was friendly. If you met one Alvaro, you'd meet all three. Gloria was Arturo's equal when it came to finances. She was savvy and kept the ladies coming back. Many admired her. She built her shop up from the ground floor."

The sound of crying in the audience threatened to drown out his words.

He leaned into the mic. "I will miss them, as I'm sure everyone here will. And when we're upset or stressed, it helps to speak about it. That's why I invite you to share a story or two about Arturo and Gloria with the gathering." Alfredo stepped aside.

Jace watched the reactions of the mourners. Thalia straightened in her chair. Peaches flashed a grin at Rex. Would either be willing to talk and mention their suspicions about the killings? Had one of these people harbored a private need or yearning to harm the cousins?

"I'll come up." Peaches stood and dashed forward with an unsteady gait, teetering on her spiked shoes as she rushed up the steps. At the podium, she lowered the microphone. "Hi."

Surprise hit Jace. Her squeaky voice seemed a better fit for a cartoon mouse.

"I'm Peaches Galore. I remember the day I met Arturo at Gloria's salon."

"This should be interesting," he whispered to Tommie.

"He'd dropped by to say hello to his cousin." Peaches sighed into the mic. "He was crossing the floor when he saw me escorting my client to my space. I was nervous since it was my first day. Arturo stopped me, and we introduced ourselves. He shook my hand and held it. He said, 'You have the softest skin. The customers are lucky to enjoy your gentle touch.'"

She blinked several times. "Excuse me." She blotted her nose with her tissue before resuming her speech. "That day, when I was edgy and tense, Arturo made me feel special and confident." Peaches managed a brief smile. "He was always helping others." Her voice was low, solemn, and sad.

Maybe he was helping himself, Jace thought.

Peaches persisted with her memories. "He spoke to me whenever he visited Gloria's shop. He was a kind soul. I miss him." She faced his likeness. "May you find goodwill and harmony in your afterlife. I hope you didn't suffer." Her lower lip quivered, and she stepped away from the lectern and wobbled down the stairs.

Jace shifted toward Tommie while keeping his gaze on the small gathering. "Quite the tribute to our deceased. Who will match it?"

"She didn't say much about Gloria," Tommie murmured.

"Noted."

The women seated with Thalia followed Peaches up to the podium. They took turns praising the cousins and wishing them peace in the hereafter. One kidded that Gloria was setting up a beauty business in heaven with her clients who had passed on.

During the eulogies, Rex slipped his arm over Peaches's shoulders and patted the top of her arm. She sank against him.

Jace and Tommie exchanged looks with raised brows.

Alfredo returned to the mic. "We can squeeze in one more person."

"Me." Thalia's exasperated shout carried through the building. She stomped to the dais in a determined, hurried gait. At the steps, she firmly placed each foot in front of the other, revealing dark stockings under her knee-length black skirt.

Alfredo attempted to adjust the microphone for the short woman. She waved him aside and fixed the mic. He retreated, shrugging.

"I'm Thalia Alvaro, Gloria's sister and Arturo's cousin. I'm not going to rehash our relationships. I'm here to remind you that two human beings were murdered."

A buzz went up from the crowd. People squirmed in their seats. If a member of the crowd hadn't known how the two died, they did now.

"I'm offering $2,000 to whoever provides information leading to the arrest of the murderer." She ended with a shout. "The contact info is posted on a web page named Justice for the Alvaro Family. Donations to raise the reward amount will be accepted."

The scuff of chair legs scraping across the concrete floor distracted Jace. He glanced over his shoulder. A broad-chested, giant man in an onyx-colored shirt and pants settled onto a seat and scooted it out into the aisle.

"Detective Grey." Tommie's distressed mutter whispered in his ear.

Jace glimpsed the investigator. Was he tailing Tommie? Would he try to detain her again?

Beside him, Tommie sat with her gaze on the stage. Thalia was repeating the tip phone number.

As she stamped off, Alfredo dashed in and grabbed the mic. "Thank you for coming. We must be out earlier than I planned. There's a rock show scheduled for this space in a half hour. Their crew needs to get in the room. Everyone is invited to grab a coffee and a doughnut from the table on the side. Please enjoy the refreshments outside or take them with you. Don't forget, I'll be selling at the church flea market on US 1 next weekend. Stop by."

Tommie slid a glower at the detective before speaking to Jace. “I’m not hungry. Are you?”

“No. Let’s hit the road.” They stood and proceeded down the row to the main walkway.

“Did anyone strike you as suspicious or as someone who’d leave notes on windshields?” she asked.

Unfortunately, they all did. Telling her this now seemed like a bad idea. He rubbed his jaw. He turned and spotted Peaches standing alone in front of the pictures of the deceased.

“I’ll be right back.” He walked up to the blonde. “I was touched by your words. I’m Jace Jackson.”

“Lovely to meet you,” she said in her high-pitched way.

“I can tell you and Arturo were great friends. Have you heard if the police have pinpointed a suspect?”

“The cops told me little, but they asked me lots.” Peaches inhaled a deep breath before explaining. “‘Where were you?’ I was at work and then at the mall. ‘Did you have any arguments with the victims?’ I didn’t. I loved Arturo. He was my first and best friend here.” She brushed her palm across her eyes. “The cops didn’t ask much about Gloria. She and I had our little disagreements, like which brand of shampoo to order, but she was my boss. Truthfully, I never gave her a lot of thought.”

“Of course not. You had a life to live. Did you know they’d been shot?”

“Rex told me and the staff. He’s good at getting to the bottom of stuff. He made sure the autopsy was done in twenty-four hours. And I’m happy you understand about Gloria. When she died, I wasn’t sad, but no way would I want her to die.” She swept her gaze around the room. “Rex is motioning me to the food table. Are you getting a snack?”

“I’m not, but who do you think shot the cousins?”

“Gosh, who would do something that awful? I mean murder?” She gulped and shook her head.

"At least, Thalia was holding up well."

"Her business is the most important thing to her. She has nothing else. I don't believe she ever married. I'm not sure if she dated." Peaches glanced over Jace's shoulder. "I better go. Rex is pacing. I hope to see you again." She paused, waiting for his answer.

"Me too. Take care." Jace caught up with Tommie. He took her arm, guiding her toward the exit.

"Learn anything?" She slowed to a stop.

Quickly, he informed her of his conversation with Peaches and included his opinion. "Thalia and Rex stand out when we consider motives and opportunity. That assumes Peaches was genuine. My computer search revealed Thalia had one brief marriage after high school. Her name is the lone one on the salon loan."

He became aware of Grey loitering near their heels. Under his hand, Tommie's arm grew rigid.

The detective cut in front of them. "Nice of you to come, Tommie. Did you drive? When we met before, you left your car at Turtle Beach."

"I don't have to speak to you."

"Hey, we're old friends."

"Go torture another innocent person." She pressed her lips together and strode past him.

Jace followed, conscious that Grey hovered behind them. When they reached the door, Jace opened it and set the kick stopper. He motioned for Tommie to go first. She walked outside.

Grey pushed ahead of him and spun toward him. "You're Jace Jackson, aren't you? You picked Tommie up in the parking lot." The detective lingered less than a foot from Jace. "Are you driving her today too?"

Struggling not to show his annoyance, he stepped back to see over the towering man. He spotted Tommie outdoors. She looked safe, but he didn't feel comfortable with her outside alone after that poem.

Meanwhile, Grey was looking him up and down. His tongue almost hung out of his mouth. Was he expecting a confession?

"I don't remember being introduced," Jace said, keeping his tone cold.

"I make it a habit to find out who Tommie is with these days. You're a private investigator—or are you a chauffeur? I'm confused." The detective smirked.

He wouldn't let the man goad him. "I'm a man of multiple talents."

"Good of you to bring her to the memorial."

Jace watched the slim, brown-haired woman with the oversized glasses approach Tommie. He gave his attention back to the hulking man. "Do you have a point, Detective, or are you wasting time and taxpayers' money trying to intimidate law-abiding people? Don't you have a handler somewhere to keep you on a leash?"

"You're the one I'm concerned about. I bet there are a few things you don't know about Miss Murphy."

"Something in particular?" Jace challenged, ready to deny anything negative. Obviously, the man hoped to turn him against her.

"She has a pattern of hooking up with men who have run-ins with the law."

"What was Arturo Alvaro's crime?" he asked, ignoring his attempts to smear Tommie. "And with all the collectibles in his home, maybe it was a robbery gone wrong."

"We've accounted for the house's contents, but I always keep an open mind and look at all the angles. Take today. At this ceremony, our victim appeared saintly," the detective sneered. "Turns my stomach. Recently, he was under investigation for fraud. Those treasures he sold for big bucks were mainly garbage."

Jace shrugged. "Reminds me of the old saying. 'One man's trash is another man's treasure.' What is your interest in Miss Murphy?"

Grey's posture stiffened. "I don't think you'd appreciate over-paying for his junk. And I'm checking that Tommie sticks around. She was discovered at a scene with two bodies and claimed she was a buddy of one of the victims. He's dead and she's alive. Who else should I talk to?"

"Friendship doesn't give her a motive to murder."

"Let me fill you in on the antiques dealer. He also has been investigated for helping women he met online empty their bank accounts into his. In his past, he's gone by many names. You're a PI. Look him up. Pinkerton was one of his favorite aliases."

"Who pressed charges?"

Grey kicked a cigarette butt near his feet. "He's been tough to prosecute. A lot of the ladies believed in an old song, 'Stand by Your Man.' Others wanted it kept quiet that he'd used and fooled them. The cases lost speed. The guy was like Teflon. He would slip away without leaving a forwarding address. However, an out-of-town detective, who knew we were looking for him, traced him and alerted us."

"You were going to take him into custody?"

"We dug up a local victim willing to speak against him. Unfortunately, she suffered a fatal heart attack before we could bring him to court."

"You had a string of bad luck, Detective, not to mention the women he dated. Who do you think killed him?"

"Working on it. Despite taking his dates' money, Arturo died penniless. He loved to spend while his victims struggled to survive." Grey scratched his cheek. "What are you doing on a homicide, anyway? This isn't your kind of gig. You must be hard up if you're hoping to come up with a divorce case by hanging around with salon groupies. You inherited the business from your grandfather, right? You just slid into the job."

Was he hinting that Jace was a slacker?

"Jace?" Tommie stood in the open doorway.

He shoved aside his retort to the detective and signaled he'd be there in a second. As he turned away, he noticed a small cluster gathered around the snack table, watching him and Grey.

Jace pushed into the detective's personal space and spoke at a level only the two men could hear. "Don't spread lies about Tommie."

A slow, chilling smile sprouted on the husky man's lips. "Anyone familiar with her background will confirm she fits the definition of a suspect. Her boyfriend before Alvaro is sitting in a prison cell. He was a psychopath who liked his girlfriends young. The last one he murdered was around Tommie's age, but I'm sure Miss Murphy has hooked up with other failures." Grey grimaced. "Picking losers is her habit." His gaze flickered over Jace.

Annoyance ripped up his spine, along with a snicker of doubt. Tommie's involvement with men snarled in criminal activities did make her appear suspicious. First Davis. Now Arturo. She and Peaches might have a lot in common.

"Remember something?" Grey's mouth opened slightly in hungry anticipation.

"I dozed off while you were speaking."

The detective's eyes bulged, and he flushed with anger. "You could learn a thing or two if you listen. I explained how Tommie's name was linked to two men involved in deadly crimes."

"What's your main interest in her?"

"Tommie? I'm a reminder she needs to stay and cooperate with the authorities about the Alvaro murders or get hit with possible legal consequences. My office did a deal with her once. We won't a second time. Personally, I believe she's hiding things. I mean, was it a coincidence she happened to stumble across Arturo and Gloria while their bodies were still warm? That's tough to accept."

He'd had enough of the detective's theories. "Get out of my way."

"A piece of advice? Watch out for yourself, Jackson. Go back to hanging out at divorce courts to catch a little work and a few dollars. It's where guys like you belong." Grey smirked. "You wouldn't want to get caught in a situation you can't get out of." He pulled a card from his shirt pocket. "Here's my personal information. Call me when you want to talk."

"When hell freezes." Jace marched away without a glance at the detective's contact info.

"Be careful," Grey yelled at him. "She knows more than she lets on."

Jace ignored him, but he couldn't silence the doubt that the warning stirred up. In the past, Tommie had hidden a lot about her life. What was she keeping secret now?

CHAPTER THIRTEEN

The rain stopped as Tommie and Jace exited the Reese Center, but lingering black clouds threatened another downpour. He clenched his jaw, signaling he wasn't in a good mood after his conversation.

Was Jace mad at her or Grey, or both? Unease rippled through her. He rarely became angry. "What did the detective say to you?"

He gripped her elbow and guided her across the lot. "He had a few things to say about Arturo. Seems the victim wasn't as honest as he pretended."

Worry crept over her. As usual, she tried to read his body language, but she recognized only irritation. Why had the disclosure about Arturo annoyed him? Was there more he wasn't telling?

He slowed his pace. "Since Grey has time to follow us at a memorial, he might need something else to do."

"You want me to give him the rhyme from my windshield?"

"Absolutely. When a person is taken into custody for stalking, establishing a pattern of intent and harassment will be essential."

Was this what was bothering him? He did have a point. Plus, it would be nice for Grey to be occupied searching for a stalker. Maybe he'd arrest or scare her shadow away. "Okay. I'll turn that disintegrating paper over to the police. I'll let them search for whoever left it."

She grabbed the bag containing the soggy warning from his car and trotted across the lot with it. Before Grey could speak, she asked him to step aside. Once he did, she handed him the evidence, rattled off her explanation, and ended on a sour note. "We have no working cameras at the inn. No one saw anyone in the lot. You can text me your investigative results."

She paused and sent him the picture of the threat on her windshield.

Jace was leaning against his car but straightened up when she approached. "What did Grey say?"

"Nothing. I took him by surprise." She smiled brightly. "I did send him the photo of my little ditty in case he couldn't paste it together."

A white vehicle parked in a space near them. A trim young man hopped out. "Excuse me. I'm with the *Daily News*. Do you have a statement you'd like to share about Arturo or Gloria Alvaro?"

"No comment," they chimed together.

"Try the others." Jace pointed to the remaining guests and Detective Grey by the building's door.

The reporter fiddled with his phone while Jace and Tommie scrambled into his car. He turned and strode toward the remaining mourners.

He turned the key and drove to the exit. "Who was the woman with the large glasses you were talking to outside?" He braked and merged into traffic.

"That was Linda Martel, Thalia's receptionist. She used to work for Gloria. We agreed it might storm, and Arturo's and Gloria's deaths were hard to understand. Linda said if I ever wanted a salon appointment, to stop by, and she'd fit me in." Tommie shrugged.

The Reese building disappeared. Frowning over his thoughts, Jace wrinkled his brow.

They should discuss the people at the memorial, but she had to find out what was going on with Jace. Had he found out something that involved her? Tommie's pulse quickened. "Did Grey explain why he was here?"

"Not really." Jace kept his eyes on the road. "Did you know Arturo was conning the ladies he dated?"

The question startled her. "Did you or Grey bring up Arturo?"

"The detective claimed Arturo was emptying the bank accounts of his dates and charging high prices on antiques that were, in reality, junk. The last we know, but it's another confirmation that Arturo wasn't as honest as he pretended. What did Arturo tell you about these ladies?" He gripped the wheel, and tense lines around his mouth.

Uneasy, she wet her lips and chose her words with care. "He didn't confess to robbing women if that's what you mean. Why would he speak to me about such things?"

Jace sent her a stern look.

He wasn't satisfied with her answer. She clasped her damp hands in her lap. "Arturo admitted he'd signed up for a few fifty-plus online dating sites. He told me he'd met a lot of women on the Internet, but none he cared for deeply. At his age, he was taking it slow, although his female companions wanted to rush the relationship. Besides, he'd been married three times and wasn't eager to add number four. All his marriages took place when he was in his twenties and thirties."

"Did he mention a particular lady or wife?" The creases on his face deepened.

Where was this conversation headed? Anxiety fluttered in her chest. "Except for that incident where he gave back their money, he never offered details about his online sales or women." Uncomfortable, she glanced at the side mirror. Grey wasn't in sight. What would Jace ask next? Would he drop her case if he learned the truth?

"I found the Alvaro siblings' social media sites." He pressed the accelerator. "Gloria and Thalia each had a minimal presence online. They'd posted pictures of their businesses with the basic data. I checked for arrests. No records of any. Both owned modest homes and cars. Gloria retained her property in her split from Rex. I talked to the neighbors of each, who stated the ladies kept to themselves. In my computer searches, individual small savings accounts turned up with moderate incomes and no history of debt." He flashed her a look. "Can you add anything?"

"You covered it. Arturo described the sisters as too busy working to socialize. I can understand Gloria feeling stretched. Three people used to run her salon. When Thalia and Rex left, she did it all alone. Maybe she didn't have the income to hire additional workers."

Jace threw her a quick glance. "If Arturo's goal was to use seniors with a few dollars, he must have had exceptions when it came to young, pretty females. That could mean a bigger suspect pool."

She raised one shoulder. "Who knows if he would have continued to see me?"

Minutes passed while he seemed to mull over the facts or the traffic. With any luck, he was picturing her as an innocent bystander.

She searched for a different person of interest to discuss. "Peaches stood out to me."

His death grip on the steering wheel lessened. “She was interesting. Her remarks about how Arturo charmed the ladies make me wonder if he attracted the wrong one on a senior dating site.”

“It’s tough to imagine an old lady shooting him.” Relief eased through her over the change in topic. “That means his vengeful girlfriend could be as old as Gigi.”

Jace drove in silence, a crease of concern etched in his forehead.

Was he done asking her questions she didn’t want to answer? She could predict his next step. He’d Google and explore senior match websites as soon as he settled in his home office.

She’d have nothing to brood over. Right? She hadn’t murdered anyone or planned to con another woman. He’d prove she hadn’t shot Arturo and Gloria, and they’d go their separate ways.

That was good. His car seemed awfully cramped. She extended her legs as much as possible. All this talk about older women reminded her she still hadn’t heard from her mom lately. She earned a meager paycheck at the 24/7 Mart, but it barely paid her way. Knowing her mother, she’d contact Tommie for a handout shortly, unless she’d found someone else.

Tommie resisted a sigh. Her mom had been doing well handling the money from her aunt before her self-destructive tendencies took over. She’d bought fashionable clothes. Worn makeup. Gotten her hair styled. She’d seemed happy until she’d followed the usual spiral downward. She drank too much and handed out money to help any friend with a sad tale. Since her recent decline, she’d looked worse than ever.

They needed to have an intimate chat—the last thing Tommie wanted to do. Too bad she always experienced this compulsion to save her mom.

Jace touched her knee. “Remember something?”

His touch made a zip straight to her chest. She opened her mouth, but she didn't trust herself to speak. Had he felt it? And why now, when her world tilted toward a second crash, was she getting these vibes?

I'm overthinking the situation. "Nada."

To her relief, they were at the inn. He insisted on walking her upstairs and to her room. Picasso greeted them when they entered.

Tommie shut the door and blinked in surprise. Dog supplies stood against the wall by the entry. "Where did the huge supply of Yummy Canine Meals come from? It's enough for a month. And a leash?" She turned to him.

He shrugged. "Little dog elves?"

She couldn't stop her grin. "Admit it. Picasso is the best."

"I almost like him."

Picasso ambled to him and sat by Jace's foot. He scratched behind the dog's ears.

"Thanks for going today and the gifts." She motioned at the presents.

His expression sobered. "You can call or text me. Anytime. You're not alone, Tommie."

His words swirled around near her heart. Heat flooded her cheeks and warned her she was blushing. She crossed to the table and set her purse down. She fiddled inside it to hide the effect he was having on her.

His gesture was for the dog, not you, her conscience cautioned.

Straightening, Tommie guessed he was about to leave. "I'm sure you're off to do whatever a PI does. How's the investigation involving the couple at the diner progressing?"

"Finished."

"Wonderful. Let me help you with my case. I can—"

"Not a chance."

She raised her palms in the air. "No problem. I also have stuff to do. Since our suspect list is growing, I'll create a chart using their names and connections. I'll share."

He patted his notebook in his shirt pocket. "I have mine."

Would he show her his? A new alarm seized her. Would his records reveal holes in her story? Her guilt refused to rest.

He walked to the door while Picasso barked and whimpered.

Jace hesitated. "Something wrong with him?"

"He must want you to stay." She'd be glad if he did.

"Picasso is a dog. Don't get carried away." He paced closer to the doorway. "Remember, you can contact me whenever." He exited without waiting for her answer.

She stood in the middle of the room. Now she was alone—except for Picasso. Worries tumbled back into her mind. How would she ever get any sleep, knowing her stalker and/or the shooter who'd left the sick rhyme on her windshield could be close? Yes, tonight all the lights would be on, and she'd be awake, straining to hear people creeping around in the hallway.

Her phone buzzed. Maybe it was her mom. She checked the screen for a name. It was unknown again. She deleted the message. What was going on with her mother? She wasn't usually this silent. As much as she disliked the idea, she couldn't put off a talk any longer.

First, the dog had to go out. As she snapped the vest on Picasso, she made a decision. She owed Jace the truth, the whole story. He'd get it. Soon. She grabbed a knife from the drawer for protection, and she and Picasso walked out of her studio.

CHAPTER FOURTEEN

The sun shone high in the sky when Jace shut the passenger door for Tommie. Her day at the Whale's Spout Restaurant was over. The eatery was closed. Empty tables filled the patio, where diners loved to feast on the homemade breakfasts until the afternoon.

In the past few days, he had driven Tommie to and from her job and home. During the rides, she'd chatted up her suspect chart with enthusiasm. Today would be the same as the rest. He'd fill her in on a few things pertaining to the investigation and in today's newspaper. No signs or gifts from her stalker lowered his wariness over her situation a degree.

"I've got big news." She ran a hand over her hair. "While I was waiting for you, Grey forwarded me an email with the lab results from the sick poem left on my car."

"They were fast."

"Don't get too excited. The report noted no DNA or prints were found and listed the type of paper, ink, and something about the pH level of the rainfall."

"It was a long shot from the beginning." He hadn't held

much hope of a break. On the sidewalk, a woman pushed a little dog in a stroller. Was that what normal life was like? He resisted shaking his head.

Tommie shifted toward him. "Grey did send two of his men to canvass the neighborhood and the inn because of my lovely rhyme. The officers didn't get any leads. Not an unexpected outcome. Oh, and he wrote a few terse words about reporting a possible crime ASAP."

Jace searched for a positive comment. "We haven't seen leaks in the media that you discovered the murder victims. That's a plus."

"It is. Best of all, the jingle vehicle has been a no-show lately."

Tommie was safe. He breathed in the scents of bacon and coffee lingering around her. "Hmm, you remind me of breakfast foods."

"I bet you say that to all the women who work the early shift," she teased.

"You've uncovered my secret." Stray wisps of her hair had sprung free of the elastic and framed her face. Her cheeks were rosy and matched her lips, which seemed to call to him. He tensed his hands on the wheel and fell back on small talk. "Meet any interesting customers?"

"My workday would have gone better without the man who walked into me while he was texting on his phone. I spilled the mug of tea I was carrying. At least I didn't burn myself." She pointed to the brown stains on her formfitting blouse.

Was his tongue hanging out? He forced himself to watch the traffic.

"Everything else was the usual," she said. "How about you? Did you do any new computer searches?" She gripped the strap of the seat belt across her chest.

He had delayed it for as long as possible. "Your picture was in the daily paper."

"What?" Her jaw dropped open. "Why?"

"The reporter must have snapped it at the Reese Center when you were getting in my car. He wrote an article rehashing the murders. Obviously, he'd nothing new." Jace swiped up his cell from the console and handed it to her. "It's in the local news section with a warning that citizens should take care with a gunman lurking about."

"Everyone knows Arturo was shot now. If only someone knew the name of the shooter." She scrolled, stopped, and held the screen up as she read the caption out loud, "'Mourners gather at the Alvaro memorial.'" She frowned as she continued in silence with the rest of the piece. When she finished, she set his phone in the cup holder. Her lower lip quivered. She shut her mouth tight.

"A lot of people don't bother to buy papers these days," he said, attempting to make her feel better.

"I'm identified as the attendee who was the former girlfriend of a homicidal ex-police chief." She expelled a breath. "Don't worry, Jackson. I'm used to it. I won't throw a fit or cry."

"The reporter was going for dirt. He didn't succeed."

"I'm okay. Believe me. Tell me more about what you did."

"I pulled up my databases that collect public information on late payments, money issues, past criminal accusations, and convictions from statistics—"

"Jace." She raised her palm. "Maybe you can omit the search details and highlight the main results."

He steered in and out of the passing lane before answering. "I discovered an interesting fact. Arturo had filed for bankruptcy on his business. He must have been attempting to sell for fast money or before the bank repossessed his property."

"I'd guess he piled up a lot of overdue bills." She tapped a finger on her chin. "When Arturo described the items he sold at the co-op, his tone changed. He had a sincere way of speaking, almost tender, like he and his merchandise were intimate friends. He loved to share the history of an object. Yes, he was skilled at pulling in customers."

"He could market. He also overspent and was in the red."

Her brows pinched together. "I bet he could have been president if he'd hired an accountant."

"Remember, he was a con man." Had Tommie been so taken in by Arturo's folksy act that she excused his dishonest ways? Jace concentrated on the steady traffic until he recalled Linda Martel.

"I looked up your friend, the salon receptionist you met at the memorial."

"Linda?" Tommie glued her attention to him. "What was her story?"

"She grew up in Spring Hill, Florida. She worked as an administrator at a mall shop. A year and a half ago, she landed in Sebastian. Her life revolves around work. Little popped up about her personally. She appears to have relocated to get better jobs. I'd categorize her under acquaintances of Arturo, not an inner-circle buddy."

"You mean nothing illegal turned up on her?" Tommie clarified.

"Right. Since the members of the salon crowd are our prime suspects, she'll remain on our list."

"Are we keeping Alfredo on our radar?"

"I stopped at the Barn Grill before I picked you up. The staff confirmed Alfredo and his flea market buddies spent the evening of the murders at the restaurant."

"He's innocent?"

"A strong possibility. Why would he wait all these months

after their big fight to shoot Arturo? Besides, Alfredo recovered from the business split and is doing okay."

Tommie nodded. "I agree with you."

"Alfredo fits with Linda in the less-likely shooter group." Jace steered around a corner, and the inn appeared. He escorted her upstairs.

She unlocked and cracked her door open. "Want to come in?" Her mouth curved up in a tantalizing smile.

The fragrance of food that had clung to her faded. He instantly was enveloped by her natural flowery scent, her warmth, and the inviting glow in her eyes. A familiar tug to trail after her urged him to say yes. He scrubbed a hand through his hair. Wouldn't hurt to stay a little while. "You can share your poster of suspicious characters. I hope you're not hiding your big discoveries."

She bit her lip, and patches of red colored her cheeks. "About the—"

A loud sneeze drew his gaze lower. Picasso had wedged his snout between the door and the frame. His nose twitched. His huge body pushed forward, shoving the opening wider.

"Our greeter is here." Jace nodded at the animal. "How are you, boy?"

The dog whined and barked enthusiastically at Jace.

"Picasso, shush." She shook her finger at him. "You'll disturb everyone."

The animal's ears drooped.

"I'm sure he needs to go out," she said.

What had he been thinking? The two of them alone in her small space wasn't the best idea. "What were you saying before Picasso interrupted?"

"Nothing important." She fidgeted with the top button of her blouse.

"Don't worry. I remember tomorrow is one of your days off. I won't show up. Let me take the dog."

Seconds later, he and Picasso were outdoors. The canine was cooperative and did his thing. Jace quickly returned him to Tommie. After brief goodbyes, he headed to his car.

He traveled the familiar way to his house, passing a yard of flowering purple flowers in bloom. They reminded him of Alicia. She'd kept a vase of fresh lavender blossoms on the kitchen table. He should have warned her decorations wouldn't turn him into the kind of man she wanted.

The pain he'd experienced when she'd driven away was gone. Now he was left with the sense that he'd failed to hold together their relationship. Were they ever meant to be a couple? He'd never felt a crazy love like in romantic stories.

Those men did anything for a woman. They chased them to foreign cities or to isolated cabins in the wilderness, all in the name of that strange emotion. That wasn't him. Nope, and he hadn't changed. He'd go home, check his notes, and search for the missing pieces to solve the Alvaro puzzle.

The next day, he rolled out of bed eager and determined to get to work. He'd discovered little up to this point. Now he was on his way to Gloria's salon. Maybe someone had the urge to gossip about their former employer, her cousin, or the people around them. Which one shot their friends Arturo and Gloria? No definite answers spun in his mind.

He drove down Route 510 as the late-morning sun shone in a clear blue sky, promising a dry day. Would the good weather bring out customers to Gloria's Beauty Cuts? Tommie would have enjoyed talking to clients and employees, but she could easily arouse suspicions about herself. She wasn't always careful when she spoke.

Jace hadn't gone far when Gigi called. She apologized for bothering him and asked if he'd pick up a bag of sugar for her.

Knowing his grandmother, he didn't quite believe her request. She hoarded baking goods.

Did she really run out of sweetener, or did she want to find out about Tommie and the case? Gigi had always mothered the girl, treating her like another grandchild.

Jace was certain of one thing about Miss Murphy. She wasn't a child. Her teasing smile on those inviting lips and the spark in her eyes cropped up in his thoughts. The beep of a car horn interrupted his daydream. The red light had become green.

The stop at the Publix Super Market took longer than he planned. A crowd was stocking up for the Thanksgiving celebration. Seizing the sucrose and a package of coffee for himself, he joined a line. Luckily, the queue moved forward without any delays.

Outside, he hopped in his sports utility. He'd call Tommie. Then he could reassure Gigi that he was checking on her. Her voicemail answered. Where was she? Walking Picasso? He left a message that he was exploring leads but had nothing solid.

Back on the road, he arrived in Star Pointe Crossings. Little had changed in the community since his last visit. He passed by his parents' home. It stood lifeless until they returned. A quarter mile down the street, he turned into his grandmother's U-shaped drive decorated with three small scarecrows. As usual, he rang her doorbell before using his key to enter.

In the entry area, her purse lay on the cherry sideboard table. A vase and his baby picture sat on either side of it. She was here.

"Hello?" he yelled.

"Jace?" His grandmother emerged from the hall, hurrying across the glossy tile floor to greet him.

Her white hair was perfectly cut and coiffured. He used to wonder if it was ever messed up after sleeping. She was dressed in an ivory, button-down shirt and black pants. Her clothes smelled fresh from the laundry. She wore an apron when she cooked. Today's was a pumpkin-orange color with the saying, "The best things in life are sweet."

She hugged him. "You came quickly."

"I aim to please." He inhaled a whiff. "Did you already bake? Smells delicious." Apparently, she hadn't needed the ingredient he'd bought. He flashed her a skeptical look.

"You won't believe what happened when I searched through the food boxes in my pantry." She held up her hands. "I found my sweetener, but I can never have too much." She took the shopping bag from him. "C'mon to the kitchen. We'll get your money for the stop, and don't say no."

Gigi's home was spotless. Her island-style furniture in the front room looked unused. She reserved the space for holiday celebrations or the women's social group.

"Next time, I'll remind you to look behind the mixes and canned goods." His instincts were correct. She'd brought him here for one of her gabfests.

"You're always helpful, Jace." She handed him a wad of bills, which he pocketed without a glance. She always overpaid him. He'd given up protesting her reimbursements. "You must sample my cheesecake. I'm trying out a new recipe for Thanksgiving."

She lived for special occasions. They provided her with a chance to experiment with different combinations of ingredients. Since his parents were away on their trip, he alone would taste and comment on all the dishes she served. He'd better start fasting.

"I promise to eat whatever you've baked for our feast. Today, I'm booked."

"I'll fix you a piece to go." She led him to the table. "You must peek at my latest creation before I cut it up. I'll grab it from the fridge."

She left him standing by the dinette, covered with a familiar ivory tablecloth that caught any spills or spots during a meal.

Had she really cooked recently? With her compulsion to clean, it was tough to tell. The sole visible sign of mixing and stirring was a gleaming glass bowl by the farmhouse sink. Neither the pendant lights nor the sunshine streaming through the nook windows revealed a speck of dust. Comforting aromas of vanilla and cinnamon teased his nose. He swore Gigi sprayed the flavorings in the air.

She returned, carrying a pie plate. "I drizzled caramel on top since you love that flavor. Are you sure you can't stay a few minutes?"

"Positive."

She set the dessert on a sparkling, white marble counter. She picked up a knife lying by the crumb crust dish and slid it across the pie. "How was the Alvaro memorial? You did go, didn't you?"

"I went. Thanks for sending us the post."

"Were many people there?"

"Mostly salon employees."

"Services for the departed are always gloomy." She nodded knowingly.

"I escorted Tommie to the service. Did you read about her in the paper? They're still calling her Arturo's girlfriend."

"I've been busy cooking and didn't see the newspaper. On the day she visited me, she explained he was an acquaintance she'd found dead when she went to his house. Terrible. She was afraid that the police would label her as a suspect. I hope she takes extra precautions for herself. We have a killer running loose." She placed her utensil on the counter. "How is she doing?"

"Tommie's fine, Gigi." He searched for a reassuring comment. "She got a dog."

His grandmother furrowed her narrow brows. "Her mother never let her have one when she was a child. I'm glad she has someone. Besides us. Did she tell you much about Arturo? She was shaken and skipped a lot of details when we spoke."

He measured his words before answering. "Tommie met him at the Artisan Co-op. She was evaluating a surfboard for him and returning it when he was killed."

"Arturo was a surfer? I can't picture the man on the television ad riding a wave."

"His cousin owned the board and wanted to sell it. Arturo was helping her."

Gigi's mouth curved upward. "I bet Tommie would eat cheesecake. You can bring her a slice."

Gigi believed food could cure any problem. And what did she know concerning the victims? She'd probably heard a book full of rumors about Tommie and Arturo at one of her social groups. Were any of them true? "Got any scoop on Arturo?"

She shrugged. "He worked with a partner, Alfredo Russo. They expanded into a store in Sebastian and sold at expensive antique shows until the men separated their businesses."

She laid a finger on her chin. "Let me see, what else did I hear? After the men split, Alfredo sold at the large indoor marketplace and at a monthly church flea market. Arturo appeared at vintage markets, rented spots in co-ops, and offered his wares online." She grabbed a cake server from a drawer and lifted the pieces. "Everything I said is common knowledge, dear."

"Maybe I should attend a meeting with you and catch up on the stories circulating." They might say more if he encouraged them in person.

She patted his arm. "Only if you want them to fix you up with a date."

"I'll pass. Have any nitty-gritty on Arturo's personal life?"

She walked to the closet and seized two plastic containers. "He had three wives and many girlfriends in between the weddings. He married the financially comfortable ladies. He eventually left them all." She put the sweets in the plastic containers.

"What about his cousin Gloria Alvaro? Did your friends have any interesting tidbits about her?"

"They brought her up." She pressed down on the lids that refused to shut. "Can you help me, Jace?"

He sensed she wanted to change the topic. He snapped the covers on for her.

"Thank you, dear."

"And Gloria?" he prompted, pressing her to continue.

"I do remember a bit about her." Gigi pursed her lips. "There were a few rumors concerning Arturo and his cousin Gloria."

"Such as?" He raised a brow. Could he hope for a lead from his grandmother?

"This is gossip," she warned. "How should I say it?"

"I'm sure it's nothing too shocking, is it?"

"All right. Some believed the two cousins were . . . a little too much into each other. Why don't you sit while I talk?" She waved at a seat. "I'll lend you my cooler, and the dessert will stay chilled. Your car will be warm from sitting in the drive."

She was determined to keep him at her house for a bit. Did she have useful scoops or nebulous hearsay? He surrendered. Reluctantly, he pulled out a chair. *The cousins were a little too much into each other.*

Was she saying what he thought?

CHAPTER FIFTEEN

In Tommie's studio, her day off seemed endless. She'd recycled her problems through her brain continually. Thoughts of Jace came up often. He'd gone out of his way for her, and he deserved the truth—all of it.

She had to explain her relationship with Arturo before he learned about it elsewhere. She had to keep her word to be open and tell him all the details of her case.

First, she had to engage in a heart-to-heart discussion with her mom. That wouldn't be easy. Yet, despite the sinking sensation in her stomach, she wasn't changing her mind. Growing up, she'd worked around her parent's moods and obstinacy. Conversations didn't exist. Her mom lived in denial and hid parts of her life to avoid judgments and legal snarls. Tommie needed all her skills to persuade her to do something she didn't want to do.

She grabbed her pet's harness and the leather leash from the top of the dog's bag of food and put it on him. "You're stylin'. Later, I'll put your chow in a cabinet."

Picasso let out a yip.

"I agree. The bag is heavy and fine where it is. Forget I mentioned the idea of moving it. Let's go."

Once in the stairway, the dog took the lead. The stale smell settled around them. The odor never got better. She inhaled small breaths and hurried to keep up. At the bottom of the steps, they rushed out the exit. Fresh air.

Picasso led the way to her car. She checked out the interior before opening up. They hopped in. Her phone rang. The ID read Unknown. She clicked it off. Robocall? A bad premonition formed in her head, but she dismissed it.

She followed Old Dixie Highway into Vero Beach and did a quick detour to order at a drive-through before she rejoined the traffic. Near a crumbling, concrete industrial building, she turned down a side alley. She parked at the curb of the fading blue-frame house. Metal hurricane shutters covered the windows. Maybe today her mom would consent to remove them.

Nah, that wouldn't happen. The lawn was full of weeds and overgrown grass. What was her mom's rent? Didn't matter. She was lucky to have a roof above her head. Nearby, an old, three-story brick structure was tagged with spray paint. Most of the glass panes were broken or nonexistent. A chill on the back of her neck urged her to rush to the entryway.

Say hello. Discuss and solve the problem. Get out. The sun beat down on her through the windshield. The weather had done a turnaround. The day was unusually hot for autumn. Without the AC humming, her car would become a heat trap. She'd bring the dog inside.

"Let's go, Picasso." She led him to the entrance and knocked.

The honk of car horns and whizzing traffic from the main street drifted toward her. Seconds passed. As she stood in the sun, sweat coated her skin. She fisted her hand for a loud pounding while shouting, "Hey, it's me, Tommie. I have a burger for you. And money."

The door snapped open. Her mother, dressed in pink short-shorts and a dingy white halter top, squinted at her. "Tommie?"

"Hi, Mom. Did you lose your glasses again?" Her eyelids were red and puffy, as though she'd been crying or rubbing them. She wore heavy eyeliner. Did she think cosmetics would hide the obvious signs that she looked bad?

"The lenses seemed weak. I must need my eyes checked. Did you notice my hair?" She fingered the ends touching her shoulders.

From a distance, the black inserts would blend into her shoulder-length bob, but not up close. How had a woman who barely paid her bills bought the pieces? Did she have a little cash left over from Aunt Sissy? Better not to ask.

"Yeah, your hair is long." Leave it to her mom to be more interested in her extensions than in inviting her daughter in. "Uh, nice."

She ran her fingers through her purchased strands and sobered. "I didn't expect you. Did something happen?" She swept a glance over the area.

"Are you expecting company?" Tommie inched toward the entry. Not a soul was in sight. Was someone out there?

"I was checking to see if anyone was in your car."

She was acting strange, even for her. Tommie felt an urge to get behind solid walls. "Nobody is with me." She handed over the takeout. "Here's lunch or breakfast. A ten-dollar bill is in the bag."

Her mother peered into the brown sack. "You're a good girl. I can always count on you. If I still had Aunt Sissy's inheritance, I'd pay you back for the meals, the rides, and the loans. I'm sorry I can't help you get a new apartment. I—" She sniffed.

"Please, stop." An uneasy sensation itched at her. She hated watching her mom cry. And she loathed standing around in a derelict neighborhood.

Be firm. Pitying her mom was how she got into these predicaments. "You explained about the money. Multiple times."

Her mother rubbed the spot between her brows with an unsteady hand. "I didn't tell you what happened at the store where I worked."

Uh-oh. The day was about to grow worse. "I can guess."

"They were terrible to me. I had to quit. The management was giving me the worst shifts. I told my boss I didn't own a car, and it wasn't safe to walk home alone after dark. Other people who drove could have taken my hours. I got the ones no one wanted. Since my manager wouldn't change my schedule, I stopped going in."

No job meant she'd be homeless soon. Tommie inhaled a deep breath, trying to control her stress.

"I'll get another. Don't worry, baby."

Tommie had heard her worthless reassurances before, but she had a pressing topic to discuss. "Can I come in? It's hot outside."

"What's that animal you got with you?" Her mother drew back like he was snarling at her.

"His name is Picasso. He's friendly and won't hurt you."

"Fine, but he can't stay. He's got lots of fur, and I'm allergic."

"He's mine, and I won't hang around long."

"Well, I can't keep him, in case you were looking for someone to take him." She stepped aside for them to enter.

Relieved, Tommie led Picasso across the threshold into the living room. From behind her came the clicking sound of locks sliding into place. How many had she installed? Four? No. Five. Who'd rob this dump?

Nothing had changed from the last time Tommie had dropped by. In the corner sat a cardboard box containing a flat-screen television that had never been hung. A sofa and two chairs popular in the sixties crowded together around the carton.

"You overdid the bolts, don't you think?" Tommie asked as the final tick of metal announced her mom was finished.

"Not with the friends of the ex-police chief around. The man wants revenge, and if he can hurt me, he hurts you."

Tommie perched on the end of the frayed upholstered couch, wishing she wasn't there. Her mother was right, but sitting locked up and worrying worsened her fears. She'd rely on her pep talk. "Roy is in prison. We'll be okay."

"I hope that's true. I'll put the food in the fridge." Her mom left with the bag and returned empty-handed. She chose a barrel-shaped seat and sat. "Any leads for a better job?"

A slice of disappointment flashed through Tommie. "I wish."

"You'll get one. You're a hard worker. Anyone would be lucky to employ you."

Picasso leaned against her legs. His warm, furry body comforted her.

"Why did you get a dog? Animals are a lot of work." She sniffed. "My nose is stuffing up."

"We've only been inside a few minutes."

"He's huge. I can barely breathe."

"I'll get your allergy pills. Are they in the medicine cabinet?" Tommie waited for an answer.

"First shelf. Bring me a glass of water to take the meds."

Did her mother really have a reaction to canines, or was she automatically falling into her complaint mode? Tommie bent and patted her dog to hide her regret that her mom never changed. "I'll be a second, Picasso."

He looked up at her with his happy expression, his mouth open, his tongue out.

"Where did you get him? He's going to be expensive to feed."

"He was homeless, and I always wanted a dog. We were a perfect match." She should jump into the reason for her visit.

"Did you read about the shootings involving Arturo Alvaro and his cousin?"

"I saw the headlines on my phone. I can't believe he's gone and killed in his own house. Murdered. And Gloria too. God save us." She rocked back and forth in her chair.

"It's scary," Tommie admitted, ducking into the six-by-six-foot bathroom a few feet away.

Their conversation triggered her memory of that night. The dimness of the study. The fragrance of flowers. Arturo motionless on the floor. His lifeless stare at the ceiling. Tommie gripped her hands together. *I'm safe, and I'm at my mother's home. Safe.* Inhaling deep breaths, she leaned against the wall. Gradually, the fear eased.

She gawked at her reflection in the cabinet mirror. Sweat had broken out on her pasty-white skin. She turned the handle of the faucet and splashed the cool water on her cheeks. Better.

With a steady hand, she opened the cupboard. A box fell out into the sink. She scooped it up. It was labeled Ocean Lure Cosmetics. Something was written in a foreign language at the bottom of the box. She peeked inside. It was her parent's mascara. Tommie placed it back on the shelf and discovered the medication behind a pile of combs. She filled a glass on the counter, grabbed the meds, and returned to the other room.

Her mom washed down her pills with a gulp of her drink before sinking into her seat. "Have the cops caught the killer?" She blanched on her last word.

"No one's been arrested, so far."

The older woman clutched her chest. "Lord save us. Our homes used to be safe. Not now."

Tommie straightened and studied her. Her mother's real hair was straggly and dull. It stood out among the extensions.

Her mother rubbed a spot above her eye. "I remember Arturo from his TV commercial. He spoke in a strong and soothing fashion. But he wasn't honest. He bought people's discards for pennies and resold everything as antiques for a bundle of cash." She tightened her mouth. "Maybe a customer was unhappy he'd been overcharged and got revenge."

"Unhappiness doesn't cover it." Tommie sat and twisted the end of Picasso's leash.

"May he rest in peace wherever he went. I have my own idea of where he is." Her mom pursed her lips and looked down.

Time to confess. Tommie raised her chin. "The police found me at his place the night of the murder. I think they listed me as a person of interest."

"What were you doing there?" she demanded. "I warned you he wasn't honest. Did you talk to the law? About me?" She snagged Tommie's wrist.

"I was giving him an estimate on a surfboard." Tommie broke away from her grip. "Jace is looking into the deaths to solve the crimes and prove my innocence. I never mentioned you to anyone."

"Jace Jackson? He's a good boy."

Bracing herself, Tommie ignored her doubts. "You need to tell him about Arturo. I can't keep your secrets, or mine, any longer."

Her mom stiffened. "I will not."

CHAPTER SIXTEEN

Tommie perched on the end of the sofa cushion. "Mom, your talk with Jace will be confidential."

"I know nothing, and you promised not to discuss me and Arturo. If the police find out I was involved in a crooked scheme, they'll read my record and send me back to jail. I can't be dragged into his murder."

"You can help, and you're off probation now," Tommie pointed out.

Tears overflowed and ran down her mom's hollow cheeks. She paused, rubbed her hand across her face, and straightened. "Jace Jackson is super straight. A hurricane wind couldn't bend the guy. He'll turn me in to the authorities."

"You were in for a DUI, not robbing a bank."

"With my history, the law won't give me a break."

"I'll have Jace swear not to reveal your secret. He'll keep it. He's dependable. Remember how good he was to you? He gave you lots of rides and cash when you had none. Now it's time to be there for him by giving him all the details."

"I didn't think you knew about the loans." Her mother locked her fingers together as if in prayer. "Please, baby. No way can I live in a cell again. I'm claustrophobic. I can't breathe in that little space."

"You might lead Jace to the sick person who shot Arturo and Gloria," Tommie coaxed, doing her best to remain calm. "You'll be a hero."

"Bad things happen to people who squeal on others. I'm not a fool."

How could she get through to her mom? She'd sworn to stay sober, and that hadn't happened. Even the threat of imprisonment if she had another DUI conviction hadn't deterred her from drinking. Her mom had successfully completed her recent probationary period because she hadn't been caught drunk.

Picasso rested his chin on Tommie's knee and stared up at her. He seemed to say, "What can you do?"

"Why would someone kill Arturo?" she persisted.

"He robbed women." Her mom folded her arms. "Don't mix me up in any murders."

Tommie's head throbbed from trying to reason with her. She'd try a different tack. "Who was mad at him or Gloria?"

Her mom's forehead dissolved into thought lines. "His old partner, Alfredo, wasn't happy with him. But he was better off without him, or that's how it looked. Everyone heard about Thalia and Gloria's fallout. Arturo was on Gloria's side in the fight." Her lips twitched tight. "Probably no one will get money off his death. He had a pile of debts. I learned too late that Arturo loved to play, but not pay."

Tommie resisted blowing out a breath of frustration. Her mom had the same recycled tales to offer.

"Gloria had a bad divorce," her mom mumbled aloud. "Her ex, Rex, didn't seem the killing type, though. I've seen him around."

Tommie's phone buzzed in her pocket. She fished it out and read the text from Jace. *Where are you?*

"Who is it?" her mom asked.

"It's Jace." Her spirits lifted with hope. Hurriedly, she composed an invite and sent it to him.

Two seconds later, he answered. She scanned the return message before speaking. "He's in the area and on his way to your house."

"A maniac is running around shooting people. Can he bring me another set of locks?" Her mother bit her lip.

"You have plenty." Tommie pushed the curtains aside on the front window to try to catch sight of him. The metal shutters blocked her view. She couldn't watch from here. "Mom, it's a bad idea to seal yourself inside. What if you had a fire, and the window was the only way to escape?"

"I'd run through the flames to the back door."

And end up a crispy critter. She decided not to argue. "I'll take the dog—" She spelled the next word. "O-u-t."

"Don't. This neighborhood isn't safe. It's scary in the daylight or in the nighttime. Walking home alone in the dark gave me shivers up my back. I was thinking of getting one of those alerts like Arturo. You can get the safety kind."

"How long did he have his device?"

"I'm not sure. I saw it by accident when he had to test the gadget. I was with him. He tried to hide the fact he had a bad heart, especially from his young girlfriends. He didn't want folks to label him old because of it."

"Can you name any of the women?" Mentally, Tommie crossed her fingers.

"Didn't know them." Her mom's hand went to her throat. "He had too many. Can't the animal go out by himself?"

Picasso barked and wagged his tail.

"Not now," Tommie told the dog. She turned back to her

mom. She was lying about remembering names. Over the years, Tommie had noticed her mother gripping her throat when she lied under pressure. Yup, Yvette Miller had a tell. Her mom's body language spoke loud and clear.

"Arturo wouldn't wear an alert around his neck and ruin his brawny look." Mom's thin mouth twisted in a grimace. "He wore his on a leather wristband and hoped his dates would mistake the device for a fitness tracker. Now you can get the monitors on your cell phones. He should have upgraded."

Maybe her mother could be helpful. "Who was on his emergency team?"

"He had a few buddies who did CPR. The EMS building is two blocks from Manatee Lake Estates in the firehouse substation."

"Was a volunteer police officer on his crew?"

"Knowing Arturo, he had a dozen paid and unpaid. I'm sure he believed they'd deliver him to the hospital faster."

Picasso flopped down beside Tommie. She and her mom sat in silence. Finally, the sound of an engine pulling into the drive alerted her that Jace had arrived. She raced to unbolt the five locks, with her mom shouting cautions at her.

She opened up. Jace marched inside in his khaki shorts and gray tee. His purposeful, cool stride almost made her acknowledge how happy she was to see him.

I will not throw myself at him and thank him for showing up. He'll discover soon enough that I've kept secrets from him. He might think I'm dishonest every time I move my lips. No, he was fair. He'd listen.

Jace stopped by the dog and petted him.

Act normal. She relaxed her fisted hands and gestured at the dog. "He acts like he hasn't seen you in weeks. Any breaks on the case?"

"I was at a shop where Arturo sold some of his antiques. Seems Grey's men interviewed the vendors yesterday. Anyway, according to the owner, nothing out of the ordinary happened the day of the shooting, and he told the cops the same. However, Arturo was two months behind on his rent. In fact, his last payment bounced, and the landlord planned to ask him to leave. I'm afraid the man must have had a ton of creditors on his doorstep"

Across the room, her mother sat with her gaze pointed to the floor.

He approached her. "How are you, Mrs. Miller?"

She lifted her head. "Remember, you can call me by my first name, Yvette."

"Mom has something to tell you," Tommie announced, making one of her split-second decisions. "You'll want to hear it. Sit yourself down." She nodded at the empty barrel chair while she remained standing.

"I'm not breaking a tie between you two?" He sat on the cushion's edge and raised his eyebrows at her.

Tommie was done with her mom's theatrics. Her neck and shoulders ached from tensing them. She held up a finger for him to wait and fixed a disapproving stare on her mom. "Enlighten Jace about your experience with dating on Starting Point Match."

Her mom opened her mouth and stopped. She seemed to be deciding whether to speak or to sink into stonewall silence.

Tommie placed a hand on her hip. "Jace, ask who she met online."

He sat up straight. "What's going on?"

Her mom fastened her scowl on him. "Who shot Arturo and Gloria?"

"No news yet, Yvette. Do you have a lead for me?"

"I reminded my daughter that the world was full of unpredictable crazies." Her mother nervously tapped her fingers together in front of her. "Two people dead. Who will be next?"

"That's the big question." Tommie was finished with keeping

secrets. "We need to take precautions. In the meantime, you can help us find whoever hurt the Alvaro cousins."

"Told ya," Mom mumbled. "I got zip for you."

Stay calm. "You can steer Jace in the right direction. Maybe your story can fill a hole or two."

"Am I protected by confidentiality?" Mom bent forward. "Anything I say can't leak to a living soul."

Tommie knelt beside her. "When we catch the person who killed Arturo and Gloria, you'll be able to get rid of the metal shutters and one or two locks."

"I'm not taking them off. All kinds of derelicts are roaming the streets."

She'd try another approach. "You were Arturo's victim. Now you can be a hero."

"Did you know him, Yvette?" Jace pushed to his feet.

"I'm not free to speak."

Tommie stood. "If you don't tell him now, I'll—"

"Let me explain." Jace approached her mother. "A murderer is walking around and could strike again. The next causality could be you or your daughter. You want to protect yourself and her, don't you? She's already gotten a death threat."

"It was from that ex-policeman." Nervously, her mom wrapped a strand of fake hair around her finger. "He threatened to punish her for testifying against him."

Tommie searched her brain for a way to get her mother to reveal the truth. "People are dead. I can't keep quiet any longer. Confess what happened to Aunt Sissy's inheritance, or I'm going to call your former probation officer."

"No need to fuss or act dramatic." Her mom patted one of her extensions. "Arturo and I met on the dating site Starting Point Match, for adults fifty and older."

Tommie blinked. Had the warning worked? Her mom was confessing? She was unpredictable, as usual.

"We went out a couple of times to eat and cruised around on his sailboat. He drove me to his beautiful home full of antiques. After two weeks, he told me he loved me. A day later, he was excited about a deal I could get in on if I acted fast."

She stared off into space and continued. "I was guaranteed to earn double my money back in a month. Arturo swore he'd repay me if I lost anything. All I had to do was trust him."

She swallowed before continuing. "I did. He cautioned if the news got out, everyone would scramble for a cut of the action and the profits. The more investors, the smaller the payout." She gazed down at the worn, yellowed tile. "I handed him all I had." Her lips quivered. "And he broke up with me. The cash return never came."

"How much?" Jace asked, now at attention.

"He took the money I had left from selling my aunt's house. I had about 40,000 after paying bills and buying things I needed. I tried contacting him. He ghosted me. Finally, he texted that the transaction fell through. He couldn't reimburse me. His loss had been too great. I realized nothing Arturo had said was true. I was the biggest fool on earth, believing he had a secret winning product."

"Police?" Jace raised his brows.

"And have them investigate me in a most-likely crooked scheme? Pass. I'm sorry, Tommie. I know you counted on me giving you some of that money to start your new life."

"Mom, please stop apologizing." The inheritance had given her mother a new life. She had no longer had to scrounge or worry about becoming homeless. Now it was gone. Stolen. An ache grew in Tommie's chest. She knelt beside her mom and squeezed her hand. "You did the right thing, telling him."

Jace paced the floor before pausing near Tommie. Confusion, disappointment, and anger flashed across his face. "You knew this, and you didn't tell me? She's one of his victims. You told a lie of omission. And knowing Arturo was a thief, you agreed to dinner at his home. You put yourself in a position that turned you into a prime suspect in two murders."

His accusations rattled her. Here, it was. The moment she'd dreaded. And she saw something else that she hadn't wanted to. Under the confusion and anger, she recognized glimmers of hurt in his voice.

She rose on her shaky legs. "I promised my mother I wouldn't repeat her story to anyone. Instead, I asked her to explain." Did he understand? Would he forgive her?

"I'm not a stranger you hired." He clenched his teeth. "I made a risky career move to homicide because I thought you trusted me. I was wrong. You have hidden facts that lead to a motive for killing. Were you afraid someone else you hired would learn the truth but not me?" His eyes widened. "You were counting on getting part of the inheritance that Arturo stole."

The shock and pain in his eyes shook her. "I didn't consider anyone but you." She searched for words to soothe him. She simply repeated the fact. "Arturo stole from my mother."

"And you get revenge for your stolen money by shooting him? That's how it could look to the cops."

"Who will die next?" Her mom mumbled and rocked herself back and forth in her seat, distracting Tommie and Jace.

"Yvette." He stepped up to her. "Do you have the names of other supposed investors? Where were you the night Arturo was shot?"

"I don't know who invested, and I was home by myself when Arturo was killed." She folded her arms. "He broke my heart."

Jace turned to Tommie. "You didn't tell me the whole story because you didn't believe in me." His voice was cold and hard. "We're done here." He walked away.

She squeezed her hands until they hurt. "Jace?"

He didn't answer but continued walking.

How could she make him understand? Uncertain, she stood frozen. The soft click of the door echoed in her ears. The sound of his car starting warned her he was driving off. What should she do?

Her mom burst into loud sobs.

Tommie crouched beside her and patted her mother's arm. How had her own good intentions caused everything to fall apart? Now Jace was gone. She had to explain and get him to understand and forgive her. How would she convince him?

CHAPTER SEVENTEEN

Tommie sat at her kitchen table. Her brain felt fogged in from lack of sleep. Worries over her last meeting with Jace had kept her awake. He'd walked away from her when he'd learned she was keeping secrets from him. Her best friend. How could she fix her mistake? She'd no clue. She couldn't go back in time.

Absently, Tommie sipped the coffee. Yuck, cold. She pushed away from the table to dump her drink and wrap up her uneaten muffin. She was too upset to eat. The clock on the stove told her she'd spent forever sitting and searching for a solution. She wished she could be like Picasso. He'd eaten, gone for his morning outing, and was now on the sofa napping.

Her mind repeatedly wandered to the look of hurt in Jace's eyes and his angry words. She'd wounded him on a personal level she hadn't imagined.

What would she do in a world without him? Even when they'd been out of touch, she'd known she could find him. Now he'd cut her out totally, not answering her messages or calls. She didn't blame him. His inbox was probably on overload because of her.

She paced to her suspect poster propped on her bureau. If she could come up with a solid lead for him, he might forgive her, or at least not ghost her. Wrong. She had to live her life honestly, prove that she'd changed or was trying to change and could solve her own problems.

Her hope sank as she studied the familiar list of possible shooters. She'd drawn lines to connect each related person. She stared at the crisscross. *Think.* What or who stood out the most?

Of course, the obvious connection was the salon, which was one big work family. She'd go there. Excited, she seized her purse and slung it over her shoulder. She patted Picasso and reassured him she'd return soon.

Her mood lifted as she rode the elevator to the lobby. Peaches, Linda, or Thalia could have the answers she needed. She dug out her keys and fisted them as she stopped on the ground floor and trotted across the tiles. Johnny, the desk clerk, nodded to her. The man alternated shifts with another worker, but he always seemed to be at the inn.

She checked the time while walking to her car. The business should be open. She pocketed her phone. As she crossed the pavement, something about her vehicle snagged all her attention. Was it crooked? She slowed as she approached. The rear passenger side was lower than the other. She had a flat. The slices in the tire were obvious. Were they deliberate?

Bending down, she ran her finger along the cut marks on the rubber sidewall. *Remain calm. Don't let fear control you.* Straightening, she rubbed the spot over her pounding heart. She scanned the area, hoping to glimpse someone. The street was quiet. Whoever had done it was gone by now.

She gritted her teeth. She had no clue how to change a tire.

YouTube must have a video that would teach her. How fast could she learn? She glanced at her messages. No scary texts, and nothing from Jace. Without her car, she was going nowhere.

* * *

At his kitchen table, Jace tried to block thoughts of Tommie while he worked on his computer. He avoided opening anything from her. Instead, he read an email from his parents, who'd reconnected with old colleagues on the West Coast. Their message was full of details about museums, sightseeing tours, and the great accomplishments of their friends and families, who'd become Silicon Valley successes.

His promise to solve the homicides and make his folks proud hovered in the back of his mind. No way could he keep his vow if he quit the Alvaro investigation.

Except he couldn't forget Tommie had concealed important facts about her own case. The inheritance that Arturo had scammed was a fortune to both women, and her own mother had dated Arturo. Worse, she'd been one of his victims. The law would believe that Tommie was motivated to help her mom get revenge since she'd planned to share a portion of the cash.

Why hadn't Tommie confided in him? They'd known each other for years. Yet, he kept returning to the question of why she'd hired him in the first place. Her reasons seemed obvious. He'd been cheap, and she could hide the facts from him. The truth stung.

He wrestled with his ideas. If Gigi asked him to hold on to a secret connected to a crime, would he? That analogy didn't work. His grandmother becoming involved in a murder was ridiculous. Perhaps he was being unreasonable and taking it too personally.

He pictured Tommie with that mischievous, inviting smile.

And when he announced the name of the killer, she'd lean over to him and—

Enough. He closed his eyes. The attraction and frustration that Thomasina sparked in him returned. He fisted his hand, trying to check his emotions. Sitting at home wasn't helping. He should get out. Talk to people.

Grey's mocking words floated to him. *Go back to hanging at divorce court to catch a little work and a few dollars. It's where guys like you belong.*

Jace heard his grandfather. *How dare he slander my grandson? He can do anything he puts his mind to. Forget what I said about this shooting being too messy. Time to prove that know-nothing, blowhard detective wrong.*

That was what he needed to do, but he'd watch his step. Grey was a smart man. He wouldn't let him antagonize him. Thalia Alvaro was next on his interview list. How receptive would she be to him? He'd find out. Grey and his men couldn't be far behind in their discoveries. Minutes were pressing.

He drove down Roseland to the intersection of US 1. Thalia's Tranquil Salon and Day Spa sat on the corner where a chain drugstore had once stood. Pocketing his keys, he climbed out. A breeze blew the scent of the barbecue restaurant across the street to tease his nose. The aroma was the best advertising and draw for the eatery.

He walked through the salon's business entrance, a hallway, and into a waiting area. Wood-paneled walls and dim ceiling lights set a calm atmosphere. Lavender replaced the fragrance of slow-cooked meat. An electric fireplace drew his attention to a cream sofa and two matching chairs facing the fake flames. A middle-aged woman sat in one, scanning a page of haircuts in a magazine.

He passed under a wide, arched doorway to the reception

desk. An employee in a pink smock and large glasses sat on a stool on the other side of a waist-high counter. She was listening to the client in front of her. She must be Linda Martel, Thalia's receptionist. Tommie had spoken to her at the memorial, but he'd caught only a glimpse of her at the Reese Center. Studying her, he guessed Linda was older than Peaches and younger than Thalia. Somewhere approaching forty.

Her customer's back was to him. She had thick, black, wavy hair to her shoulders. She leaned against the countertop, wearing dark capri pants that displayed her long, lean legs, and a beige shirt that showed off her tanned, toned arms.

He would have recognized her anywhere. Tommie. Good grief, what was she doing here? She was the last person he'd expected to run into. He strode over to her. "Getting a beauty treatment?"

She whirled to him. "Jace?" She blinked several times and blushed. "I was inquiring about an appointment, and Linda and I started chatting."

"Hello. How can I assist you?" The receptionist smiled and scanned him up and down with obvious approval.

Tommie's brows snapped inward as she took in Linda's sudden attentiveness toward him. "He's a friend." She hooked her thumb at him. "Nice to see you again, Jace." Her blush deepened. "I was asking Linda if she could direct me to someone who might take Gloria's longboard."

"How about giving it to Rex?" he asked, while fuming. First, Tommie had revealed she hadn't been honest with him. Now, she was nosing around and likely stirring up the suspicions of a possible suspect. She'd broken both her promises to him. Of course, the last didn't count since he didn't work for her. He shoved that thought aside.

Linda laughed. "I'm sure Rex doesn't want a surfboard. He rarely goes to the beach."

He noted the glow of curiosity on the woman's face. Maybe he could use her interest. He flashed his best grin. "I'm Jace Jackson. I guessed we missed a formal introduction at the Alvaro service."

She extended her hand, which sported a collection of pretty silver rings. Her jewelry was a striking contrast to her plain looks. "You're the PI."

"I am." He shook and stepped back, breaking contact. "Let me offer my sympathies to you on the loss of Arturo and Gloria. Carrying on with a tragedy weighing on you is tough. I admire your ability to keep working. How's Gloria's staff doing?"

"Her place is closed. Possibly forever." Her lower lip trembled. "We're all in shock." She grabbed a tissue from a box on the counter and dabbed her heavily mascaraed eyelashes.

Tommie patted the receptionist's arm and turned to him. "Linda worked for Gloria before transferring to this salon."

The receptionist could be an encyclopedia on the victim. He placed his palms on the desktop and bent toward her. "Must be twice as hard."

Linda shrugged and waved at the reception room. "When I started here, everything was lovelier because it was new. But I was sad for Gloria. She never updated and was behind the times. Her business was more a walk-in barbershop."

"If you were her employee," Tommie said, "you saw Arturo a lot."

"Well, he stopped by often to see his cousin. He was pleasant. I admit, he loved talking to Peaches. I didn't know him like she did."

Tommie nodded. "Understood."

Jace forced himself to focus on the receptionist. "How's your boss handling the shootings?"

Linda threw a peek at the door behind her. "Thalia is in her office and supposedly taking it easy. No one has seen her since she went inside when she arrived. That's unusual. She's usually cruises around and makes sure our clients are happy." Linda pressed against the counter and motioned them to her. "She told us she fainted when she heard her sister was dead. Good thing she and Rex were working on the books, and she wasn't by herself."

"Scary," Tommie said.

"Stressful." That's exactly how he felt with Tommie beside him. He did his best to stay rooted to his spot near her. "Were they alone when the shooting happened?"

"She and Rex routinely grab takeout at the end of the week and go over the numbers while eating. He always locks the building doors."

Gloria's ex and Thalia sealed away together. This image brought up lots of possibilities. "How did Rex handle the news of the deaths? It must have been a blow for him."

"I think he was distracted by Thalia. Rex thought she'd suffered a heart attack. He was going to call an ambulance, but she regained consciousness and refused to get checked out."

Tommie's eyes widened. "Did the police tell her on the phone?"

"No one said how they got the word." Linda paused and massaged her forehead. "Customers have been calling, and we've gotten deliveries of cards, flowers, and food. Most of the gifts are in the break room." She jabbed a finger at the hallway table. A collection of bouquets decorated the console center. Plates of snacks rested around the vases. "Our patrons are very thoughtful."

He was glad he wasn't sensitive to the scents. "People are generous."

"They are. We're booked solid for later in the day." She tapped her pen on the desk for a moment. "A couple of weeks ago, a vandal shot out Thalia's rear car window while it was in our lot. Some of our employees are whispering that the murderer did it and was practicing on her first. I mean, who knows?" She shuddered. "Thalia reported the vandalism, but no arrests have been made."

"Terrible, isn't it, Jace?" Tommie injected.

"Horrible," he agreed. "Any security cameras on the property?"

Linda paled. "We have nothing. When the building was remodeled, they reviewed the budget. Thalia cut the monitors as a cost-saver."

"She presented a strong front at the memorial," Jace noted.

Linda bobbed her head. "She tries to be a model for us. She told an employee she spoke to a police detective after most of us left."

"Grey?" Tommie moved a foot from the desk.

"Is that his name? We were hoping he would announce an arrest was imminent, but Thalia hasn't shared details with us. Everyone is worried about her." Linda released a shaky breath. "She thought it would be better if the spa stayed open, but it's been hard. No one talks about anything else. I wish we'd temporarily shut down."

Jace scooted the tissue box under Linda's chin.

"Everyone is upset." The receptionist blew her nose.

"Who would hurt a person who ran a salon?" Tommie probed.

"No one I know." A tear trickled down Linda's cheek. She brushed it away. "When I worked for Gloria, she was critical, especially if you messed up. She could be nice if she was in a good mood, but she had a lot of problems and rarely smiled. I felt bad for her."

"Money issues?" he suggested.

Linda's lower lip turned under. "Mostly fights with her sister. She and Thalia competed over everything. If one bought something, the other had to have either the same product or an upgraded version. They reminded me of feuding twins. Gloria was barely a year older. A lot of customers confused the two until Thalia dyed her hair silver."

"Did the two sisters fight over men?" Tommie asked, wide-eyed.

Linda peeked around before continuing. "Gloria was super upset when she and Rex split, although she initiated the divorce. She announced she couldn't take another second of his cheating."

Tommie frowned. "He doesn't sound like good husband material."

"There was a bit of goodness in him." The receptionist rushed to explain. "People might not agree with my opinion, but Gloria owed some responsibility for their breakup. She never had a spare moment for her husband. The business was her whole life." She paused to wipe her cheeks. "Rex refused to budge from their house until the settlement was inked. Gloria blamed him for any little thing that went wrong during that time."

"What happened in the end?"

"Rex lost his share of the shop and their home in the divorce. Gloria still wasn't happy. She could be petty. When he moved out, he forgot his scissors and combs. She threw them in the dumpster. Those things aren't cheap."

Jace ran through his mental catalog of motives for the Alvaro deaths. Had the crime been inspired by greed, a revenge scheme, or a combo of each? The image of Peaches leaning into Rex at the memorial sharpened in his mind. "Does Peaches enjoy working here?"

"She's popular with clients, and she thought she'd bring in a larger paycheck at Thalia's. Besides, she wouldn't stay with Rex's ex."

Tommie laid a palm on the counter. "Are the two dating?"

"Ew." Linda drew back. "She's his daughter."

"Daughter?" He hadn't predicted that one. He might bump her up on his interview list. "Was Gloria her mom?"

"Rex and Peaches didn't meet until last year, when she found him. It's all documented by DNA. Her mother has been married to someone else for almost fifteen years." Linda wet her lips as though she couldn't wait for the juicy gossip. "Rex doesn't like people to know. It's an open secret no one talks about if they want to keep their job. Don't mention what I told you. Anyway, that's why Peaches calls him by his name. I think having a kid makes him feel old."

"I had no idea," Tommie said. "Was Gloria aware Peaches was Rex's child?"

"Your guess is as good as mine. We didn't talk about him since it upset her."

Jace considered that Rex most likely preferred that his girlfriends and his ex were unaware of the truth. "How—"

The loud squeak of hinges pulled their attention to the office door.

Thalia paused in the opening. Her glare flitted from Linda to them. "Can I help you?"

"We wished to express our sympathy," Tommie said. "And I need a hair appointment. I'm Tommie Murphy."

Thalia approached the counter. "You both were at the Reese Center." She pointed at Tommie. Her eyes sparked with anger. "You, Miss Murphy, came to see me about a dog and a surfboard." She raised a thin, penciled eyebrow. "Listen, I have no desire to take in a pet, no matter who owned it, or a board for the water." Irritation radiated off her shoulders.

Tommie stayed in place and shifted nervously from foot to foot. "I understand."

Thalia scowled at Jace. "You're the private investigator. Are you at my salon to gather evidence to try to prove I killed my sister?"

He switched to a different tack. "I believe you loved Gloria and didn't hurt her."

"Bah." She winced, but the stress lines on her forehead eased. "I've spoken to a lawyer. He informed me not to speak to anyone about the murders. And you!" She aimed her finger at Tommie again. "Seems like I'm not the main one under suspicion." She stomped to her office and turned to them. "Linda, schedule Miss Murphy. She needs to go."

"Of course, Thalia." The receptionist gave her attention to Tommie. "Did you have a preference? We have lots of talented employees."

"Give her Peaches's first opening," Thalia ordered.

Linda scrolled for a second on her computer. "A week from today, Peaches is available at two p.m." She filled out the appointment notice and passed it to Tommie.

"See you in a few days, Linda." Her expression tightened. "Jace."

Thalia stood, watching Tommie cross to the exit.

He held his ground. Was the woman guilty or innocent? "I'll leave my contact number and email for you, Miss Alvaro. I'm available if you want to meet about anything at all." He seized a business card from his pocket. When she didn't show any interest, he dropped it on the counter. "Take care." He strode away from the reception desk.

"Come back soon," Linda called in a singsong, flirtatious voice.

He raised a hand and kept walking. Was Tommie gone yet? He wasn't ready to discuss yesterday with her, but it wasn't safe for her out walking around.

The heat surrounded him as he stepped outside the salon. The door clicked shut behind him. His mind bounced to Tommie and her private agenda. His temper sparked, and he did his best to control it. He scanned the lot for her hatchback. No signs of her. He marched to the side of the building. No Tommie.

His anger faded as he hopped into his car. She'd left. Unfortunately, he was experiencing a strong urge to find her.

CHAPTER EIGHTEEN

Jace started his vehicle at the salon. It was clear Tommie was going to be meddling in the investigation and not staying in her studio apartment. Dangerous. That also meant their paths would cross. They needed to talk.

He drove to the exit to merge into traffic and spotted her. She was walking down the sidewalk. Had her old car died? With his flashers blinking, he pulled out and glided along beside her.

She startled and splayed a hand over her chest. “Don’t sneak up on people, Jackson.”

Cars steered into the passing lane and zipped by him. He lowered the passenger window. “Where’s your car?”

“I took the bus. I had a flat tire.”

“I’ll park, and you can hop in.” He headed to a nearby lot and found a spot.

She approached him and rested her folded arms on the car’s frame. “I can take the bus home.”

“I’m here. Get in.”

She studied his expression, probably searching for anger. Shadows under her eyes told him she’d been suffering insomnia.

She reached for the handle and hesitated. “Are you sure?”

He tapped the unlock button.

She climbed inside and hugged the door. “I shouldn't have hidden my mom's secret or mine from you.” She stared at her hands in her lap. “I was wrong. Everything was woven together, despite how I attempted to deal with parts of my life separately. I wanted to tell you about Arturo and my mother. First, I had to think how to break the news to you. I decided Mom had to be the one to disclose her Alvaro connection.”

“Tommie.” He held up a palm to stop her nonstop confession. “I can't do my job if my client isn't honest with me.” He fought his rising annoyance. “Not all my clients have been straight with me, but I expected more from you. And why were you at Thalia's today and strolling around in the open when you've gotten a threat?”

She opened and closed her mouth as though she'd argue and changed her mind. “I was working on snagging a lead, to prove I was a capable person. I guess the idea didn't work out.” Her shoulders sank downward.

Her sincerity cracked his resolve, but twinges of his temper warned him not to forgive her. “You should have trusted me. I'm not a stranger you hired from the Internet. We've known each other for years.” He'd hit on what bothered him the most. “Why wouldn't you confide in me, your friend?”

She lifted her head. “I've always tried to keep my mistakes private. Lately, I've been doing my best to fix them.” She looked up from staring at her lap. “My biggest secret has always been my mom. I never let people grasp how dysfunctional she was. I couldn't explain her behavior as a kid. I'm not sure if I can now. If she got into trouble, I worked to get her out of the jam before anyone learned how she operated.”

“The past is over. You don't have to go through difficult periods alone.”

She shifted to sit with her back to the door and gazed at him. “Others can be harsh. Even you and Gigi didn’t know the whole story.”

He refrained from commenting, sensing she’d continue.

She curled her fingers into her palms. “I grew up fearing she'd be reported to social services, and they'd take me away. The thought terrified me. She’s my only family. As I got older, she was a constant embarrassment because of her problems.” Tommie raised her chin. “But she’s my mom.” She clenched her hands on her knees. “And I will handle the situation.”

Her mouth set in a line of determination. She met his gaze. “Believe . . . me?” Her voice shook on the last word, betraying her stress and a pain he hadn’t expected.

He fought the urge to tell her he understood. It was okay. Slow down. First, he had to make her understand. “Listen. After Alicia and my pal cheated on me, I realized one thing. I can’t deal with dishonesty from my so-called friends again.”

“I promise you won’t regret giving me a second chance.” She placed her hand on his arm. “Will you?”

The whiz of passing cars, the honks of horns, and a dog barking filled the quiet between them while he wrestled with his answer. He was keenly aware of the warmth of her palm and that she was waiting for him to speak.

“Jace?” The plea in her words made him long to stretch across his seat to reassure her. Worse, he felt that tug of something he didn’t want to decipher whenever she was around. *Careful.*

“What about Arturo and your mother?” he asked to avoid the growing impulse to console her. “I don’t have the full picture.”

She sat back and broke their contact, causing him regret and relief.

“Well, my mom was devastated that she fell for his con, especially since they dated for a short time. She thought she was too smart to be taken advantage of. Now she looked like the fool of the year."

"Why did you go to his house, Tommie? He was a crook." He struggled to hold his temper. Why had she put herself in such a dangerous position?

"I assumed I could guilt him into returning at least part of Mom's money. I had no clue he was broke." She paused and seemed to reflect for a moment. "As a last resort, I would have threatened to report him to the law."

Jace opened his mouth to interrupt, and she rushed to add, "I know now legal pressure wouldn't have worked. He'd have slipped away. He was a pro."

"And you couldn't go to the police because your mother was on probation for her DUI. She was worried about going to jail again if she was investigated for her connection to a con man."

"I'm glad you understand. There was a chance they would learn Arturo was into ripping people off and think she was involved in his shady business. And I fell for the way Arturo gushed about his valuable antiques. I expected he'd sell one or two and give me the cash he stole from Mom. I guess my mom and I are alike. We both act on ideas before we understand the whole situation." She folded her arms over her chest and frowned.

"Your plan could be interpreted as blackmail, Tommie." Did she understand her situation?

"I wanted to get my mom's investment back." She fisted her hand on her knee. "That was fair."

"Fair or not, the cops might disagree over a few legalities, but let's set aside motives for now." Jace watched a woman stroll past them, holding the hand of a small child. A picture of simple trust. He refocused on their conversation. "Did Yvette provide you with any new details about Arturo? Did they really meet online?"

"In my aunt Sissy's obit, my mom listed her name as the sole living relative, which suggested she'd inherit whatever was left behind. I wondered if Arturo found her through my aunt's death announcement and located her on the dating site."

"Scam artists have used the scheme for years."

"I should have explained to you that she knew Arturo. What a mess." She rubbed her forehead. "Please, forget my mom and the investigation. I want us to be friends. That's all. Never mind my case."

Her words caused that ache in his chest. He gripped the bottom of the steering wheel to avoid touching her and struggled with how to make her understand how he felt. "Sometimes I think about when we were kids, and your mother didn't come home. We rode our bikes around searching for her. You were upset and anxious."

"I get it. You were worried that I would get arrested like I was worried about my mom being arrested or hurt. And Gigi didn't allow us to go far to look," she reminded him.

"No, she didn't."

"If Mom didn't come home, I went to your grandmother's. You guys were the best. I can't count the times Mom couldn't take me to after-school events. You and Gigi took me. I haven't forgotten." She squared her shoulders. "But Jace, it's time to solve my own problems."

"You don't have to tackle everything by yourself. That's why you hired me, and it's important you understand our agreement."

"I can do better, Jace. I promise." Her pledge rang with sincerity. She leaned toward him. "I miss you. My friend."

The sweet smell of her lotion or shampoo floated around him, teasing, pushing him to kiss away the concern on her face. *Stop.* What was wrong with him? He cared about her. That's what was wrong with him. And she'd called him a friend? He'd called her the same. Why was he irritated?

"Will you forgive me?" She peered up at him. "I will not to let my mom involve me in her issues, and I'll be completely honest and open with you."

Get back on track. He reined in his emotions. "Let's stay grounded. You're a suspect, according to what Grey told me at the memorial, which means bigger discoveries and blows may be coming."

"Are you saying I should let the authorities handle the investigation? I bet they'd as soon arrest me and label the case closed." Frowning, she sat back against the door

Tommie arrested? In an instant, he wanted to return to the way things had been before the scene at her mom's house. That meant forgiving her. If he didn't, was he prepared to walk away from the job and her? Could he forget the years they'd shared and the childhood memories? What if she was charged with the murders? He instinctively knew he wouldn't be able to forgive himself if she went to prison because he hadn't done everything he could for her.

He gave her a stern look. "No secrets," he ordered. "Did Arturo know you were one of his victim's daughters?"

"He didn't. My mom and I have a pact. She doesn't acknowledge me, and I do my best to get along without her unless she's in one of her bad ways."

"Why would you be a secret?"

"She and Rex have something in common. She believes an adult daughter makes her appear old and ruins her image. My mom is a lover of denial. Remember, she uses my stepfather's last name. I was never positive they married. She thinks others respect her if she has a missus title."

Her mother had lots of odd notions he didn't have a lifetime to discuss. "Do we have an understanding?"

"We do. I will be as transparent as plastic wrap." When he hesitated, she jumped in. "I am forever thankful for all you've done. Believe me." She held out her hand.

"You're certain there is nothing else to reveal? Did your mom go out with Alfredo or Rex or Thalia or—"

"I've not a syllable to add."

He took her hand, and they quickly shook.

"To a new beginning." She lowered her tensed shoulders. "Can I ask which person you'll investigate next?"

"Let's fix your car first." Getting her home was a priority. Being confined together in his vehicle brought up ideas he shouldn't have.

He drove to the Yellow Flamingo Inn. In the lot, he pulled up behind her car. The rear left tire had gone completely flat. They hopped out. He inspected the damage while sensing he was letting her off too easily for keeping secrets, but refusing to help her wasn't an option.

When he straightened and told her he'd fix it. She sent him a bright smile that reflected the light of gratitude and happiness in her blue eyes.

His doubts vanished. For an instant. He heard his grandfather lecturing. *Always stay emotionally detached from your clients' cases.*

Too bad he hadn't followed his advice. He'd do better.

CHAPTER
NINETEEN

While Jace cleaned up in Tommie's bathroom, the sun was sliding toward the afternoon side of the sky. He'd put the new tire was on her car. She'd sent an online report and images of the flat to the police and the inn manager.

Now, as he walked into the main room, he found her slumped beside Picasso, sharing the sofa and watching TV. They needed a break. "Gigi gave me two desserts. I'll pick them up, and we can ride to the park and enjoy her cooking. We'll bring the big guy with us."

"You had me at 'desserts.'" She got the dog's leash. "Let's go."

After a quick stop to collect Gigi's cheesecake, they arrived at Riverview Park. They strolled around the grassy grounds where the city held free events. The docks that jetted out from the narrow shore for fishing or observing the manatees were empty. Picasso sniffed the area and studied the dogs parading by on their leashes.

When they finished stretching their legs, she settled at a picnic table under a wooden pavilion. Jace brought the ice chest over from his car and sat on the bench across from her. It was a perfect place for a work pause.

He drew out a wrapped bone for Picasso, lying near his feet. He turned and admired the serenity of the river. Speedboats cruised past the island in the middle of the water. Two sailboats raced off to somewhere. The light breeze puffed out the white sails.

Tommie perched her sunglasses on her nose and took in the idyllic spot. “Arturo loved sailing.”

“The authorities must have confiscated his craft and any funds he had left.” Jace glanced toward the shouts of children in the fenced playground. Hardwood trees sheltered three preschoolers climbing and running around a green slide. He guessed the young women grouped by the swings were the moms or family sitters.

Facing her again, he remembered he hadn’t filled her in on his conversation with his grandmother. “I didn’t get a chance to tell you what I learned from Gigi the other day.”

“What did she say?” Tommie straightened in her seat.

“Well, this is gossip.” As he lifted the lid off the cooler, he grabbed a container and handed it, along with a napkin and plastic fork, to her.

“That makes it more interesting.” Her mouth curved upward for the first time all day.

“Arturo and Gloria were sleeping together.” He removed the soft lid on his dessert and inhaled the scent of the caramel topping.

She blinked twice. “Wow, that’s important, isn’t it?”

“For sure. Remember, Gloria dated Alfredo. I bet Rex didn’t like hearing rumors about his ex-wife’s lifestyle.”

“Rex could be the shooter?” She frowned. “You’ve done a great job investigating, but everyone has a motive, weak or strong." Her eyes lit. "I found out a few things from Linda at the spa." She poised her fork over her food.

He dug into his helping. "That was a different kind of situation. Thalia wanted to throw us out, but she didn't because she'd lose money on your haircut."

"She's thrifty. Listen to what I learned from Linda. When the sisters had the big argument on their final day together, Thalia was screaming that she wished her sister had never been born or died at birth."

Jace's attention sharpened. "And Gloria is dead, and her sister had her wish granted—in a sick, delayed way."

"The remaining Alvaro could be the murderer."

"We've got one problem. She claimed she was with Rex the evening of the murders." He rubbed his chin.

"And if they were guilty," Tommie said, "why didn't Thalia and Rex go out in public after the shooting to give themselves an alibi and witnesses?"

"Maybe they believed keeping to their usual routine was enough. A decent defense attorney would convince a judge and jury that Thalia hoping her sister died was angry talk and nothing else." The investigation was as clear as mud pies. Jace flicked a graham cracker crumb onto the ground for a bird. "Who is protecting who in this crisscross of relationships?"

Tommie dug into her dessert. "Thalia could still be in shock or in denial of her feelings. Deep down, she could have loved Gloria."

Why was she defending Thalia? "She and Gloria were jealous, resentful competitors. Why not get rid of her?"

Tommie nudged him with her fingertips. "You and I will be all right, won't we?"

As much as he tried to ignore her touch, the emotion in her words pulled him toward her. A blue jay swooped to the grass, snatched the morsel, and flew off as he gathered his thoughts. "If you're open and honest, we'll be okay."

"I will be." She moved her hand away. Her eyes clouded. "I'm worried my mom doesn't have an alibi for the night of the shootings. The good news is she doesn't drive, and Arturo's house was too far to walk. I guess she could have arranged transportation if she was determined to murder him. Though my mom is rarely that motivated."

"We can't underestimate that the police will or may have found out about your mother and Arturo. Now, how will they use their discovery?"

On the playground, the kids laughed. At the table, Tommie ate quietly.

Jace searched for a topic that would distract her from worrying about Yvette. The image of Peaches snuggled up to Rex floated in his mind. "Hey, how about Peaches and Rex at the memorial? He wasn't quite an example of a fatherly role model, was he?"

"I thought he was her date," she confessed. "My bad. I'm glad I'm not a member of their family tree."

"The salon group had a lot of rotten limbs." The breeze carried the laughs of an excited child on the swings. "And I'll talk to Peaches and get a better sense of her guilt or innocence."

"I can do it." Tommie gestured at herself. "Peaches is cutting my hair. I'll chat her up and find out if she has any witnesses to back up her claim of shopping."

"No." He scooped up a mouthful of cheesecake to keep from arguing.

"We can go over everything I'll say." She smiled brightly. "What could go wrong?"

Picasso lifted his twitching nose as if catching a disagreeable scent.

"The dog has answered." Jace raised a palm in the air. "And didn't you pledge to stay out of the case?"

"Think about it. It's a simple cut."

"What's the matter with your hair? I like it that way."

She leaned toward him. "You do?"

Somehow, he'd touched on something deeper than he'd meant. Her warm, teasing voice caught and focused his attention on her. The bobbing boats, the lingering sweet taste of the dessert, and the children's shouts of happiness faded.

Her long fingers brushed a curl from her cheek, sending a swirl of heat through his gut. Under that button-up shirt, her chest rose and fell. A lone functioning fragment of his brain cautioned he was in danger, sinking fast. He didn't listen.

He covered her hand resting on the table. She gaped at him until a spark in her eyes appeared and urged him closer. He leaned against the hard tabletop to give her a quick kiss as a wind gust tossed their napkins and utensils between their faces.

Jace jumped into action. He collected and stuffed everything in the plastic bag. As she watched him, she kept her feelings to herself.

Okay, he wasn't doing well with his resolution of keeping their relationship on a business level. This was his chance to reset the mood. "You're invited for supper tomorrow at Gigi's. She told me to ask you. I'll pick you up around seven."

He threw the trash in the cooler to take home. He'd almost slipped up and kissed her. What was happening? For a man who regarded himself as a professional in control of his emotions, he'd fallen in over his head. Worse, he had no net to catch him.

CHAPTER TWENTY

The outdoor lamppost by Tommie's window lit the studio. The digital clock on the stove glowed 11:55 p.m. as she lay in her bed, unable to catch a wink. Her muscles ached from lack of rest, but her mind wouldn't shut off. Flashes of the day, especially of Jace almost kissing her, rotated through her brain. She tried to turn over, but Picasso was snoring on her legs.

The AC clicked off. Good. She was nearly chilled in her ivory sleep tank top and shorts. Ice cubes from the refrigerator ice maker clunked into their tray.

Think positive thoughts. Tomorrow, Jace would pick her up for Gigi's dinner. She'd taken out the dress she would wear, clean and fresh from the laundry. Hopefully, her choice would make an impression on him. She smiled to herself as Picasso stirred.

"It's not daylight yet, boy."

His ears perked up. He stared at the door and pointed his nostrils upward, sniffing.

Was someone passing by? She sat up, straining to hear over

the normal sounds of the inn—pipes knocking and electrical appliances buzzing.

Picasso's nose twitched.

The soft pad of footsteps outside her room forced her to freeze when she opened her mouth to reassure her pet. The steps moved closer to her doorway and paused. She pulled the sheet to her chin. Was she imagining things? She held her breath and heard the fridge hum in the silence.

She exhaled. What was wrong with her? People came and left the inn during all hours. Perhaps a fellow resident was being considerate and tiptoeing.

Swishes of clothing in rhythm with a body's movements drew her attention to the hall again. Was a stranger roaming around? The skin on the back of her neck prickled. The deadbolt was on. Should she yell or peek out?

The dog growled a warning and scooted off the bed.

The impulse to pull the covers over her head gripped her. *Stay calm.* The dog had sensed her nerves. That's all. "Hel-lo?" She sat up. "Anybody?"

No answer or shuffle of shoes. Was the person gone, or was somebody looming in the corridor, waiting for the moment she'd slide the lock and look out?

Picasso scratched at the old wooden doorframe and whined. Tommie bet one strong push against her flimsy entry, and it would fly open. Shaking, she rolled off the mattress. "Sit," she whispered to the dog.

She hurried across the cool tiles to a cabinet drawer and snatched a steak knife. Standing an inch from her entrance, she yelled, "I've called the police. You better leave."

The whir of an appliance answered. She positioned her body to block anyone from bursting in. Perspiration poured over her brow. She slid the bolt and winced at the metallic click. In one hand, she pointed her weapon down. With the other, she cracked the door wide enough to peer out.

The low ceiling lights of an empty hall droned in the silence. "Hello?"

Gulping, she stuck her head out and searched the beige-tiled corridor. There was no mechanical whine from the elevator signaling it was in use. Across the hallway, the fire door to the stairs was shut. All was clear.

Relieved, she locked up. She stroked the dog's soft fur and willed herself to stop imagining the worst.

Picasso eyed her.

She had overreacted. In the light of day, would she think she'd been foolish or that she should have opened sooner to discover if anybody was outside her room?

She switched on the lamp and tucked the knife under the edge of her mattress. Armed, she crawled into bed to wait for daylight and the answers.

* * *

The big evening had arrived. In her studio, Tommie ended her pacing and gaped at the digital clock: 7:03 p.m. A boxed security camera had been delivered five minutes ago. She'd look at it later. Jace must have ordered it. He'd be here any second. Should she bring up the mysterious, noise in the passageway? What would he do? She knew the answer. He'd interview the inn's guests and the desk clerk to determine if anyone had crept around during the bewitching hour.

She wasn't up for that and had worked out her own theory. It was simple. A resident got off on the wrong floor. Most likely, the person exited the elevator after drinking a little too much or wasn't paying attention. To be safe, she'd sleep with the blade beneath her mattress again.

She walked across the tile to the side window and back to the table. Forget the inn's creaks and swishes. She had dinner to go to. Why was she nervous? They'd enjoy a casual, small gathering. She and Gigi weren't strangers. And it wasn't like Jace was taking her home to "meet the parents or grandparents." Everyone understood what that meant.

"Why didn't I drive us there?" she asked Picasso. "Jace picking me up feels date-ish."

On the sofa, the dog blinked at her.

"Right. Go and enjoy. I'm glad you concur." She patted him. "Gigi will love you. I can see your pretty eyes now that I brushed you." Tommie clutched her hands together. She sank onto the cushion. The dog lay beside her.

At the knock, she tensed. "Who is it?"

"Jace."

He was here. She ran to the bathroom and examined her reflection. Her hair was under control, the rest of her wasn't. Her face was a sickly white with splotches of red on her cheeks.

"Tommie?"

"Coming." She ran to let him in. Picasso nudged in front of her, wagging his tail.

She turned the lock, held the door open, and invited him in. "Hey, my security camera arrived today. I haven't—" Quickly, she took in his expression. He wasn't frowning or tightening his jaw. Both positive signs.

She tapped her fingers against her thigh while he stood, staring at her. "Everything okay?"

"Uh-huh." He lowered his gaze and continued scoping her out.

"What's wrong?" She forced herself to relax her raised shoulders to hide her worries.

"You're wearing a dress."

She ran a hand down the blue, shapely, stretchy fabric, avoiding his gawking. Did he think she'd overdone it?

The uncomfortable truth rose in her mind. Jace was escorting her to his grandmother's, not because it was his job, but because Gigi wanted him to bring her.

He was still gaping at her.

"I wore a dress to Arturo's memorial."

"It was . . . different." He studied her.

She looked perfect—if they were attending an opera. Well, she didn't have time to completely change. "Should I take off the necklace?" She hooked her finger around the gold chain with glinting indigo stones and pulled it away from her. The jewelry reminded her of the day she'd met Arturo at the co-op. She'd planned to connect the two-dollar purchase to a happier occasion at Gigi's home. Looked like that wasn't happening.

His features eased. "Don't bother. You look nice."

Nice? She'd picked the outfit especially for their evening. She thought he would like it better than her usual capri pants.

But this was her buddy, Jace. She'd been kidding herself. She turned to shove a chair into the table and hide her disappointment. Yes, but yesterday at the park had felt different. *Come into reality*. He probably hadn't been going to kiss her. More likely, she'd had a twig or a bug in her hair, he'd been about to grab.

Sitting by Jace, Picasso whimpered.

"You're handsome too." He scratched the dog behind his ear.

"He wants his vest. I gave him a bath, and I was letting him dry before I put it back on."

"I'll get it." He seized the red fabric from the counter. "The dog harness would fit a baby elephant."

"You're sure it's okay he comes too?"

"Gigi loves animals." He snapped on the leash.

"And I'm not expected to bring an appetizer, or drink, or my blood?" Didn't a guest usually arrive with a dish? Would

Gigi expect food? Tommie was an adult now, not the lonely kid looking for a safe spot to stay. She'd goofed on her clothing. She couldn't afford to make another mistake, no matter how small.

"My grandmother will pile the food on the plate. I bet Picasso will run from her."

"The dog ate. Though I can't guarantee he won't use his sad whimpers to score a snack." She scooped up her purse and keys. "I'm set."

Jace stood aside for her to go first. She locked up, and they went down the stairs. Their feet and paws padded in the empty staircase.

"Do you have anything to add from your computer searches?" she asked, eager to get out of the stairwell.

He paused to answer. "We can talk in the car. But I'm convinced the cousins' deaths were personally motivated. We should examine if you need to tighten your safety precautions."

"What does that mean exactly?" She looked downward. One flight left.

"During periods of stress or anger, grievances can become magnified and extend to others, including you. To be safe, I'll continue driving you to and from your job."

In the lot, he opened the car doors for her and Picasso. The dog jumped into the rear, and she climbed in the front.

It didn't hurt that the servers at the Whale's Spout had quizzed her about the cool-looking dude picking her up and dropping her off.

"He's a former neighbor, helping me out," she'd told them.

Many had exchanged silent, disbelieving looks, and Tommie had shrugged and held back her smile.

Jace slamming his car door ended her memories of work. As they cruised along, Picasso sat upright by his window, seeming fascinated by the scenery lit by streetlamps.

“When Arturo and I first met,” she said to Jace, “he portrayed himself as the friendly, grandfatherly type.”

“You didn’t think he’d expect more than conversation from you?”

“He would have needed a reminder or two to stay in the friend zone, but I could handle him.” Had she been wrong?

“Risky move.” He frowned. “The fact he stole money from your mother should have been a huge red flag that he was a crook.”

“As I told you, I hoped to make a deal with him.” She crossed and uncrossed her legs, unable to get comfortable. “Any other news on the case before we eat?” She might as well go for total indigestion.

“I met with the president of the Manatee Lake Estates Homeowners Association today.”

Her interest sharpened. "What happened?"

CHAPTER TWENTY-ONE

"Well?" Tommie prompted.

Jace threw her a glance. "I didn't learn anything earthshaking, except the HOA president of Manatee Lake Estates told me they don't have a security guard. That means the figure you saw immediately after the murders wasn't an employee."

"I wish I could give you a better description. I was shocked when a person ran in front of me."

"It was a traumatic situation. The president of the group also confirmed the alert headquarters was a quarter of a mile away and that's why Arturo's team arrived quickly."

The wail of the sirens and flashing lights shot through her mind. "Do you think the mysterious person in black planned to hijack my clunker because it would be quicker than a hike to a getaway car?"

"A possibility."

Jace cruised down a side street and passed the dollar store. The gates of Gigi's community appeared. He punched in the code on the black box. The entry slowly swung open. He drove to Gigi's circular drive and parked.

Tommie hopped out and opened Picasso's door. The dog ran to sniff the flowers bordering the home.

"One final question." She joined him at the hood of the car. "How could Arturo have fooled everyone?"

"He had years of practice with his past victims. From my computer searches, I've learned most of his targets had little to no family, and he acted fast in the romance department. Consider yourself lucky you weren't one of his casualties. You took a big risk."

She tugged at the neckline of her dress, which had become uncomfortably tight. "I was determined to get my mom's money back, and I thought she'd be grateful to me."

He sent her a glance of disbelief and cleared his throat. "Let's set the subject aside. Remember, we hang loose tonight. Let's go in." Jace whistled for the dog, who ran to join them.

He rang the bell. After a second, he pulled his key from his pocket and inserted it. "Gigi must be busy fussing over the food. I bet she's doing last-minute arrangements." He ushered them into the hall.

Picasso set to work, sniffing the tiled floor like a bloodhound.

"Hello," he yelled in his usual greeting. "Tommie and I are here."

The AC hummed in the quiet. The dog raised his snout. His nostrils trembled in the air.

Jace stuffed his key away. "She's probably in the kitchen." He strode through the formal living room.

Tommie and Picasso followed. She'd forgotten how spotless and neat Gigi kept her house. The aqua-colored furniture and the crisp, off-white drapes looked brand new.

"Gigi," he called and paused in the dining nook with three windows. A bare glass tabletop sat under a silver pendant lamp.

"I'll check the pantry." He marched into the adjoining space and returned. "She's not in there."

A familiar handwritten note taped to the refrigerator snagged Tommie's attention. "She left a message." She pointed to the memo with relief and curiosity.

He snatched the paper and read aloud:

"'Dear Jace and Tommie, my friend Clara was having severe pains. I'm driving her to the ER. Your meals are in the fridge. Please forgive me for running off. Love, Gigi. PS: I expect to be home late. You know hospitals.'"

"She had to be upset if she changed her dinner plans and didn't contact us." Tommie shooed away Picasso, who was snooping around the table. The dog had the advantage of being level with the furnishings. Gigi wouldn't appreciate it if he smeared nose slime on the glass top.

He opened the fridge. "Gigi spared a few minutes to store and label our food." He grabbed two plastic containers and turned.

She found herself a centimeter from him. How had he gotten this close? Heat from his wide chest soaked through her thin dress. His gaze traveled up and down her form. She held her breath, hoping to slow the rhythm of her fast-beating heart.

Without thinking, she reached up and brushed his overgrown hair back. Surprised, he raised his brows. Why had she done that? Suddenly, she was too aware they were alone. The faint odor of clean soap and the fresh smell of the damp night air lingered on his clothes and skin.

His eyes burned with an intense light as he stepped up to her. Her nerve endings sizzled. All her dark, shadowy problems disappeared."Jace," she finally whispered.

He fingered a stray curl before his lips touched hers, full and tempting. A nervous energy flowed through her. T*his was it, the step over the friendship line.* She slid her hand up to his broad shoulder, holding on to him and his heat. His lips brushed hers.

Her pulse was pounding, and her thoughts scattered. In the distance, Picasso whined. *Not now*, she managed to think.

Something wet nudged her elbow, followed by Picasso's big body pushing between them.

Jace retreated a step. "Uh." He ran a hand over his jaw. "I believe your animal is after the food."

Oh no. Her pet had stuck his head in the open refrigerator.

He ordered Picasso to move and shut the door.

Her dog sure could kill a moment. A damp smudge on her leg caught her attention. Ew, was that dog drool? She grabbed a paper towel and wiped the wet spot.

Jace watched her. "Are you all right?" He rubbed his jaw. "Afraid I stepped over the line. It won't happen again."

"Okay." She bit her lip. She'd dreamed about kissing him, and now it had ended, barely happened. Not that it hadn't been wonderful, but too short, a tease. She wanted more.

He seemed to regret it. He had changed the subject and was talking about cuisine and the dog. And why had he apologized because he was a professional and not acting like one? Was that his excuse?

His cell buzzed in his pocket. "It must be a text from Gigi." He pulled out his phone and read the screen. "She's staying with Clara at her house tonight. Clara's well enough to come home but needs another test. It can't be done until tomorrow. Gigi wants to be certain we'll eat."

He shoved away his phone. "I should go check on the ladies. I'll bring you to the inn first." He texted his grandmother a short text and walked to a cabinet to snatch a bag to carry their food.

Picasso looked up at Tommie as if to ask what was going on.

So much for their evening. "I'll run a cloth over the table and fridge where the dog scouted around. Would you mind taking him out while I do it? He'd enjoy stretching his legs in the fenced yard."

"No problem." He handed over the plastic bag, whistled for the dog, and he and Picasso went out the rear slider.

She let out a deep breath. She needed to get control of her emotions. They'd briefly locked their lips. No big deal. People kissed each other all the time. It was a common gesture. She didn't live in the Victorian era. Besides, she wouldn't kid herself. He wasn't going to hang out with her once the police arrested someone for Arturo's murder. He had to work, and she'd be restarting her life. Yes, she'd be a model platonic friend—if he stood six or twenty feet from her.

In minutes, Picasso and Jace returned. She put their meals in the sack. The three of them tramped to the car and hopped in. During the drive, they talked about Gigi, her sick chum, and the delicious cuisine's aroma.

He parked in the lot of the Yellow Flamingo Inn. Yup, forget a romantic evening. Disappointed and eager to get away, she climbed out before he did. She waited as he snatched her meal, leashed Picasso and let him out of the rear.

"Thank Gigi and tell Clara I'm thinking of her." She leveled her gaze on the food. "I can't wait to taste Gigi's cooking."

"I'll go in with you."

"Don't bother."

"Hey, enough strange things have gone on. C'mon." He tightened his grip on her dinner and nodded to the building. "Set?"

What would happen at her door? Nothing. Her nerves twanged and twinged as he escorted her.

She barely noticed the musty odor in the stairwell. The thought of saying goodbye at her rental occupied her mind. The end of their not-a-date night was proving he wasn't that into her.

They paused outside her studio while she dug out the key. Picasso sat near her feet.

Jace crowded up behind her with the leftovers. "Too bad dinner ended before we had a chance to eat."

Get away fast. She unlocked the door and pushed it ajar as she turned to him. "Thanks for the ride." She edged backward into her room and held out her hand for her supper.

"I'm trying to say—" He peered over her head and frowned. "Tommie."

"What?" Had she forgotten to turn off the coffeemaker?

"Did I miss that you moved the dog food to your couch?" He went around her and followed a trail of canine chow on the floor to the pulled-out sofa bed. Picasso's bag of chow sat on the mattress.

She stepped inside. Her blankets, pillows, and sheets were twisted together on the flooring. The cabinets and the bureau were open. Her clothing lay in mussed heaps in the drawers.

Huh? She tried to understand what had happened. "Somebody searched through my stuff. Why? Who?" A shiver of panic chilled her back.

She massaged her temple and expelled a breath. Tonight had become a huge, throbbing headache. A premonition warned her problems were about to grow worse.

CHAPTER TWENTY-TWO

Tommie turned to Jace, her eyes bulging. "I can't believe someone messed up my place."

He laid a hand on her arm. "You and Picasso stay where you are while I look around."

The dog thumped his tail on the tile and sat by her feet.

She grabbed Jace's elbow. "Last night, I thought I heard somebody loitering in the hallway near my studio. I yelled that I had called the police, and when I opened the door, the hall was empty."

"Why didn't you tell me before now?" He struggled with his rising frustration.

"I brushed it off as a resident out late. Besides, what could you have done?" She glanced at the package by the sink. "The box with the security camera is still here."

"Too bad it's not working." He looked at her. "If you'd texted me, I'd have come over and made sure no one was hiding out in the building."

Nervously, she played with the links of the necklace. "I don't expect you to run over whenever I hear a noise. Anyway, whoever was walking around probably would have been gone when you arrived."

"I can at least check your room." He couldn't ignore the worry in his gut. "I'll be quick." He put her meal on the counter and stepped around the heap of bedding on the floor.

"Shouldn't I inspect it?" She shrugged. "It's my stuff."

"Direct me." He drew his Beretta from his pocket. Her place was small. He doubted a normal-sized human could hide in the small space.

"The man with the gun wins the discussion. And since when do you carry a gun? I thought that was your wallet."

"You'd be amazed at the size of modern-day firearms. They're easy to conceal and carry." He cautiously strode toward the bed and peered underneath. No one. "The next time you think a stalker is at the inn, don't peek out. Text me or call the 911."

"I'll remember." She pointed to the bureau. "The burglar went through my drawers. I'll need to wash everything. I mean, it's too disgusting to wear my things after a scummy stranger handled them." She wrung her hands. "Why move the bag of Picasso's food to my bed?"

"To get our attention, I'd guess." He hovered over the chunks of dog chow on the mattress. "Your crook used the nuggets to spell out 'sweet dreams.'"

"I'll have nightmares for sure. I don't get what anyone expected to find of value."

"Usually, money, drugs, anything to sell, or to frighten you." Books lay scattered across the tile. The closet was open. Inside, her clothes and hangers were thrown to the floor. In the bathroom, he yanked on the shower door. The stall was empty. Over-the-counter meds, toothpaste, and cosmetics had been brushed out of the medicine cabinet and into the sink.

"Did you have any prescription pills?" he asked, returning to the main room.

"None." She wet her dry lips. "Finished?"

"Almost." He glanced in the fridge. "All is clear." He walked back to her and studied the lock. "Not much to prevent a person from entering. A credit card would be strong enough to force the latch." He lowered his weapon. "I don't suppose the inn owns a working interior camera?"

"You deduced correctly." Her gaze jumped around the mess while she shook her head. Picasso sat and watched beside her. "The scum rifled through my personal belongings and left a message to frighten me. How creepy can you get?"

"We'll catch who did this," he assured her.

For an instant, she pressed the heels of her palms to her forehead before composing herself. "The lowlife must have been watching me. How else would someone know I was gone?" She shivered. "I hope it wasn't a renter living in the inn. Maybe the creep wanted to break in while I was sleeping, and I scared him off." She squeezed her eyes shut as though the chaos would disappear.

He slid an arm around her and settled his palm on the indent of her waist. She relaxed a fraction. She seemed thinner, leaning against him. He stared down at her soft lips he'd barely touched. *Stop.*

He sought the invisible wall that kept him on the professional side, but he only managed to loosen his hold on her.

She inhaled a deep breath and pulled away. "I'm taking pictures." She grabbed her phone.

"Did you have any cash hidden in a drawer?"

"I didn't, and a thief searching for valuables at the Yellow Flamingo doesn't make sense. If I had something worth stealing, would I live at this inn?" She raised her cell and stood near the doorway, clicking photos of the kitchen space.

"People well-off sometimes stay in cheap lodging." He took in the limited footage, the secondhand appliances, and the old furniture. *Cross out money as the reason she was targeted.*

"If you've hidden anything that's not legal, dig it out and toss it before we call the police. They'll be looking for motive," he cautioned.

"I don't have drugs or stolen goods."

He ignored her comment and pressed on. "Did Aunt Sissy leave you a family heirloom?"

"Nothing."

"Did you buy matching earrings for your necklace that might be worth money?"

"No. You're persistent."

"I'm reminding you that the law will go through your room." He didn't need another surprise like the one at her mother's home.

She fingered her necklace. "I wish I owned something of value. This chain was created of rose gold, not very expensive. The center cluster is shiny blue glass that I pretend is a sapphire. I bought it because I liked it, and Arturo offered me fifty cents off the two-dollar price. A deal."

His interest sharpened at the name—Arturo, not a good connection. What did the intruder want? He ran a second glance over the furnishings. A piece of white was sticking out from under the box spring near the headboard. What was it? He strode across the tile floor and shoved the mattress down a couple of inches to reveal white paper.

"Is it more dog food?" She tapped her foot.

"Not sure." He grabbed a bunch of tissues from a box on the counter and to use while pulling out the gift. "I don't need my prints on the evidence," he explained when she gave him a puzzled look. He pulled out an envelope. "Yours?"

"Definitely not. Open it up quick." She crowded up to him with Picasso following her.

He set his latest discovery on the countertop and shut the door. "The contents might upset you."

"I discovered dead bodies. I can take it. Hurry." She stood by his side, peering at the new discovery. Next to her, Picasso flopped down with a grunt.

Jace wasn't certain if she was telling the complete truth, but he wasn't arguing. Using his makeshift hand coverings, he pulled out two folded newspaper clippings. He smoothed the larger paper, dated three weeks before Arturo's death, on the laminated surface of the counter.

Jace and Tommie stared at a newsprint picture of Arturo in front of an artisan canopy sheltering his antiques. The headline read, "Weekend Craftsmen's Fair at Riverview Park." A black circle rimmed in red was drawn on his forehead.

"The news never reported he was shot in the head," she said in a hoarse whisper.

"Maybe it leaked. Are you okay? Can I get you a glass of water?"

She waved the offer away. "I can't believe this." She wiped a shaking hand across her brow. "If Grey had found the article in my room, he'd have accused me of saving a souvenir of the killing." She scanned down to a smaller photo. "I recognize Arturo's customer." Her lower lip trembled. "It's my mom."

Jace studied the image. He had to admit the woman did look like Yvette Miller. The couple was standing a hair's width from each other, and Arturo had his hand on her waist.

"I bet the reporter thought she was a casual shopper, but the shooter realized she was more than that. Once Grey saw the pictures, he'd want to reinterview me and my mother. Who could predict what my mom would say, especially if she'd been drinking? We can't call the cops."

She had a point. In an interview, Yvette's rash nature and uncensored answers could damage both women. The less Yvette was involved, the better. "Let's see the next clipping."

She opened to the picture of herself snapped outside the memorial for Arturo and Gloria. A black circle rimmed in red was drawn on her forehead.

She paled. "I need to sit."

Jace gripped her elbow, guiding her to the chair. He brought her water.

She sipped, and slowly, the color returned to her cheeks. "I'm better."

"Call Grey now?"

"No." Her mouth tightened with resolution.

"Fine. I'll give the clippings to my buddy who works at a lab. He'll examine the material for latent prints and DNA. We would have one problem. If he finds anything, and we want to hand the papers over to the cops, they could claim the evidence was contaminated since we broke the chain of custody."

"Grey would as soon take me into custody. He'd say I messed up my own room to throw the suspicion off myself. I'm thinking the crook wants me to report the break-in. Remind the detective I'm a prime person of interest."

"I'll go with your decision."

"I vote no law. Besides, nothing was stolen. And how will the inn react? Remember their unhelpful response to my flat tire and the not-so-lovely rhyme on my windshield?"

He snapped to a decision. "We're getting out of here. Now. Get what you need."

"I agree." Studying the mess on the floor, she gripped her hands together. "I can stay at my mom's."

Yvette's neighborhood? "Bad idea." He stuffed the news articles in the envelope and shoved it and the tissues in his pocket. "I'll make a phone call."

"You're right, but I should touch base with her." Tommie disappeared into the bathroom to speak in private.

Picasso leaped to his feet to sit by Jace's side. He pulled out his cell and tapped on Gigi's number.

His grandmother answered immediately. She reassured him that her friend felt well, and she couldn't wait to get done with her last test. "The doctors believe Clara suffered from gastric distress," Gigi rushed to tell him. "How are you and Tommie?"

"I'm happy to hear Clara is improving, and Tommie and I had quite an evening. We brought the meals you left to the inn. We arrived to find her room broken into and trashed. Nothing appears to be missing, and we're fine."

"Oh dear! I'm glad you and the crook didn't meet up. Did you report the crime to the police?"

"Not yet. Tommie needs a safe place ASAP." When they met again for cheesecake, he'd confess the entire story. He paced back to a sitting Picasso.

"Who'd do such a terrible thing?" his grandmother asked. "Tommie doesn't own anything expensive, does she?"

"Probably teenagers looking for change. That's all she has." Would she accept his white lie?

"The inn is lovely to drive past, but not to live in. It's too dangerous for her to stay there."

Gigi's firm comment gave him the opening he wanted. "Can she stay at your house?"

"Why, yes, what a wonderful idea. I should have thought of it. She can pack a bag and come over. You can use your old bedroom. I would worry if she was alone."

He'd be with Tommie 24/7. His concentration skittered in a different direction as he tried to tune in to his grandmother, who continued to talk.

"Jace? Jace? Are you listening?"

"I am, Gigi. Tell Clara we're pulling for her. You both take care." He tapped the end button.

He met Tommie as she exited the bathroom. "How's Yvette?"

"Mom was the same. She asked to use my credit card to order food. I told her to be careful and not to go out."

"I spoke to Gigi. You can crash in her guest room."

"How's Clara?" Tommie circled her pile of bedding on the floor.

"She's better. Might not be too serious. Gigi will drive her to and back from the exam tomorrow."

"That's a relief. Your grandmother is always thoughtful. I'll have to thank her for the room." She glanced at the shambles. "I should clean."

"Not now." He wasn't letting her linger a second longer at the inn.

"I guess I can pick it up later."

"You're not thinking of staying at the inn again?" Was she for real? "If Gigi learns you plan to continue living at the Yellow Flamingo, she'll be calling and texting every hour with concerns."

Tommie rubbed her shoulder as though she'd slept on her mother's lumpy furniture. "I guess I'm done here."

"Grab a few things. I'll bring you back to get the rest."

She rounded up her clothes and food for Picasso. Jace escorted her and the animal down the stairs to the parking lot.

They crossed to his car. "Picasso can hang out with you. I'll bunk in my old room."

"You're staying too?"

Was she unhappy with his decision? It didn't matter. He wasn't leaving her alone. He motioned to the open passenger side. "Are you getting in or admiring my doorman skills?"

"I should drive." She took an alarmed step away. "You don't suppose the slime broke into my hatchback, do you?"

"I'm repeating myself, but is there something valuable in your vehicle?"

"Zip." She held out her empty palms.

He shut her door and let the dog hop in the rear. "I'll look for you. Key."

"I'm a grown woman and can examine my own car."

She sounded firm. She must be better. "We'll trade. You tend to the dog, and I'll do the inspection."

She dug out her keychain and held on to it. "We'll compromise. We'll go together. I'll come back to the Yellow Flamingo to scrub and pack my things later."

They trudged to her parking spot. An uncomfortable sensation grew in Jace's gut. The useless camera above the entry was aimed at him.

He pressed up against the passenger window of her vehicle. Nothing appeared disturbed. He turned to her. "Hey, since we're unsure when you'll return, I should get the surfboard. We aren't a hundred percent positive if the board has a connection to the shootings or not."

She dug out the locker key and rattled off a brief direction and number for her storage unit.

Jace jogged off and returned in minutes and returned the key. "I'll fit the board in my car and follow you."

"Fine." Tommie hit the unlock button on the fob and slid into her seat.

He signaled when he was ready, and she drove to the exit as he followed her. The big question remained stuck in his head. Who had trashed her room? Maybe he was near, watching or following them to his grandmother's house.

CHAPTER TWENTY-THREE

Tommie and Jace strolled in step through the dunes. The sun reflected off the blue water as a seagull swooped overhead. He hesitated on the white sand and turned to her. His quiet, thoughtful eyes skimmed over her, and his mouth curved into a brief but dazzling smile that caused a funny jolt in her stomach.

She woke from the dream slowly and found she was at Gigi's house. Darn, she'd much rather be on the beach with Jace. Oh well, she had to concentrate on the real world.

Now fully awake, she took in the bright cobalt and yellow walls of Gigi's guest room. The longboard leaned against the closet door where Jace had left it last night. She glanced at the digital clock on the bed stand: 7:37 a.m. Thank goodness, her boss had agreed to give her a few days off when Tommie had called and explained her housing situation.

Inhaling a deep breath, she enjoyed the home's cinnamon and vanilla fragrances that soothed her. The scents reminded her of childhood.

Looking out the double windows, she searched for the

sunshine. The sun peeked through the gray clouds and disappeared. Picasso raced by, chasing a squirrel. Tommie sighed. He liked Gigi's too. And if the dog was outside, Jace must be up.

She'd better rise and shine. She'd lots to do and problems to sort out. Mentally, she ticked them off. *First, check for any messages from Mom. Buy a spare. Clean the mess at the inn. Read the ads for a new rental. Prove to Jace, I'm not hiding anything else. Wow, a full day.*

After the dirtbag had invaded her private space, she was itching to get her life in order. Besides, accomplishing the little things she could control offered comfort.

She left the bed and hopped under the warm spray of water in the bath. Twenty-five minutes later, she'd dried off and dressed in the beige capris and a taupe top she'd brought with her. She grabbed her cell from the bureau and hit the familiar numbers. Her mother's familiar, groggy morning voice answered. After a short conversation, she assured herself everything was as good as could be expected. Tommie disconnected. She stuffed the phone in a pocket.

The tempting odors of bacon and eggs drifted to her as she walked into the hallway. Jace was plating her food when she entered the breakfast nook. He looked homey and handsome.

She pulled up a chair. "Are you psychic? How did you know I was up?"

"Electronic waves in the air." He crossed the tile floor to let in the dog before adding, "And I heard the shower."

Picasso wolfed down his chow from a bowl near the counter.

What had he given the dog to eat? She wouldn't ask. The contents disappeared in a gulp. Finished, Picasso settled by the glass slider.

Jace sat beside her at the table. The woodsy, citrus scent of soap loitered around him. His overlong, damp hair provided him with a windy beach look. Her heart gave a small flutter.

He raised his orange juice and asked, “How did you sleep?”

“I guess I was exhausted. I don’t recall much after slipping under the covers.” Except she’d been imagining them together on the shore and was glad to feel safe. She repressed a sigh.

He set his tumbler on his placemat. “The mattress should be comfortable. Gigi buys the best.” He stabbed a piece of bacon on his plate.

Her phone rang in her pocket. She dug it out. The name of Thalia’s shop appeared on her screen. “It’s the salon calling me.” She clicked the button. “Hello.”

“Morning. This is Linda at the Tranquil Salon and Spa. Am I speaking to Tommie Murphy?”

“You are.”

“Peaches has an opening at ten today if you can come in earlier for your haircut.”

“Super. I’ll take it, Linda.”

“We have an introductory half hour massage for new customers. Discounts are ten percent. I can set one up for right after your cut. You won’t believe how it relieves stress.”

“Do it,” Tommie said, shoving aside concern for cost. “I’ll see you soon.” She hit end.

“You’re going to Thalia’s?” Jace’s pointed tone, revealed his irritation. “Is that a good idea?”

“You’re kidding? I can find out the news straight from Peaches’s lips. Linda scheduled me for ten, followed by an hour with a masseuse.”

“Have you considered everyone at there knows you hired an investigator? Why would they tell you anything? They’re a tight, clannish group. Last time, Thalia accused me of trying to frame her and practically threw us out.”

“What goes on between a customer and her stylist is different. It’s like a priest and his parishioner in the confessional. It’s free gossip and has no consequences. I doubt I'll get much while being massaged. We'll see."

"Your plan is risky."

"C'mon, Jackson. Do you think Peaches will attack me with her scissors?" She dismissed him with a flip of her hand. "Don't get paranoid on me." She drained her mug and snuck a peek at him. Would he thank her with a kiss when she returned with a scoop?

He frowned at her over the toast he brought to his lips.

Maybe not. He wasn't reading her thoughts, was he? He'd done it enough in the past. Heat flooded her cheeks.

"I'm not sure Thalia is honest." He put down his food. "I recall a rumor that Rex had a secret account he used to set up their hair business. When I ran a credit check on him, nothing financially significant showed up. I've checked on his current accounts, too, and there's nothing unusual in the past five years. I wonder where Rex saved the money he tapped to finance the salon?"

"Under a mattress?"

"Remember what we found under yours. And why didn't Gloria take Rex back to court? He couldn't have revealed his true worth during the divorce proceedings."

"I'd guess that Gloria wanted to get on with her life and not rehash the legal scene. Thalia, must have taken the cash and didn't use a bank."

"I'm warning you, something is off at that place. None of the staff we've met are model citizens. It's likely one of the women killed Arturo and Gloria. I'd bet everyone in their tight group has a good suspicion who took their lives "

"Exactly. Now is my chance to find out which one. Linda told us their clients were asking her about the murders. I'm no different from the rest except I'll be careful not to accuse anyone." When he remained silent, she explained, "I can't sit around staring at my suspect poster, which I left at the inn, by the way."

"Understood. I can drop you off at the salon since I'm going to an appointment for an estimate on the surfboard. When I'm done, I'll pick you up. How much time do you need?"

She opened her mouth to protest but decided not to raise the issue. After all, he'd agreed to her cut with Peaches, though this trade-off, bargaining stuff wasn't perfect. She suggested a time, and he gave her a nod.

They ate breakfast and cleaned up. Tommie scooted off and made her bed. Finished, she grabbed her pocketbook and checked for her credit card. It was safely tucked away in her wallet. She must be near her credit limit. She'd worry later. After bagging her clothes, she slung her purse across her shoulder. Picasso tailed her as she strode through the hall to the kitchen.

Jace stuffed his phone in his pocket as she joined him. "I talked to Gigi. She and Clara are fine, and I loaded the board onto my car's roof. Let's go."

The dog barked and tagged along at his heels.

He stopped by the entry and fished out his keys. "Big guy, you can't go."

Tommie sidestepped to the door. "Picasso is definitely better off here. He can't stay in a hot car while you're inside."

Jace peered down at him. "He's wearing his unhappy-puppy expression."

She laid her palm over her chest. "You're turning into a dog lover."

"Let's not go crazy." He nodded at her paper bag. "What are you doing?"

"You can drop me off at the inn after my haircut and massage. I can't live here forever."

"Spending a week or two is different from moving in. My grandmother is comfortable at her friend's. She didn't expect you to run off today. Find a decent apartment first. Don't hurry. Gigi loves to help others. She has plenty of room. Honestly, no one can guarantee your safety at the inn."

He handed her an extra key. "I doubt you'll need this, but in case you go outside, you won't have to worry about locking yourself out of Gigi's house."

She hesitated but took his offering. They walked to his car. His words about the Yellow Flamingo were chilling. She hopped into his front seat.

The traffic was light on Roseland Road. In the sky, the sun played hide-and-seek behind the clouds. The AC blasted in the car. Jace parked in a spot by the salon entry.

"Pull up to the door. Don't bother parking."

"No way. I think I should hang around for a while and check things out." He shut off the car and rested his palm on the handle.

She opened her door. "We'll compromise—again. You can walk me to the entrance, and when I enter, you can take off. Text me when you come back, and I'll meet you in the lot. You won't have to sit in front of the fake fireplace with the ladies. I won't wander if I get done before you arrive. Scout's Honor."

"It's a plan." He climbed out and met her by the car's bumper.

"Walking me two yards is ridiculous," she grumbled as they strode to the entryway.

"Humor me."

She paused before entering. "I'll take it from here."

"Be careful."

Her pulse picked up. She wished he hadn't reminded her. "I will."

He started to protest but stopped and smoothed his expression. "Good luck with the hair thing." He wagged a finger in the air. “Your job is to listen.” He spun on his heel and marched to his vehicle.

She walked inside. He just didn’t understand girl talk. What could go wrong? She glanced out the glass in the door and caught sight of Jace leaving. Her sense of security slumped a notch.

***

Jace drove into a corner parking space at Gloria’s Beauty Cuts. He hopped out and scanned the lot. The shop looked closed. Except for a red convertible near the entrance, nobody else seemed to be around. The top was down. Large boxes filled the passenger side of the two-seater. The top flaps were missing on one, revealing the contents.

He strode over and read the labels. They were all Ocean Lure products and decorated with a beach scene. He peered up at the camera at the front of the building. Was it recording him?

Rex appeared in the doorway. He balanced three cartons in his arms while holding the door with his hip.

“Hey, wait up.” Jace raced to help him and grabbed the handle.

As always, Rex wore a Hawaiian shirt. His ponytail was pulled above the back strap of his Gators baseball cap. “They’re not open.”

“I guessed from the lack of customers,” Jace admitted.

Rex crossed to his convertible.

Jace shadowed him. “I don’t believe we’ve met.”

Rex frowned. “You’re the private investigator. You showed up with Arturo’s latest girlfriend at the Reese Center.” He shoved the containers into his car.

“Tommie?” Was her relationship with the victim more than she’d told him?

"That's what we called her at the salon." Rex dusted off his chest. "Arturo was a collector of the ladies. He also preferred a certain type. Young or old, usually on the rebound, lonely, and eager to return his advances, usually cash rich."

Tommie had zero in her savings account. Maybe Arturo had an actual romantic interest in her that she hadn't realized.

"Your surfer friend and the homicidal ex-police chief had a thing going. I'm sure Arturo believed with her past that she didn't have a lot of friends or choices. Nobody likes to hang around murderers or their buddies. He assumed she'd be amenable to dinner or a ride on his boat. He'd show her his antique collections and get whatever she had to offer."

Jace fought the urge to punch the guy. "Did you warn Peaches?"

The man pursed his lips. "Peaches and Arturo kind of helped each other. She loved his attention, and Arturo hated being alone. She had one flaw—no money. Their relationship was over in a month or two. I didn't keep track." He shrugged. "The couple were both aware they were placeholders until something better came along. That's why they remained on good terms, unlike the rest of his exes."

"Didn't anyone call him on his behavior?"

Rex swept off his hat and smoothed the top of his hair before replacing the cap. "Gloria said he learned to live that way. His parents split when he was a kid, and neither of them had room for him in their separate lives. He grew up living with any relative who would take him in. As an adult, he bounced from female to female. Anyway, Gloria and Thalia excused him because of his past. He probably told his sob story to plenty of ladies."

"Nothing wrong with spending time with a pretty girl," Jace lied, forcing a grin. "I'm Jace Jackson, in case you didn't hear." He extended his hand.

They shook while Rex considered him. “Are you working for the surfer?”

“I’m not free to confirm or deny. My clients are confidential. And her name is Tommie.”

“Who hired you was easy enough to guess. What’s on your mind, Jackson?”

“I assume Arturo met many women through Gloria.”

Rex’s lips thinned to a straight line. “Why do you think he met his dates here?”

The man didn’t come across as cooperative. “At the memorial, Peaches said he liked to visit Gloria and was friendly with everyone. Seems it would have been simple to meet available females when he stopped by.”

“I never tracked where he found his lady friends. For the record, my salon isn’t a pickup club.”

“Understood.” The man was touchy about Jace’s assumption. “I was thinking the shooter could have been an ex-girlfriend who held a grudge. Not someone Arturo met at your workplace,” he said quickly. “Maybe she and Arturo had a bad breakup. Let’s be honest. Most folks go out on a bad date or two during their years.”

“I suppose. Gloria thought Arturo had signed up on several dating websites, and he sold junk to lots of customers online. One of them might have felt shafted, except he would return their money rather than face criminal action.” Rex reached into his car and grabbed a package of cigarettes from the dashboard.

He emptied out one and stuck it in the corner of his mouth, unlit. “Trying to quit.” He tossed the smokes into his car. “As for Arturo, a lady might have been angry at him. He didn’t hold on to them long.”

“Anybody in particular?” Jace pressed. “I could check her out. Take the pressure off the rest of you guys.”

Confusion flashed in Rex’s eyes. “What do you mean?”

"The police always target family and friends first in a homicide."

"I didn't care for their suspicious questions," he spat. "Those detectives tried to pass them off as routine."

"If you believe a former girlfriend shot Arturo and Gloria, I could investigate her and turn in the relevant evidence. Point the law in the right direction."

"You're fishing for clients, aren't you?" Rex kicked a butt on the ground. "I don't want negative publicity like a murder associated with me."

"If what you tell me leads to an arrest, I can collect the money from the tip line. You and I can split the reward. What do you say? You could get a chunk of the cash, and I'll keep your name out of it, unless you're looking for hype."

"Completely confidential?" Rex pressed.

"Absolutely." Jace wondered if the man would stick to his word.

"What do you need?"

"Where were you the night of the shootings?"

"Thalia and I did the books. Nobody else touches them, and no one was with us. I picked up scallops and fries at Big Shrimpy's drive-through around seven. When I got back, we locked the doors and went to work. We ate while we crunched the numbers."

His alibi matched Thalia's. They could have planned their excuses. "I heard a rumor that a killer was after the salon workers. Do you think the gossip is true?"

Rex studied the passing traffic. "Stranger things have happened. A few people get upset if they're unhappy with their cuts." He grinned, revealing perfect white teeth. "Usually, the mad ones don't tip the stylists, rather than shoot the owner."

"True." Jace gestured to the building. "Who's going to run Gloria's now? Thalia?"

"Nah, the place needs total updating, too expensive. Gloria was old-school and too cheap to change. She was having problems keeping up, replacing worn furniture, and giving out pay raises. Thalia wouldn't make much of a profit if she ran it. She'll sell and pay the bills. I'm taking leftover products to the flea market. The ladies love our cosmetics and prices. Alfredo sells them for a percentage. No sense leaving the packages here to rot."

"Smart idea."

Rex pulled his car door open and hesitated. "Now that I recall Arturo's exes, I bet an old girlfriend is to blame for the shootings. He could hide his flaws for a short while, but not forever. That could be why he ditched the women quick—before they saw his faults."

The theory might be worth exploring. "Who in particular comes to mind?" Could be a long, winding list.

Rex's features lit up. "I'm not sure if I should say a name."

"I'll keep it quiet."

"Linda Martel. She was Gloria's receptionist. She works for us now. I remember a story that she went out with Arturo before your surfer."

Jace remembered the girl's flirtatious response to him the other day.

"Thalia told me she'd heard the gossip that Linda and Arturo had gotten together. Later, she said it wasn't true. She thought Linda created the buzz herself to appear attractive to men. Sounded strange to me, but that's women." Rex's phone pinged. He walked away to speak in private on his cell.

Linda hadn't brought up dating Arturo when Jace had spoken to her.

Rex ended his call and returned. "Uh, I talked to Peaches. I had it wrong. Linda and Arturo didn't date." He jumped into his Camaro. "And I'm not paying you anything for investigating."

Jace edged up to him. "Do the police suspect Linda?"

"Why not?" Rex reversed his convertible out of the spot and stopped. "Everybody is suspicious of everyone. Like I am of you."

"Does that mean we don't have a deal?"

"You are correct, Mr. PI. We do not." In seconds, he blended into traffic and disappeared.

Jace hopped into his car. That was an unusual interview. He pulled out his phone and searched for Gloria's brand of makeup.

A recent link with the headline "FDA Bans Ocean Lure Cosmetics" popped up. A quick read confirmed the US government had placed many of the ingredients used by the Asian manufacturer on its prohibited list. Thalia and Rex had to know what had happened to their product. They were going for money over health.

The company sounded shady. The corporation was accused of selling prisoners' hair, removed by force, and using the inmates as guinea pigs for the new cosmetic lines.

Nice knowing the business had no morals. And neither did Thalia nor Rex. Hurriedly, he sent a message to Tommie about the banned products and warned her not to try any.

A bad inkling about Rex sank through Jace. He'd drive to Big Shrimpy's Restaurant, flash his license to look official, and confirm Rex's alibi. He had time before he met his surfboard expert, Lucas Davis.

The flashing light of caution about the salon popped up in his mind again. He wouldn't be late picking up Tommie.

CHAPTER TWENTY-FOUR

Linda greeted Tommie in her chirpy manner. "Glad you could come today. Ordinarily, I post cancellations on Facebook, but I remembered you were eager to get a cut. I'll buzz Peaches to tell her you've arrived."

In the waiting area, a senior citizen rose from the sofa and traipsed to the back with a stylist. No one else was around. Good time to quiz Linda before Peaches showed up. Maybe between the two women, she'd get a lead. "How's everything?" Tommie gave the receptionist a bright smile.

"Well, we were booked up for a few days after Gloria died," Linda said. "Everyone was in shock. And they came to have their hair or nails done, get massages, and calm themselves by talking about the shootings at the salon. Now that the early curiosity and first blow have worn off, we're in a lull, except for Peaches. The customers love her perkiness."

Tommie jumped right into trying to find answers. "I bet she got a raise when she transferred to Thalia's. Money can make you cheerful."

"Rex believes she's our best beautician. Kind of irks the other girls. They work as hard as she does. I'm thankful I'm at the desk and not in competition."

"I guess the days aren't always sunny at Thalia's." That was lame. She'd do better.

"I'm hoping the business picks up." Linda bent forward and whispered, "Thalia's been coming out front a lot. She pretends she has to get something, but she's bored. Sometimes, she's spying. She acts as though her employees are goofing off, and she'll catch them. Everybody looks super busy and avoids her when she appears. All the workers have been dusting, sweeping, and tossing stuff. We should win an award for cleanest business." Linda glanced toward the hallway. "There's Peaches."

The young woman approached from a side door. Peaches was dressed in a light lavender blouse. Her hair color matched her top. Her black, high-heeled sandals tapped on the floor.

"Hi, Tommie. I'm happy you could join us on such short notice."

Tommie's phone vibrated in her pocket. She plucked it out and perused Jace's message about Ocean Lure.

"Any problems?" Peaches raised her brushed-up eyebrows.

"Spam." Tommie pocketed her cell. "I'm glad Linda thought of me. I've heard you're tough to get an appointment with."

"I stay busy. Come this way."

"See you when you're done," Linda said from behind the counter.

Peaches led Tommie behind six-foot dividers. She showed her a hook for her purse and tossed a hand at her styling chair. Tommie studied the space as she eased into the seat. A wall mirror hung above a cabinet. Tools and bottles were stacked on top of the metal cupboard. All her gear was neon pink trimmed in purple.

"Before it slips my mind," Tommie said, "my mom used all

her Ocean Lure mascara and wanted me to buy a tube. Do you sell it?" She'd like to look at the product.

"We stopped selling that brand. The distributor wasn't reliable. Shipments took forever to arrive, and the company never delivered the amount we ordered." Peaches straightened the line of hair products on top of her cupboard before turning back to her.

"My mom will be disappointed. She loves it." Well, she couldn't help Jace with more details on the makeup. Although now that she'd read his message, she'd predict he wouldn't approve of her asking Peaches about the product.

Peaches wrapped the vinyl apron over Tommie. "In the end, we lucked out. We carry a better label now. I can get a sample for you when I finish."

"I'll talk to my mom about it. You own such a pretty collection of combs. Did you pay extra for those pink shears?" Tommie nodded at the shelf.

"Stlyin' isn't cheap. I buy everything I use. Sometimes, other workers borrow mine and accidentally forget to return my things. To remind them, I bought fluorescent ones. I can spot anyone using my stuff from thirty feet away. I planned to tack up a sign, 'No Sharing,' but Rex warned me no one pays attention to a notice."

"The colors are a smart idea." Hmm, how could she change the topic? Jace did it easily.

"I always introduce myself to my new clients." The young woman stood behind Tommie and spoke to her reflection in the glass in a quick, rote manner. "As you know, I'm Peaches. I bet you're wondering if that's a nickname. No, it isn't. My mother named me after the fruit because all she craved was peaches while she was pregnant. She usually only ate sweets. She told me I was responsible for keeping her healthy during her nine-month wait."

Was the tale true, or was Peaches being . . . Peaches? "You have quite a story. You could have been a Candy or a Sweetie, depending on your mom's eating habits."

A wrinkle of dislike formed between the hairdresser's brows. "She wouldn't call me anything unhealthy. I love to tell my customers I was a hero before I was born. I kept my mom fit. Can I ask you a question?"

Now she had Tommie's attention and curiosity. "Shoot."

"Who cut your hair last?"

"Uh, probably me while I looked in the mirror. I guess that makes it a home business." Tommie smiled.

The stylist's lips slid into a line of disapproval. "You could use some advice."

"If it's free, go for it." Was the young woman going to recommend an extra-expensive, chic hairdo? Any workplace with the word *salon* in the title was bound to charge a lot.

"You have good, thick hair. People would pay to have it."

Her mother and her weave came to mind.

"But you're wearing it wrong." Peaches shook her head. "The style should complement a person's face."

A teen walked past the opening. Half of her skull was shaved. The top strands were combed over. An uneasy dread flooded Tommie. "I don't like drastic changes. Clip a little off for a trim."

"I aim to please." Peaches grabbed her pink shears.

Tommie stared at her reflection and winced at the snip and tumble of a long black lock onto the floor. What did Peaches consider a short cut? *Stop worrying and find answers.* "I had a break-in at my rental the other day."

"How? Who?" Peaches shot in front of her. Her scissors pointed up in the air. "Were you around when they broke in? Did you call the police? Did they arrest somebody?"

Tommie hadn't expected her strong reaction. "I lived at the

Yellow Flamingo Inn. I wasn't around during the crime. No one has been arrested."

"Any leads?" Peaches asked, leaning forward.

"None. Have you had problems with robberies in your neighborhood?"

"No, but since Gloria and Arturo were murdered, I've been having nightmares. In one dream, I was looking for Arturo. I was running and screaming for him in the salon. Someone was chasing us, and I'd lost sight of him." Peaches paused, her eyelids lowered. "I ran into my cubicle, and I found him in this chair. He was dead."

"This one?" Ew. Tommie yanked her hand off the arm of the seat. "What happened next?"

"I woke up."

"That was a scary story." Why had she shared her tale? Did Peaches want to frighten her? "I'm glad it wasn't real."

"Me too." Peaches seemed calm and plunged back into her job.

Snip, snip filled Tommie's ears.

She inhaled deeply and asked, "Why do you think Arturo was killed here in your dream? Didn't he hang out at Gloria's?" Was it a subliminal message?

"No clue. He and Gloria were buds, but Arturo informed me she had a lot of anxiety. Her doctor wanted to prescribe her meds. She refused them. She probably worried people would think she was weak or not too smart. Thalia is kind of like her sister. She's overcritical, except when she's around Rex. She says he had a bad life because of Gloria."

Under her vinyl cape, Tommie braced herself. "Who would shoot Arturo and Gloria?"

Peaches's expression was grim. "I believe it was an evil person."

"You mean an ex-wife or lover?"

"I wish I had the answer." The wrinkles in the hairdresser's forehead smoothed. "Once, Thalia was mad at Arturo. She said nobody liked him. Hardly anyone believed her. Arturo was sweet. Lower your chin."

Tommie followed the direction and lifted her gaze.

"Can I ask you something?" Peaches stared at Tommie's reflection.

"You can." Was she about to pitch a shampoo or disclose another dream?

"Is it true you were first to find Arturo at his house? Makes sense." Peaches nodded. "You were his girlfriend."

The interview seemed to be going in the wrong direction. "I did. And we were friends. Did the police ask for your alibi?"

"They asked lots. I told them I shopped at the Vero Beach Mall and went home. We had rushes all day long at work. I was exhausted and picked up a salad to eat from the fast-food court."

Tommie was beginning to appreciate how hard Jace worked, and she wished her stylist cut faster.

Peaches pursed her lips. "His former partner, Alfredo, could have hurt him. The two had a terrible fight, and the men never spoke to each other again. Of course, that was a while ago. If only I could speak to Arturo. I'd be happy."

"What happened between them?" Would she have a lot to say about the rift?

Peaches inhaled a breath. "Arturo bought an expensive painting and left it in their shop when they closed. The next day, it had vanished. Alfredo had been the one locking up. Arturo was convinced he had stolen it. Nothing else was missing, and no signs of a broken door or window lock."

"Why did Alfredo hold the memorial?"

"He was pretending he cared and hoped he'd fool the cops. You can ask Linda. She keeps up with what's happening like birthdays or boyfriends." Peaches laid her finger on her lips.

"Hmm, I didn't know about the meal with his flea market buddies. That will clear him."

Tommie's awareness sharpened. "Did Linda date Arturo?"

The young woman cut in front of the chair. "Who spread that lie?" Her cheeks flushed, and her mouth turned into a line of anger.

"I'm not sure. I must be confused," Tommie said to calm the stylist. "Linda and Arturo weren't a couple."

Peaches stamped her foot. "People are such gossips." She hacked off an additional hunk of Tommie's hair. "Linda has a boyfriend in her hometown. She wouldn't cheat on him."

Tommie leaned over the seat's arm, trying to see in the mirror the patch behind her ear. Shouldn't Peaches cut in another spot? She caught a glimpse of herself in the glass. Yikes, Peaches had cut like three inches in one section. Had she meant to hack off that much? Tommie put up a hand. "Will you work on the right side soon?"

Peaches blew out a sigh of frustration. "I get upset when I hear all the rumors around here. Linda does repeat a lot of the tittle-tattle. Don't tell anyone, especially Thalia. She lectures us on talking nice to everyone. Once, Linda told a client I couldn't come in because I had lice. I've never had them." She pumped the chair higher and higher. Her bottom lip pouted out. "I had mosquito bites."

"Yeah, that was mean. Can you finish?" *Before I'm bald.*

Peaches stared at Tommie's reflection. "Everybody thinks this job is easy. It's hard! I stand on my feet all day long. And some clients are cheap with tips."

"Peaches," a woman shouted.

Tommie whipped her attention to the cubby opening.

Thalia stood at the entrance. Her hands were clamped at her sides, her body rigid. "Please step out for a moment. I wish to speak to you." She stepped aside for the hairstylist to exit.

Peaches marched to her boss.

Thalia narrows her eyes at Tommie. Recognition glinted in her eyes and disappeared. "We'll be a second. Can I get you a water?"

She shook her head as cold anxiety hit her. She should have kept her mouth shut. Peaches was an emotional person, easily riled.

Thalia stomped away behind the dividers.

Tommie hurried to the mirror and gazed into the glass, prodding her lopsided style. She finger-parted a lump of hair to hide the uneven cut.

"You are not allowed to yell at a patron," Thalia hissed outside the movable walls.

Tommie crept toward the women.

"I've spoken to you several times about the importance of attitude."

"It's not my fault. Everyone is repeating horrible things about me."

"They won't stop," Thalia insisted, "if you give us a bad reputation. Didn't you recognize your client? She hired an investigator who's been asking questions all over the city that make us look guilty. And she was the girlfriend of our crooked ex-police chief. Your unacceptable behavior ends today. You're suspended. Without pay."

"You don't understand. I—"

"Immediately."

"I'm tired of you ordering me around. You're nasty. I'm leaving, and I'll tell Rex what you said to me. My father won't be happy."

That was right. Peaches's dad had a stake in the salon.

Peaches rounded the divider before Tommie could dodge out of her way. The stylist ignored her and grabbed a large tote bag from the bottom of the cabinet. With one hand, she swept all the tools off the shelves and into the bag. Wheeling around, she exited the cubby.

Thalia walked into the cubicle. Her arms were folded. "I will send another girl over to you. Peaches had an emergency."

"I'm set." Tommie would finish the cut at home. Pulling off the plastic bib, she pitched it on the chair. She seized her purse.

Linda entered the cubbyhole. "Can I help?"

"Please escort Ms. Murphy out, Linda."

"Don't bother." Tommie rushed past them.

The receptionist shadowed her through the hallway. "Hold up." She hurried to catch her. "I'm sorry about Peaches and Thalia. They can irritate each other. Since Arturo died, Peaches has become oversensitive. I'm not sure if she misses his attention or him." She stared off into space as she asked, "What about your massage?"

"Cancel it." Tommie halted at the door. Wait. Her car wasn't here, and rain loomed in the sky. Jace was working. Her mind darted to Peaches's dream. The shooter had chased Arturo in the salon. Was a sniper hiding out in the building? *Great.* She turned to Linda. "Where's the nearest bus stop?"

"I'll give you a lift," she said. "I'll get one of the girls to cover for me. I'll explain to Thalia your ride wasn't around. Everyone on the floor heard Peaches yelling. She was just unlucky that Thalia came out of her office when she did."

"She kind of lost it. Is that normal—for her?"

Linda moved closer to Tommie. "When Peaches learned Gloria and Arturo were . . . dating, Peaches acted upset. No one knew why. They weren't a love match. Peaches liked Arturo because he complimented her often and treated her to expensive restaurant meals. No one believed they'd last long. And Thalia was especially mad at her sister for taking her relationship with Arturo to 'another level.' She kept accidentally running into

Gloria and lecturing her. Gloria finally gave up seeing him, but of course they stayed friendly."

"Linda, you're up on everything that's happening. Did you go out with him to eat or anything?"

"Me? Never. Yuck. I'll swear on a Bible." She looked at Tommie and covered her mouth briefly with her palm as though the words were distasteful. "Oops, I forgot you went out with him. Honest."

"We were friends."

"Got it. Let me drive you. Okay?"

The walk to the bus seemed less appealing by the second. "I accept the offer."

"I'll get my keys." She turned and raced off.

Tommie pulled out her phone to send Jace a message about the change in plans. The screen was black. Huh? Had she charged it recently? When had she paid her bill? *Months* ago. Oh no. The truth sank in. Her service provider had cut her off. She shoved her cell in her pocket.

Tommie walked outside to meet Linda. A dark SUV entered the lot and cruised up to her. Grey? His window wound down. Where had he come from? Was he tracking her?

"Tommie Murphy, why are you always hanging around this place?"

"Why are you here?" Should she duck inside?

"Doing my job. Interviews. Since you're standing in front of me, I'll ask you about your mother."

Her mom? *Stonewall him.* "No comment."

"I'm not a reporter. I'm investigating two homicides." His tone was hard and cool.

Had he discovered her mom had gone out with Arturo, or that he'd fleeced her? "My mom didn't kill him."

Be careful. Don't let him goad you into talking.

The wind picked up. Stray cold drops of water hit her.

"Your mother might have had someone else do it for her."

She felt her jaw drop. Did he mean she was the shooter?

A toot of a horn tore her attention from the detective. A sleek black car rounded the corner of the building. Linda? Had to be. Tommie raced toward the vehicle.

A cloudburst beat down on her as she struggled to hold the door open against a gust. She tumbled into the passenger seat.

"You got a little wet." Linda shifted her gaze from Tommie's drenched clothes to the SUV and back. "Was that a friend?"

"He was nobody."

Grey drove to the side to park.

In the car, the locks set with a click. Tommie winced. She knew little about the receptionist, except that she was friendly and hadn't dated Arturo.

Linda steered out of the lot. "What's your address?"

"Star Pointe Crossings Boulevard." Had she gathered enough scoop today to prove herself to Jace?

The rain pounded on the roof. Peaches's odd story resurfaced in Tommie's thoughts. *I found Arturo in this chair. He was dead.*

Had the dream been brought on by stress over the murder of her buddy, or did the dream reflect the young woman's guilty conscience?

CHAPTER TWENTY-FIVE

Jace parked near the ocean-blue cottage with a weedless green lawn. The drive had been a smooth one under the gray clouds. He hoped getting the surfboard appraised would be as simple. If it was worth a decent amount of money, it could have been a motive in the killings. That's why he'd gone with one of the best assessors for the task, Lucas Davis.

Did the man harbor any resentment against Tommie for planting the drugs on him? Jace was about to find out. He checked his phone. His source at the police department was contacting him. He must have news. He scrolled to the message.

Ballistics ID'd a 9 mm Luger as the weapon in the Alvaro homicides. Close-range shootings. No defensive wounds on either victim. Background checks revealed the deceased male had held routine indemnity policies for himself and his property. His plans had lapsed due to nonpayment. The female casualty had no personal insurance, but she did have standard coverage on her home and store with a large deductible.

Jace didn't respond. The fewer communications sent

between him and his informant, the better. He considered the updated information. The gun was one commonly used in crimes. *Close-range* and *no defensive wounds* suggested the shooter had been allowed to enter and/or had taken the victims by surprise. Both options were possible. He'd ruled out monetary gain as a likely cause. Jace's searches had turned up that Gloria had had two mortgages on her business. And Arturo was bankrupt.

The gush of the beach waves floated over the dunes. His thoughts snapped back to the present as he untied the surfboard on the car's roof. He inhaled the fruity aroma from the pink and cream, blooming flowers edging the fenced yard. In the distance, he spotted a huge yellow house. Pretty place.

He unloaded the board and carried it across the lush grass toward the sun-bleached gate. Tommie would love this spot. She would not have been happy if she had discovered he was meeting the son of ex-chief Davis without her. She'd have bugged him to let her tag along. Listening to her say, "I'm sorry for trying to frame you for drug possession" wouldn't be in keeping with the tone of today's meeting. It was a miracle Lucas had agreed to meet him.

There wasn't a more knowledgeable surfer than Lucas Davis in the county, maybe in the state. Growing up, he'd lived on the sand and ocean, most likely because no one had watched over him.

Jace lifted the wrought-iron knocker on the wooden door.

The knob jiggled. The entry swung open enough for a tall, blond man with a scruffy jaw to stare out at him. He wore a white T-shirt. His hair was cut short.

"Lucas Davis? I'm Jace Jackson." He extended his hand.

The surfer dropped a glance at the board before they shook. "Welcome."

"Should I take off my shoes?" He eyeballed his host's bare feet.

"Not necessary." He shrugged. "Whatever makes you comfortable rules in our home."

Relieved over his friendliness, Jace added, "You probably don't remember me. You were ahead of me in high school."

"You played on the basketball team."

"Yeah, I was the scrawny rebounder. I gained a few pounds."

"We don't run around like we did in those teen years. Come in." Lucas sidestepped from the entry.

Jace entered a snug room with a dark orange sofa and a wicker chair. The space flowed into the kitchen area. The aroma of coffee greeted him.

"Can I offer you a drink?"

"I'm good." Jace stood the board up in front of him. "I wasn't sure until you contacted me yesterday if our meeting was on."

A flicker of wariness crossed Lucas's face. "After your first text, I almost told you to find another person. Tommie Murphy is not a name I care to hear."

The guy was direct and getting the conflict out in the open. "I understand. She swore you were the best surfboard expert."

Lucas scrutinized the longboard while speaking. "I expect you know the story. Tommie planted drugs in my car because my father wanted me in jail and out of his way. He used her to do it."

"You might not believe me, but she's sorry for what she did."

"Most people who get tangled up with my dad are. Too bad she didn't realize the kind of man he was beforehand. Does she comprehend the situation now?"

"Completely. If you give her a chance, she'll apologize, and she's sincere."

He raised an eyebrow. "Did she ask for me to do the appraisal?"

"She wasn't aware of our appointment. I think if you let her apologize, you won't regret it."

"I'll take it under consideration."

"I can't blame you for avoiding her. Tommie was my next-door neighbor for several years. We grew up together, and I learned long ago that she has a way of getting involved in bad situations. Staying out of her path was my solution."

Lucas threw a hand at him. "Yet, here you are."

"She has good intentions." And for some unexplained reason, if she was injured, he was too. "She has it set in her mind that she must admit responsibility for hurting others before she leaves."

"Where's she going?"

"I'm not sure." He'd avoided thinking about the day they'd say goodbye. "She's hoping to get a fresh start somewhere."

"You're mixed up with the surfboard . . . how exactly?"

"Did anyone ever tell you that you should be a cop?" Jace joked.

"Many regretted my time on the force, especially my father."

Jace's humor had hit a sore spot. He hastened to put them back on track. "As I stated when I contacted you, I'm her investigator."

"Are you also her intermediary, testing the waters for her?"

"I need to get an estimate on the longboard. Consider the rest of our conversation white noise you can tune out if you choose."

"Let's get down to business." Lucas clapped his hands. "As for Tommie, I wish her the best of luck in her future. Holding on to grudges causes problems for everyone. I met with you today because Mia, my better half, informed me that acknowledging you, Tommie's friend, would be part of moving on. I'm beginning to understand."

"Women sometimes talk in this mysterious lingo. Now, about the surfboard . . ." Uneasy, Jace steered away from discussion of hot topics. "Tommie believes it's not too valuable. She told me it's used with a lot of dings and cuts. What were your first impressions?"

"Nicks give character. Mia says I'm a surf-o-holic, but she understands. She has her own thing about books." He picked up the board and held it under his arm and nodded. "Good for beginners or catching a wave on smooth water."

"A pro wouldn't use it?"

"I might, depending on the conditions. What did the buyer pay for it?"

"No clue." Jace shrugged.

Lucas ran his palm over the fiberglass and squeezed a section. "Someone did a decent repair job on a break, and I'd pay $250."

"Not a board worth dying for?"

"Definitely not. Come check out my collection." He leaned the longboard against the fridge and walked into the adjoining quarters.

Jace followed him past an iron, spiral staircase and through the open doorway.

Lucas stopped and flung his arms out at his sides. His s glowed with pride.

Surfboards of various shapes and colors were mounted on the white wall. Rows and rows of them. Books filled the opposite wall.

"You can guess which displays are mine and which are Mia's." He grinned. "She's an editor. She copyedited most of those manuscripts. The rest are her personal reads."

"The collections are amazing." Jace wandered to the tomes. All sizes and genres overflowed the shelves. "This looks like a store." At the other end of the room, two cream recliners and a wicker coffee table stood by the double windows, offering a view of the dunes.

"Who did Tommie get the board from, or shouldn't I ask?" Lucas raised one eyebrow.

"It was from a friend of a friend. She wants to return it or sell it, but she hasn't found any takers. A person broke into her place at the Yellow Flamingo and left her a threatening message. I hope to rule out the burglar wasn't looking for this board."

Lucas held up two fingers. "I'll give you a couple of reasons a thief could want it. The surfboard had sentimental value, or maybe the perv was trying to hurt Tommie by violating her individual space. Any cameras in the residence? Neighbors note any strangers or hear dogs barking at an unusual time?"

"No working electronic surveillance was available. It was an under-the-radar event, not reported. I emailed the desk clerk earlier today."

"Did he answer?"

"He confirmed no disturbances or curious goings-on occurred at the inn that evening."

"I haven't heard any scuttlebutt on the street about a stolen longboard either. I'd say it's not a hot property." Lucas tapped his fingertips on his thigh. "Let me look at the board again." They went back into the kitchen. He ran his palm over the repaired section. "Might have been cut deliberately." He walked to the window and studied the longboard in the direct light. "Yup, it's a nice straight slash. There's a chance it was accidental. Though it seems suspicious to me. Something could be inside."

"Drugs?"

"A powder or a crystal form would easily fit."

"How do we find out?"

"X-ray. Know any techs who'd help you out?" Lucas asked.

"That list comes up empty." Who would have hidden dope in the board? Arturo? Rex? Gloria? Thalia? Peaches? An unknown? Had the money for the possibly concealed shipment come from Arturo's victims?

"If Tommie doesn't mind another patch-up, I can cut it open and look. I'll fix it afterward." He shook the board. "Don't hear anything. On the other hand, if you were shipping illegal goods, you'd make sure it didn't sound like a saltshaker."

Lucas raised an eyebrow. "I have a proposal. If she doesn't want the longboard, I'll buy and donate the plank to a kid who has always wanted to surf but can't afford the sport."

Jace would have to ask her about selling. "Can you do the cutting job now?"

"Definitely."

Jace was certain which choice she'd pick.

CHAPTER TWENTY-SIX

Jace drove through the torrent to pick up Tommie. Once in the lot, he sent her a text that he was outside and asked if she'd be out soon. She should be done, and he'd a lot to tell her. He stared at the entry. Raindrops splattered on his window and distorted his view.

He put on the wipers and checked his phone. He found a time-out error response about his bounced message to Tommie. What was going on? He'd call that receptionist, Linda. A quick Google search provided the shop's number. The salon recording instructed him to leave a voicemail, and an employee would get in touch.

Had Tommie's appointments run late? Tapping on his steering wheel, he ed his decision. *Forget this.* He dashed through the storm and inside.

At the reception counter, a dark-haired, young female in a pink smock looked at him as he wiped water off his hair. "Can I help you?"

Where was Linda? "I'm picking up Tommie Murphy. She was seeing Peaches and a masseuse."

"I'm filling in. I'll check." The woman disappeared for a few minutes before returning to her chair. "Miss Murphy left after seeing Peaches. She canceled her massage."

Impatient, he shuffled closer. "Did she say how she was getting home?"

"Uh, no. I was told she was Miss Galore's last appointment today." She wrote something on a piece of paper while speaking.

"Did Peaches give Tommie a ride?"

"I doubt it." The temp pursed her lips and shrugged. "Your friend could have caught the bus." Her phone rang. "I better answer that."

Dismissed, he wandered to the waiting area and tried Tommie again. He received the same error message. A sinking sensation iced his gut.

He called his grandmother's landline without any luck. Tommie wouldn't walk the dog in the rain. How long would the bus take to cross town? He was unsure. Why wouldn't she wait for him? He'd head to Star Pointe Crossings. Maybe she'd headed to the house or posted a note for him on the fridge.

Fifteen minutes later, he pulled into the U-shaped drive. Tommie's vehicle was parked in the same spot near the entry. The storm's intensity had lessened. Jace unlocked the front door and ran inside. "Tommie! Are you here?"

Picasso scampered to him from the hall. Jace patted him. "Where's Tommie, boy?"

The dog sat by his feet and yipped.

"What did you say? And what am I doing?" He rubbed the back of his neck. "Now I'm talking to an animal. Next, I'll take you everywhere, like those dog-obsessed owners." An uneasy feeling crept over him. Pulling out his gun, he systematically went from room to room.

The place was empty. Did his grandmother go with her to get

her clothes? He'd call Gigi at Clara's. He had to be careful and not upset her. *Stay calm and be vague.*

She picked up on the first ring. "Jace, I was thinking of you. How are you? How's Tommie? Have the police arrested anyone? Are you still investigating her attempted burglary?"

Tommie and his grandmother weren't together. "No news of arrests. What's the latest on Clara?" He checked his watch. He'd been at the house for almost five minutes. Tommie didn't have her car. The temp said she hadn't gone off with Peaches. Would she? Nah. They weren't buds.

"Clara had her test and is waiting for the results." Gigi said, interrupting his thoughts. "She's doing better," his grandmother continued. "I'm worried about Tommie. She's not planning on living at the inn after what happened, is she?"

They both wanted answers. "The idea is under discussion. We've lost touch. Her phone wasn't on or charged. If you hear from her, tell her I'm on my way to pick her up." That was kind of true.

"Oh dear, she's not in trouble, is she?"

"I'm sure she's okay." Could Gigi detect he was lying?

"Let me know when you catch up to her."

He reassured her and disconnected. Prickles ran up his spine. He brought up the alerts on his screen. Nothing much except for tornado watches miles away. Scanning his messages, he unearthed Tommie's old texts. Not useful.

He had to find her. What if the person who'd broken into her studio had been hovering nearby and snatched her? His insides clutched and tightened with fear.

T*hink logically*. He'd leave a message for her on the fridge and trace her steps. Why had he agreed to Tommie going to the salon?

Picasso tagged after him as he turned toward the kitchen.

The door opened, followed by the sound of rain. Jace swung

around to discover Tommie rushing inside. He stared at her until his frenzied brain registered her presence.

"Jackson, you won't believe my day. Wait till you hear what I found out."

Her hair was flat and soaking. Her clothes clung to her, showing off her small, shapely chest. *Refocus.* "Where have you been?" he demanded. "You weren't at Thalia's when I went to get you. I came back to Gigi's to double-check, and you weren't here."

"I canceled my second appointment, and Linda gave me a ride. We had to stop and hang out until the tsunami eased up. I guess that's how you beat me to the house. Linda talked and talked about attending business school and the first guy she dated and the second, or was that the third? Anyway, Peaches walked out of the salon while I was in her chair. She and Thalia had a fight, but worse—" Tommie pointed to her head. "My haircut is lopsided."

She was safe, wet, and standing in front of him. Should he hug her or lecture her?

"Wow, from your expression, I'd say you agree. Peaches did a horrible job." She attempted to fluff her hair with her fingers.

She was home. Relieved, he tugged her to him and held her tight. Her chest pressed against his.

She gawked at him in shock. "Did someone die?"

She wasn't kidnapped or lost. "When I couldn't reach you, I was afraid you were hurt."

He lifted her chin and skimmed her features. Under his stare, her cheeks flushed a deeper red. Her damp clothing seeped into his shirt and shorts. She'd never looked or felt better. He released her but couldn't budge. She wasn't leaving his sight.

She gaped at him. "I tried to call, but my phone was dead. I must have missed a payment. I thought I'd use the landline once I was dropped off, or an employee would tell you."

"You're okay" Jace didn't need any explanations. The scent of rain lingered on her and invited him to inch toward her. Fighting the urge to do more than talk, he took her hand. "That's what matters."

She blinked several times. Gradually, the confusion in her eyes vanished. A hint of a smile lingered on her mouth. "I should get a trim every day if I get this response."

He had an itch to touch her hair. He smoothed aside a wet strand of hair on her cheek. Her lips were full and tempting. How would they taste?

Without hesitation, he kissed them. They were warm and sweet. He folded his arms around her. His lips glided down her throat to her beating pulse.

A quiver in his gut set off a warning. *Enough. You're a professional who is on the job. Yank up the invisible glass wall.* Where *is it?*

There was only Tommie.

Her breath quickened. "I—"

"Shh. I don't want to have a discussion." He had to hold her for a minute longer. Maybe he'd kiss her again. Yes, he would. The idea shot through him like a bullet. Quietly, he touched his mouth to hers. She rested a hand on his shoulder and slid her other around him.

He cupped the back of her neck and angled in for an easier taste. She reminded him of the flowery fragrances at Davis's cottage. He ran his palm over her, finding and enjoying the softness of her breasts, the indent of her waist, and the rise of her hips.

She tightened her arms around him. His mind went blank. His heartbeat roared in his head.

Picasso pawed at his leg and barked.

Jace stepped away. "C'mon." He threaded his fingers through Tommie's, and they crossed the floor to the hall and to his old bedroom. He stopped by the doorway, blocking the animal at their heels. "Not this time, Picasso."

She walked inside, and he shut the door behind him.

* * *

Sometime during the afternoon, Jace had pulled the sheet over them. He remembered that much. Everything else was a long dream. Now, the sunlight was dimming in the windows. He couldn't stop staring at her. Under the blue-striped linen, his arm was wrapped around Tommie's middle, holding her to him, allowing their warmth to blend. The wild curls framing her face on the pillow urged him to run his hands through her hair.

She stirred and turned to him. "Did we miss lunch?"

"Hours ago."

She started to get up.

Quickly, he grasped her arm. "Wait. I'll bring you a snack."

Once they left their small cocoon, things would change. They'd have the frank chat about getting carried away and how living through the murder traumas had brought them together, but this wasn't everyday life. They'd separate.

"I appreciate the offer," Tommie said, interrupting his musings. "You've said that how many times when I suggested we leave the bed?" She tilted her head to the side, and her lips curved upward.

He bent toward her. "Three or was it four?" He stole a quick kiss. "Who's counting?"

"It's okay, Jace." She sat up and folded and refolded the edge of the sheet. "I understand. We were, 'caught up in the moment.'"

"Moments," he corrected.

"Right." She nodded. "I don't regret a second, but we need to get back to work."

"You must admit, we managed to mix pleasure with business. I filled you in on Rex using Alfredo to sell Gloria's leftover Ocean Lure products. I told you I confirmed Rex's food pickup alibi. That left a small window of time for him or Thalia to speed over and shoot the cousins."

"Hard to believe people would attack their own families." She scowled. "They're certainly not the loving type. I updated you on Peaches's angry response when I asked her if Linda had dated Arturo and her walkout on Thalia." She put a finger on her chin. "What else? Oh, how Grey appears to have connected my mother to Arturo. He might know Arturo conned her."

"My honest guess is yes, he knows" Jace said.

"He'll probably tie my mom and me together like Thelma and Louise." She rolled onto her side. Suddenly, she sat up, pulling the sheet with her. "I totally forgot to ask. Did you get the surfboard priced?"

"I did." He shoved upward against the headboard, and they rested shoulder to shoulder, the pillows behind them. "My man estimated the longboard to be worth $250 to $300, at the most."

"I agree. Any other information?"

"One end of the board appeared to have been cut in half and repaired."

She frowned. "I noticed it had suffered damage during its use, but someone did an excellent job repairing it. Did your expert say that affected the price?"

Fess up, his conscience ordered. "I took it to Lucas Davis."

"Lucas?" Her mouth parted in surprise. "Did you inform him you're investigating for me?"

"I did. Now where was I? Oh, Davis examined the cut. He suggested the previous owner might have wanted to hide something illegal inside."

"You're kidding." She gave his shoulder a gentle push. "How could you forget to tell me?"

"First," he said, "you went missing."

"Skip that part. Start with what happened to the longboard."

"Lucas cut it open, and we looked."

"And?" She waved her hand for him to hurry it up.

"Nothing was in it. The contents or evidence could have been cleared away, but we've no way of knowing."

"You mean the longboard once belonged to smugglers?" Her eyebrows flew up toward her hair. "Rex had it." She tapped a finger on her lips. "He was a runner?"

"Maybe Rex was the courier, or nobody was. We have no proof."

"Can't they detect particles?"

"A slight possibility, but not much, especially if the board was in the water. I'll put it in my old room. Lucas temporarily sealed the cut. He'll completely restore it in a week or two. Decide if you want to sell the longboard or keep it. And I'll give you my opinion on why Arturo had the surfboard and wanted to help Gloria. It was his hook for you."

"Me?" She pointed to her chest.

"That was how you met in person, wasn't it? "

"Yes, we met at his booth. But you're saying he wanted me to be next on his list of women. That's true, but I thought I was the initiator. What a conniver." Her frown disappeared. "I thought I was clever and meeting him for my own purpose."

"Let's be glad you arrived late for your dinner with Arturo." He kissed her cheek and held her, letting the warmth from her skin blend into his.

Clawing on the other side of the door interrupted them.

"Picasso will need to eat and go out." She grabbed the edge of the sheet. "At least he waited for you to finish your story."

"He's not that thoughtful. I took him outside two hours ago. Tommie, he's taking advantage of us."

"He's a dog. Food and walks are canine highlights. Where are my clothes?"

"I'll take him. You stay. I'll be right back." He climbed out. Retrieving his belongings from the pile of clothing on the floor, he pulled them on.

"I can't believe Lucas Davis agreed to help you. Are you sure he understood you're my investigator?"

"I am."

"Jace? Jace?"

"Gigi's here!" Tommie drew the linen to her nose.

He tossed her top to her. "It's still damp. I'll handle my grandmother."

She had her T-shirt yanked on before he stepped out of the bedroom.

He hurriedly let Picasso out onto the fenced lawn. As he shut the glass slider, Gigi appeared on the threshold of the great room.

"Jace, there you are. You never called me. I left two messages."

Guilt nipped him. He'd been . . . distracted and had forgotten that he should have texted her the news that Tommie had been found.

"Uh, I turned my phone off. Tommie's wasn't working. Her appointments were canceled, and she had to get a ride from an employee."

"Why didn't she ask to borrow a phone?"

"I guess she thought she'd see me before I went to pick her up. The storm delayed her."

"I'll remind her she can call me when she's stranded." Gigi put a hand on her hip.

"She wasn't stuck," he said, trying to minimize the situation and ease his grandmother's concern.

"Where is she?" Gigi searched the space as though she

expected to find Tommie hiding behind the sofa or a chair.

"She's safe and sound," he said, deliberately misunderstanding her question.

"Tommie should stay in touch, especially since her rental was broken into and two people have been killed."

"I'll speak to her."

"I will too. I stopped by to get clothes and food to bring to Clara's. Where did Tommie go?"

"Umm, out walking."

"Alone?"

"She stays on the loop inside the gates."

"Should she be doing that? Too many strangers are running around. We don't know who to trust. You're as bad as she is." Gigi frowned. "Honestly, Jace."

"Right. I'll get her, but first a cup of tea." He seized his grandmother's arm and led her to the pantry. He pointed to a shelf. "Your favorite brand of loose tea."

She stepped away, narrowing her eyes. "I haven't lost my memory."

"Of course not. How's Clara?" he asked, searching for a different subject. He scooped up the box.

"Since it was gastric distress, she's working on getting me to travel with her. Her health scare reminded her of the trips she'd wanted to take, and now was a good time to do them. Can you grab the vinegar also? Otherwise, I must get my stool. Clara's coffeemaker needs cleaning."

He seized the bottle for her. "You should sign up for a cruise."

"I won't go anyplace until Tommie is settled and your parents return. That's not until Christmas." She grabbed her goods from him.

"You don't have to worry about us."

"I don't, but I will. Go find the girl."

"Hello," Tommie called out.

The sound of Picasso running in the house alerted him that the dog had come in too.

He and Gigi met Tommie in the kitchen nook.

"I guess you and the dog enjoyed your stroll," he said deliberately. He raised his brows, signaling to her to go along with him.

"Picasso loves the fenced backyard." She smiled and patted him. "Gigi, you're here." She kissed her cheek.

He had to admit Tommie looked terrific. Too bad, she hadn't followed up on his clue that she'd been out walking. Somehow, she'd tamed her hair and was fully dressed, although she'd struck him as great without clothes. She seemed more composed than he felt. His grandmother's sudden appearance had thrown him back to his childhood when she'd caught him sneaking a cookie.

"Jace?"

"Hmm?" What had his grandmother asked?

"Gigi was talking about Thanksgiving," Tommie prompted.

"This Thursday is one of our annual holidays. Jace, maybe you need to rest before we celebrate."

"I will take an extra nap," he vowed, avoiding a glance at Tommie.

The older woman sighed. "Clara and her niece are joining us. Tommie, you're coming, right?"

"I should look in on my mother."

"She must join us. I insist. Now, I'll find my stuff and get out of your way." She placed her goods on the tabletop and went toward the bedroom. She paused and turned to them. "I assured Clara's niece I'd stay at her aunt's until she arrived next weekend."

"Super." Jace stood, listening to his grandmother's footsteps fade away.

"Does she know . . . about us?" Tommie whispered once she was out of sight.

"She might." Had they fooled her? "I told her you were out walking, and you're not wearing shoes. With today's temperatures, the concrete would burn your skin off."

She bit her lip. "She's kind of old-fashioned and may disapprove if we tell her the truth. Gigi's been wonderful to me. I don't like to let her down."

She was right. His grandmother would only give her blessings if they were in a serious relationship, not a one-day thing. "If it worries you, we'll keep our time together our secret."

"Appreciated, Jackson."

She agreed quickly, without a trace of regret. Why was he disappointed, not reassured?

CHAPTER
TWENTY-SEVEN

The morning was cool and cloudy. Tommie sat on the lawn chair on Gigi's lanai. Picasso lay at her feet. Jace was inside at his computer.

The chill penetrated her light blue capris and short-sleeved top. She scooped up the gray sweatshirt Jace had loaned her from her lap. She tugged it on. The fresh fragrance of his soap wrapped around her. Her heart pounded in her chest. A sense of happiness lifted her spirits as she floated on her familiar daydream of the two of them strolling along the water.

Picasso lunged at the screen and shook her from her trance. A squirrel dashed away in the yard, ending the dog's hopes. He sat and waited.

Tommie gathered up a handful of the shirt's neckline and inhaled Jace's scent. She sighed. Jace would meet Alicia No. 2 soon. She wasn't delusional about a man like him going through life alone. And she'd learned from her past relationships that she wasn't a long-hauler in the romance department.

A knot formed in her throat. She was an adult and could handle their one-night stand. She'd rather leave than have him wish they hadn't gotten together. It would be uncomfortable running into him at Publix.

Yup, they'd had their moment. Now it was time to move onward. Up to this point, they'd had no hint of an arrest in the Alvaro deaths.

Picasso crossed the concrete floor to the patio door, waiting for her to let him in.

Once in the house, the dog trotted toward the kitchen. She followed Picasso to the dining nook. The AC was silent. Jace sat in a tall-backed chair, concentrating on his laptop. His lower lip turned under in thought as he scanned the screen. He ran a hand through his overgrown hair and tapped the keys with the other. She loved watching him work. His never-give-up attitude.

She went straight to him, unable to stay away.

He looked up as she approached, and a grin pulled at his mouth.

Her heart did a flip. She sank into the seat next to him, thinking about getting a little closer. "Find anything good?"

"I've been trying to tie up loose ends to get a break. I got an email from Muriel, who works in records and data at Starting Point Match. She was responding to an interview I did with her after learning your mom and Arturo met on the senior website. At the time, Muriel wasn't too helpful. She gave me general or no answers to most of my questions."

"Why did she contact you today?"

"Well, she informed me they'd just found the name Arturo Pendleton in their file storage. I'd asked her to check for his registration under the alias Grey had reported Arturo used."

"What did she tell you?"

"Not much. He'd been a member of their dating site for three months before his death. Muriel repeated her old claim that the rest of his data was expunged. I did note that his membership overlapped your mom's." He stretched his arms over his head.

He'd been on the computer for hours and deserved a break. "It's a small step forward," Tommie encouraged.

He turned to her. "The stalker has been quiet, which might mean he or she is anticipating a perfect opportunity to strike again. You should stay on guard. How about paying Gigi and her friend a visit this afternoon?"

"We were invited to dinner?" Tommie put her hand on her stomach, imagining a table full of food. "I shouldn't have eaten a muffin this morning."

"If I tell her you're coming, she'll whip up a feast."

She hadn't cooked yet? Odd. Something was up. "She didn't ask us to come over, did she? Why would we crash Clara's home?"

"I have a potential client. A pending divorce, as usual. I'm supposed to meet him for an interview in Vero Beach. Of course, I'll finish your investigation."

"When is the appointment?"

"Today. If I go, it means you'll be alone."

"You think it's a bad idea for me to stay here on my own."

"Your last incident at the salon makes me uneasy. You ended up in the middle of a fight."

"The squabble was between Thalia and Peaches. I wasn't involved." Her time with Jace was ending. She hadn't paid him a penny, and the man had bills to pay. He needed a case.

The improved Tommie could deal with the situation. The longer she lived with him, the harder it would be when she left. And she'd be honest. She didn't do breakups well, private or professional ones. Once she and Jace parted ways, she would need space to hole up and recover.

"You should go for the job." She'd skip going to Gigi's house.

She rewound her memories to yesterday and the sizzling moments they'd shared. The tender way he'd touched her. The soft stroke of his hand that had sent tingles spiraling through her and that special light in his eyes when he'd looked at her.

He shut the laptop down with a click. She squared her shoulders. *I'm a grown woman. I can take care of myself.* "When is the interview?"

He considered her for a moment. "I'll cancel the appointment."

Tommie sat forward. "Don't. What's your schedule like?"

"I'll be gone about two hours, including travel."

"Not a problem. I'll scan the rentals and jobs online and enjoy the quiet."

He rubbed the back of his neck. His face grew serious. "Promise me you won't go to the Yellow Flamingo Inn by yourself."

"I should clean and pack my belongings. As delightful as this sweatshirt is, I kind of miss my own outfits." She splayed her fingers on the oversized neckline.

"Wait here until I return. Don't go there alone."

"I won't." She raised her palms in a temporary surrender gesture.

"Don't worry if you don't spot an apartment today. Gigi loves company."

"I don't want to become a guest who turns into a roommate. Wish me luck that something new shows up."

"It will." He covered her hand for a second.

She wanted to kiss him, but was he just consoling her? Would he miss her when everything ended? *Don't go down that path.* She resisted a sigh.

"I'll pick up Chinese on the way home." The flicker in his eyes hinted he was thinking about more than the job or food. He stood and scooped up his phone from the table and held it out to her. "Take my cell."

"I can use Gigi's landline. Besides, you shouldn't drive off without a way to call or text people. How did they do it in the olden days?"

"Don't know. Smoke signals?" He slid his cell into his pocket. "I'll call you when I get there."

"What else do you need to research online? I can help." She shouldn't have used that last word, but she hadn't been able to stop herself. A few doubts swirled in her head when he flashed his stern look at her before turning to collect his things.

She sat, listening to him rummaging around, getting whatever PIs took to meet a client. When he returned to the nook, they walked together to the entryway. He kissed her goodbye and left her wishing she were going with him.

She and Picasso stood in the hall. The dog pushed to the glass insert to watch Jace cruise away. He was gone, and she was alone. Okay, she'd lived on her own for many years. *Get to work. Find another apartment, pronto.*

As Tommie wheeled around, her gaze landed on her parked car. She wished she had a change of clothes, but she'd promised Jace she'd stay home. Hold on, she'd given her word not to go to the inn without a buddy along. Who would go with her? Rain fell, and the palms swayed in the wind.

Picasso wagged his tail and woofed.

"Out? We'll wait for the storm to pass." She crowded up to the door and peeped out. A dark car was creeping down the road. *What was up?*

The dog flopped at her feet with a large sigh.

"It's disappointing, but we'd get soaked if we went out." The odor of wet fur wasn't her favorite. Outside, the passing car was barely moving. Was it someone scoping out the house?

The landline rang. Could it be Jace? She ran to answer. "Hello."

Dead silence.

"I can't hear you. Jace?"

Heavy breathing panted in her ear.

Her neck prickled. "I'm hanging up."

She thumped down the receiver and gulped. Who was that? Maybe it was a friend of Gigi's who was slightly deaf. It could have been a random call or a sicko who enjoyed freaking out old ladies. Sickening. Unease followed her as she paced the room. It could have been a robocall.

The rain pelted the roof. Growls came from the hallway. She hurried back. Picasso was staring out the door's glass. The skulking car was cruising away. She'd been letting her imagination go wild. Who wouldn't slow down in a downpour?

Gigi's phone rang again. She stood, listening. Each persistent, old-fashioned ring notched up her anxiety.

This time it could be Jace. Had he forgotten something? Picasso raced after her and slammed to a halt when she grabbed the receiver.

"Jackson residence."

"Tommie? Is that you?"

"Mom?" She frowned. "Why are you calling Gigi?"

"To find you. I thought Jace would have told her where you were. I tried your phone. It's not working."

"Did you call before?"

"Wasn't me. Hey, can you or Jace come over?"

"Why?"

"I can't get the back door to lock. The bolt is broken."

"You should contact a locksmith."

"Tommie, I don't have the money to fix it. Besides, the frame is falling apart. Nails are sticking out. Most are bent."

"I'm not a carpenter." She massaged her shoulder where the stress was settling. The landlord was probably useless.

"I can't stay here without locks. A couple of days ago, the news broadcasted a bomb threat at a school four blocks from me. They're closing in around me. Can you nail it shut?"

"Didn't the reporter say the scare was a false alarm?" She wanted to remind her mother she lived in a spooky-looking neighborhood no matter what was happening, but she decided not to argue.

"Please. I need you."

She inhaled and exhaled before speaking. "Do you have tools?"

"I've got a hammer."

She wouldn't ask why. "Maybe Gigi stored some nails for small home repairs. Jace used to build stuff in her garage years ago. I'll head over when the storm passes."

"Thank you, baby. You're always the best." She ended the call.

Tommie hung up. The roar of the rain pounding the rooftop wormed into her thoughts. She stared out a front window at the empty street. The water fell in a sheet of gray. The wind whipped the tall grass and the branches of the oaks, the pines, and the palms.

Picasso stood next to her, his tail and ears bent downward.

"Good thing we're not outside." She was about to turn away when another car crawled toward the house, and this time, it stopped in the driveway.

CHAPTER TWENTY-EIGHT

A female slid out of the rear seat.

Tommie peered out the front-door glass. Who was that? Her shoulders tensed. Maybe it was a friend of Gigi's.

Standing by the car, a rail-thin woman straightened.

"Mom?" Tommie peeked out.

Wind blew rain against her mother. Running, she yelled to Tommie, "I can't talk ab—" A gust stole her words.

Tommie opened the door as her mom burst inside. Water rolled off the shoulders of her raincoat.

"What are you doing here? I talked to you a minute ago on the phone." Tommie took in the puddle on the tiles.

Her mother held the lapels of her button-up weather jacket together with one hand. Her other was shoved in a pocket. "I called on the way. I couldn't stay at my house with strangers stalking me, and I wanted to make sure you were home and could bring me back to fix my entryway."

She was being completely irrational. *Speak calmly and get her to leave.* Misfortune followed her mom wherever, and Tommie didn't need that at Gigi's. "I don't know who is after you. I told you I'd come over. I was waiting for the sky to clear. You're the only living soul who'd travel in this deluge."

"My driver did." Her mom shook her head, sending more droplets flying. "I spotted a car with two people driving around my place before the storm. I've seen them circling the block in the past. I think they were on a reconnaissance mission. I had to get out. Later might be too late."

What was she talking about? Her pupils were dilated. Was she on drugs? "Mom, anyone can drive by where you live. It's a public road." Now she sounded like Jace, and seconds ago, she was worried about someone driving past Gigi's home. She should attempt to believe her mom.

"I think it's Chief Davis's minions. His little army threatened to never forget. And they weren't talking about forgetting to send flowers."

If someone was hounding her mom, would the mysterious person follow her to Gigi's? Tommie jumped forward and turned the lock.

Outside, she spied the vehicle in the driveway. Tommie hesitated, trying to glimpse the man behind the wheel through the torrent and the tinted window. Tall and broad were all she could gather. Why hadn't he left? Was he waiting until the cloudburst ended? A bad feeling nibbled at her. "Why is your new friend still here?"

"I offered him a few bucks to bring me. Lend me the money to pay him. Will ya, baby?"

"Mom, I don't have any. Who is he?" She was falling deeper into her mom's problems.

Her mom wrung her hands. "We're in trouble. I gave him my word. I don't know him too well. He's a nighttime security guard for one of the buildings near me. He runs his own taxi service during the day. Can you ask Jace for the cash?"

"He's not home. Remember?"

"I don't suppose the driver would welcome an IOU or a plate of that food Jace's grandmother cooks and keeps around?"

Tommie searched deep within herself for patience but found little. "How could you do this?"

"If we ignore him, he'll scram. He won't get out in a cloudburst to yell at me."

"No. He'll call the police, or worse. Does he accept credit cards?" Tommie tried to calculate the charges on her bill. It was way too much to calculate in a minute.

"Of course he does."

Tommie marched into the bedroom, grabbed the plastic from her wallet, and returned. "It might get declined."

"Don't worry. I'll tell him it's a mistake, and we'll send him a check."

"I doubt he'll fall for your story."

"Let me deal with him." Her mom took her hand out of her pocket, revealing a hammer in her grip.

"What do you intend to do? Threaten him?" Was her mother going to attack the man to avoid paying? "You can't hit or bully him."

"Tommie, really. I had it out for you to nail the door shut. I decided I might need it for protection." She swiped the card from her grasp.

"I'll take your tool, Mom."

Grimacing, she surrendered her weapon. "Wish me luck."

Hoping they weren't on their way to jail, Tommie closed the entry. Her mom ran to the car and knocked on his window.

Tommie couldn't watch her flimflam the man. She stepped away to wait and set the hammer next to the vase on the console table. Having her zonked-out mother with her was a recipe for disaster. Uneasy, she peeked out. The street and sidewalks were empty. Homes were sealed tight. No signs of anyone. Still, she was allowing her mom to use her card, which was most likely maxed out.

The door flew open. Her mother walked inside with another gush of wind and water and pushed the entry closed. She spread her dampness by taking off her raincoat and shaking it. Picasso backed up and shook off the wetness she'd shared. The drops splattered across the floor.

Her mom turned to Tommie. "Where should I hang my coat?"

"Drape it over the bar in the laundry room, but I'll call Jace's grandmother and ask permission for you to stay."

She lifted her chin. "I'll explain to her if you want."

Yeah, her mom reporting imaginary beings were after her and how she wanted to nail her door shut for protection would sound like a normal kind of conversation. "I'm good. What happened with your ride?"

"The card worked." She smirked. "I gave him a large tip."

Picasso barked and paced.

"He has to go out."

"I can't believe you kept that dog." Her mom wrinkled her nose.

"You might have a hard time staying with your allergies."

"When the weather clears, I'll walk up to the dollar store and buy some meds."

"You have money?" Was her mom holding out on her?

"I was planning on using your card again."

"Or I can drive you back and fix the nails in your doorframe."

"You're always thinking." Her mom patted Tommie's arm. "I'll put on the teakettle and make us a cup of hot tea to warm us up."

"I'll get a towel to wipe the tiles." Tommie pictured one of them sliding and falling. "We'll go outside in a few minutes, Picasso."

The landline rang.

"It's probably Jace. I'd better answer. Mom, you can put the kettle on."

"I will if you don't mind me searching through the cabinets. It's been years since I was at Gigi's house."

"The teapot is on the stove." Tommie hurried to snap up the kitchen phone. "Hello?"

"Tommie?"

"Jace." The two tons of weight on her shoulders disappeared. "You're not driving in this weather, are you?"

"Currently in a store lot down the road, waiting for the rain to let up."

Gigi's doorbell chimed.

"I'll get it," her mom called.

"Was that Yvette?" Jace's confusion was clear. "Why is she at Gigi's?"

The sound of Picasso barking and howling came from outside. How had he gotten outdoors?

"What's the matter with the dog?"

"My mom probably let him out, and he wants to get back in. My mom is having a breakdown. She asked me to nail shut her broken door while she's inside. She's worried somebody is after her."

"Tommie. Hurry." The stress in her mother's voice signaled something was wrong.

"Jace. I have to find out what's happening. With my mom here, I bet it's not good. She tried to skip out on paying her driver a minute ago. From his size and knowing the people my mom hangs with, I'd say no one should cross him. Maybe he's back. I need to go."

Had her cabby realized the card was past its limit and returned? She hung up and entered the living room. "Mom, why are you—"

Peaches stood, holding a gun pointed at her mother. Tommie's stomach jumped up to her mouth.

On the other side of the door, Picasso howled and clawed.

"What are you doing, Peaches?" Tommie couldn't stop gaping at the firearm and the girl's finger on the trigger.

"We're waiting for Rex. Put your hands up."

She raised them in the air. "Okay, but don't aim the gun at anyone."

"I want you to listen." The muzzle wavered up and down. "People don't take me seriously. Now I'm going to make sure you do."

"I hear you. How did you find me?"

"Linda called and told me she dropped you off here yesterday. Thalia fired me."

"I thought you were only suspended."

"She sacked me later because of you."

Sweat broke out above Tommie's eyebrows. *Say something soothing.* "I'll go talk to her. I'll tell her it was my fault."

"She won't change her mind." Peaches released an exasperated breath. "She'd have to admit she was wrong. Thalia would never say those words."

"I can offer her money."

"You?" Peaches's bottom lip pouted out. "You don't have any. You dress like a thrift-store model. And you've caused more headaches than a wedding windstorm tearing at the bride's hair. Thalia won't believe anything you say. Rex explained that you and your private investigator are trying to convince the police we murdered Gloria and Arturo."

"Did you?" Yvette challenged, standing a foot from Tommie.

"Me? You're all crazy. I hate you." She waved the gun's muzzle at Tommie. "You've ruined everything. How can I get another job without a decent reference from Thalia? Get on your knees." She pointed the weapon at a spot in front of her.

Peaches planned to kill her! Dizziness attacked her. Any second, she'd pass out.

"We have a visitor." Her mother gawked out the window.

"I texted Rex to come. Everyone thinks I can't control my own life. I'll show him I can deal with a liar."

Outside, Picasso wailed.

"I'm going to be sick." Tommie leaned against the wall.

"I told you to get down. Now. You have until the count of three. One." Peaches stepped up to her. Her face was red with fury. Her full attention zeroed in on Tommie. The firearm wobbled in the air.

The dog dug at the door. The landline began to ring again. Out of the corner of her eye, Tommie glimpsed her mother, who put a finger to her lips, signaling her to be quiet. She inched forward.

"Two," Peaches cried. "I'm not fooling. I'll pull the trigger."

Her mom shouted, "Hiya!" She leaped toward them. Her palm sliced through the air and chopped across Peaches's wrist.

The gun tumbled to the floor. Tommie dove for it. Her sandals slipped on the wet tiles. Her feet went out from under her. With a thud of pain, her chest hit the flooring. She winced. The handgun lay above her head. *Get it.*

She stretched out her hand. The edge of her fingertips grazed the cold metal.

"No!" Peaches's scream echoed in the room. She jumped on Tommie's back, pinning her down. Fingernails dug into her neck. A fist pummeled her ribs. Biting her lip, Tommie strained to reach for the weapon and missed. Almost. Tears of frustration blurred her vision. Where was her mother? "Help!"

Peaches continued to pound on her. "You ruined my life."

What was her mom doing? F*orget her. Get the gun.*

Tommie pushed forward with her toes. She made millimeters of progress. Success. She grabbed the grip.

"Get away from Thomasina," Mom shouted.

A *clunk* filled the air. Tommie glanced over her shoulder as Peaches collapsed sideways and landed with a soft thump on the floor.

The door burst open and banged against the wall. Picasso ran inside, crying.

"Tommie!" Jace yelled. He was crouching beside her, supporting her until she could stand.

Picasso licked her hand as she held the downward-pointing gun.

"Are you hurt?" Jace studied her.

Stunned, she murmured, "I'm good. What about Peaches?" Why wasn't she moving?

Peaches moaned.

"She's alive." Her mom paced to and fro. "I used the vase from the table to hit her." She nodded to the urn in her hands. "Figured the hammer might have hurt her."

"That was thoughtful of you, Mom. Peaches was only trying to shoot me." Tommie leaned into Jace, her legs unsteady.

Rex appeared in the doorway and slammed to a halt. "What's going on?" His eyes widened at his daughter lying on the floor. He sprinted to Peaches and squatted next to her.

The young woman groaned and rubbed the top of her head.

"Are you all right?" Rex asked.

"Dad." She seized his arm and pulled herself up to sit. Tears streamed down her cheeks. "Tommie and the old lady attacked me."

"She tried to murder my daughter." Mom stabbed a finger at the stylist. "I bet she's responsible for Arturo's and Gloria's deaths." She glared at Rex. "You were in on the Alvaro murders, too, weren't you? And I'm *not* old."

"I had nothing to do with their shootings," Rex spat. "And

neither did Peaches. I believe her. When I walked in, Tommie was the one holding the firearm."

"Liar!" her mom hollered. "Tommie snatched your daughter's weapon as she was about to shoot her. She threatened me with it when she arrived. I'd bet money she pulled the trigger on the Alvaro cousins."

"Mom, stop." Her mother was making the situation worse. "We don't have any evidence that Peaches or Rex killed Gloria or Arturo."

Her mother's jaw fell open. "She was going to kill you before you both ended up on the floor."

"No, I wasn't," Peaches cried. "My gun doesn't have any bullets."

"There's a quick way to find out." Jace held out his palm to Tommie.

She passed the weapon to him.

He checked the chambers. "It's not loaded. That fact doesn't change that you and your father need to get off my grandmother's property. Immediately."

"You can't keep my gun." Peaches's lower lip pouted out.

"Tommie was legally in our home," Jace said, "and had the right to use self-defense. You did not."

Rex frowned and seized his daughter's arm. "Let's go." He escorted his protesting daughter from the house.

Jace, Tommie, and her mom hurried to the window.

Peaches stood in the yard, resisting Rex's tugs to move. "You'll kick yourself for treating me like trash," she yelled over her shoulder at them. "I'm innocent. Arturo was my friend. I didn't shoot anyone. Give me my weapon."

Two cruisers appeared on the street and parked at the curb. Four officers jumped out. They approached Rex and Peaches.

Her mom scrunched up her nose. "Who called the police?"

"I contacted 911 when Tommie didn't answer the phone,"

Jace announced. "I didn't bring it up when I arrived because it might have increased Peaches's tantrum in the house."

Pulling herself together, Tommie pivoted around to him. "Thank you." Her heart stumbled in her chest as she stretched upward on her toes to kiss him.

Her mother grabbed her arm. "You should ice where she punched you before the cops interview us. We'll get a frozen bag of veggies or whatever from the fridge. Come with me."

Tommie sent Jace a regretful frown and went with her mom.

CHAPTER TWENTY-NINE

An hour later, Tommie sat at the kitchen table, letting her cup of coffee grow cold. Across from her, Mom dumped three spoons of sugar into her mug and stirred.

"Are you okay?" Jace sank into the chair next to Tommie.

She gave him a reassuring smile. "I'm not up for hand-springs, but since the police escorted Peaches and Rex away, I'm much better. I finally might get some sleep. Will Peaches be charged?"

"It's possible she will be arraigned for aggravated assault and battery. A defense counsel may plead it down. She didn't help herself out on the lawn when she kept shouting threats and refused to cooperate with the officers."

"What?" Mom yelled. "That's all she'll get? Good thing I explained to the cop how she trespassed and terrorized us when he interviewed me."

"Don't fret, Yvette," Jace reassured. "I'm sure Grey has been investigating her. And I agree, Peaches is looking guilty of the Alvaro shootings. We'll hear soon what is decided."

He touched Tommie's arm, drawing her attention. "I got a

call from Gigi. A neighbor informed her two strangers and two patrolmen were arguing on her lawn in the rain. Although I made it clear we were well and safe, I'm afraid she's on her way over."

Ten minutes later, Gigi and Clara arrived. Tommie joined everyone in the formal living room. Jace gave them his edited rendition of their afternoon and repeated that everything was under control. Unfortunately, her mom announced Peaches had tried to gun them down.

Tommie cringed and hoped her mother would soften her account. No such luck. Her mom ended her dramatic story of the wrestle over the weapon by announcing she—Yvette—saved the day by smashing a vase over Peaches's head.

Gigi and Clara exchanged shocked glances.

Her mom added Rex and Peaches gunned down the cousins. Tommie hastened to clarify that was a theory and that the firearm Peaches brought with her today was empty.

The women's worried expressions eased.

A couple of Gigi's friends, who lived nearby, showed up. Jace caught them up with a shorter summary of the day. Yvette frowned but didn't speak. Tommie breathed a sigh of relief. Gigi served snacks and drinks. The hours went by with people swapping stories about the murders and past scary tales.

After an hour, Gigi's chums left. Gigi, Clara, and her mom decided to stay for the night. Jace crashed on the couch. Picasso settled beside him on the floor. Clara stayed in Jace's room. Her mom used a cot to bunk with Tommie, and Gigi retired to her own bedroom.

As much as Tommie had wished for a private moment with Jace before turning in, it was not to be. Lost in her thoughts, she couldn't sleep. She was glad the police had taken possession of Peaches's firearm, but questions remained unanswered. Had the cousins slept together like Gigi had reported? Had Peaches shot them out of spite?

Everything pointed to Peaches as the guilty person. The logical part of Tommie was calm, but the memory of the young woman pointing a gun at her, sent streaks of panic up her spine.

She jumped from her bed and locked the door.

"Don't worry, baby," her mom mumbled from her spot. "I got a knife."

At least it wasn't the hammer. With that not-quite-reassuring notion, Tommie fell asleep.

The sun was climbing above the trees when she turned over to face the window. Outside, Picasso ran after a squirrel. Jace must be up. On the bed stand, the clock numbers read nine a.m. She'd slept late. Her mother's cot was empty. She was probably eating. Tommie relaxed, and her mind wandered.

She'd send her boss another text, explaining she needed time off next week too. With luck, she'd still have a job. Tommie rose and showered. She dressed in her beige shorts and a brown shirt.

Jace was on his laptop when she entered the kitchen nook.

"Good morning." She sat next to him. Fresh fruit, muffins, and a carafe rested in the middle of the table. "Where is everybody?"

"Your mother, Gigi, and Clara went out for breakfast. I think they wanted to give you and themselves a little space to digest what has happened."

"Was Gigi aware my mom was broke?"

"No worries. My grandmother was paying." He shut off his PC.

Tommie filled her mug and held it between her palms. The fragrance and warmth from the cup comforted her. "I know you thought someone at the salon shot the cousins. Did you conclude it was Peaches?"

He straightened in his chair. "She was motivated. Arturo loved showing off an attractive, twentysomething female on his arm, and she loved the money he spent on her. She pretended she cared for him, and he did the same in reverse. When he was done with her and her new lifestyle vanished, she killed him. But could Peaches kill someone who was close to her? We need additional evidence."

Tommie felt a twinge of guilt. Hadn't she faked an interest in Arturo? She sank deeper into her seat.

"A forensic examiner will run ballistics on her weapon to determine if it was used in the Alvaro homicides," Jace said. "The DA will file the appropriate charges. You're safe now."

She wished she could shake the lingering doubts. "What about the camera at the community gate? Peaches should be on the recording as she drove through."

"She could have walked inside earlier or entered through the preserve. I'm positive Grey has viewed all the comings and goings by now."

"I thought someone was following me that evening. It must have been Peaches. She turned around when I was lost and drove to Arturo's house."

"Once there," Jace said, picking up the story, "she shot the cousins in a rage of jealousy."

"What about her shopping alibi?" Tommie asked. "And don't forget that Rex insists she's innocent."

"She might have breezed past one or two mall cameras before the shooting to provide a fake defense. Rex is standing beside her to make up for all the years they were apart, or because he believes she's not guilty."

"It's disturbing." Tommie massaged her tense, aching shoulders. "Do you think Peaches broke into my studio, or that Rex could have been involved in the killings?"

"We'll find out. Your hairdresser doesn't impress me as the type who'll keep her secrets or is too smart for the prosecutor."

"She does enjoy talking." Tommie sipped her tepid drink.

Jace pinpointed a sharp gaze on her. "Why did you flee before the Roy Davis trial?"

She wasn't proud of her past behavior, but she'd answer. "Davis told me he'd hurt my mom if I testified. The one guaranteed way to avoid the stand was to hide out. I returned from Florida when he was behind bars, and I was promised protection for my mom if I went to court. They also dropped prosecuting me for the mess with Lucas since he'd discovered and removed the drugs I'd left before his car was searched."

She clasped her hands in front of her to stop them from trembling. "Trying to get Lucas arrested was my lowest point. I've never told anyone the whole story before." She looked away, unable to bear his look of disapproval. "Since then, I've worked on changing myself."

He bent across the space between them, drawing her attention. His hand cupped the back of her neck while he gave her a deep, soul-shaking kiss. Just as unexpectedly, he released her.

She touched her tingling mouth. "You surprised me, Jace."

"You ran off to safeguard your mom. I approve."

"I'm explaining, not excusing, my actions." She picked up her cup, while thinking of the kiss, hot on her lips.

"I'll be meeting with my prospective client today in Vero Beach. The one I missed yesterday. How about we enjoy a meal at a restaurant this evening? We can forget the last twenty-four hours and relax. And if everything works out, you'll soon be free of Sebastian, Florida."

"True, I can live where nobody knows my name. If someone whispers when I walk past, I won't think they're bashing me."

"We all have regrets, Tommie, but we go onward."

Who was he kidding? "Jace, you always do what's right." She felt closer to him, and further away than ever. "And I'd love to have dinner with you, but will it be fancy? I only brought a few clothes."

"We're in Florida. Most eateries expect shorts." He sprang to his feet and shoved in his chair. "I'm heading out now. I'll get Picasso in first. Our meal will be about fun. One rule—no negative vibes allowed."

Her pulse skipped every which way with future possibilities.

"Later." He marched to the slider.

She wrapped her arms over her chest, holding on to the streak of excitement, followed by a sadness for what was ending. Jace let the dog inside. Picasso trotted behind him down the hall, and she listened to him move around, collecting his things.

He returned with her pet next to him. "Here." He handed her a phone. "It's yours and working."

"What?" She stared up at him. "You paid my cell bill?"

"Don't worry. It's on your tab."

She tapped her phone's power button. The screen lit up. Magic, but costly. "This was too much."

"You'll pay me when you can."

He obviously was suffering from amnesia about her income. "I accept, for now." She'd find a way to return his money. Tommie walked him to the entry, where she waved as he drove away. Silence pressed around her. For the first time in months, she was alone.

Picasso settled in his spot by the patio doors. She picked up the kitchen and strode to the sofa in the other room. Snatching the remote, she sat and flicked through the channels. Three minutes later, she stopped and wandered the house.

Now that everyone was gone, she missed them, especially Jace. This was how her life would soon be.

Another thought struck her. She should go to the inn and get the dress she'd worn for Gigi's dinner. But she'd promised not to go by herself. She sat at the table and scrolled to her messages.

Linda had written to her. *U & P fighting? Heard it from Rex. I got out of work early for dental appt. R U home? Need details!*

Tommie texted back. *Come over. Help me decide between 2 dresses & grab 1 from the inn.*

Linda answered. *On my way.*

Tommie clicked off. Linda would fill her in on Rex's version of yesterday. She'd checked on Picasso before she left. The dog sat by the slider, watching the birds dance on a branch. She read more emails. Unable to concentrate, she paced to the entryway, where the hum of a motor turning into the drive alerted her Linda had arrived.

Picasso ran to the hall and barked. Tommie cracked the door.

Out front, Linda tooted her horn and yelled out the open window of a faded blue sedan. "Ride with me."

"Give me a sec." Tommie ran to the guest room and grabbed her purse. Should she let Jace know what was happening? Yes. Her fingers flew over her phone's keyboard and explained that Linda's was going with her to the inn.

Her conscience clear, she hit send. In the pantry, she discovered a bone for Picasso that Jace must have bought. She handed it to him. "Have fun." She locked up and ran to her friend's car. Once she was seat-belted inside, she thanked Linda for driving.

"Glad to do it. My car isn't as nice as Thalia's, the vehicle I drove when I took you home the day of your haircut. She let me use it because Peaches yelled at you, and she thought you'd tell everyone about the fight and hurt her reputation. She hoped a comfy ride would soften anything you said about the salon." Linda started the engine and pulled onto the street. She was dressed in a light blue skirt and a white blouse, looking ready for work.

The door locks bolted into place. "Rex told the girls at the salon that Peaches wanted to scare you. She blamed you for her firing. And your mother accused him and Peaches of shooting Arturo and Gloria."

Uneasy, Tommie bit her lip. Was this a bad idea? "A few details are missing from the story."

"Hey, I've got a private spot where no one hangs out. We'll go there and gab. You won't have to worry about anyone overhearing the juicy parts." Linda stepped on the gas.

A familiar *jingle-jingle* seeped through Tommie's mind. The noise threw her back to dim mornings and her daily stalker. No, she couldn't be in the drive-by car. Lots of automobiles must make a jingling sound.

She snuck a peek at Linda, who was staring at the road. "What's that clinking noise?"

"My muffler was falling off. Replacing it would cost me a fortune. I had it wired up, but it's still a little loose. Don't panic. It won't come off. You'll get used to the racket. I don't notice it at all."

Even if she were hard of hearing, Tommie was certain she couldn't ignore it. Sweat broke out on her palms. She'd call Jace. No, she was being foolish. She shifted in her seat but couldn't get comfortable. "Where are we going?"

"To the Jungle Trail. You know the narrow dirt lane that goes for eight miles, mostly into swampy spots in the preserve? No one is around there. We can say or do whatever we please." She drove toward the Wabasso Bridge.

Tommy fought the rising dread. "I can't be gone long."

"Not a problem." Linda stared out the windshield. "I talked to Thalia. She can't believe your mother called Peaches a murderer."

Linda pushed her hair away from her eyes, and a stray ray of sunshine reflected off the shiny blue stone on her finger, catching Tommie's attention. It matched the necklace Arturo had sold Tommie. Both pieces were rose gold with a pseudo-sapphire gem.

Arturo whispered to her. *This is an excellent reproduction and part of a set. I intended to keep the collection together, but a piece was grabbed by another customer, an old flame.*

CHAPTER THIRTY

Tommie choked back panic. Maybe she was mistaken about the jewelry. She forced herself to speak. "Did you buy a new ring?"

"What?" Linda startled and then shrugged. "It's a gift from an old boyfriend. I found it in my drawer. He meant nothing to me." She briefly covered her mouth with her hand.

The gesture struck a chord in her memory. Tommie recalled the day of her disastrous haircut appointment and the ride home with Linda. Tommie had asked her if she had gone out with Arturo.

Me? Never. Yuck. I'll swear on a Bible.

And she'd put her palm over her mouth.

Arturo's and Linda's words and actions raced around in Tommie's head until they collided with the truth. Linda had a tell when she fibbed under pressure, like Tommie's mother did. She was lying now. She and Arturo had been more than friends.

Was she responsible for the Alvaro deaths? Tommie's throat was closing. How would she breathe? "I'm not feeling well," she managed to say. "We need to turn around."

"I have big plans."

An old flame, Arturo repeated, stronger this time. Tommie stared at Linda's fourth finger.

"Something the matter?" Linda's eyes narrowed to slits.

Tommie gripped her shoulder harness. "The color of the gems and the rose gold remind me of a necklace I bought from Arturo. No big deal."

Linda shot a glower at her and back at the ring. Her lips formed an O. "Um, I confess. Arturo sold it to me, and I sailed on his boat once or twice."

"You da-dated?"

"What an old expression." Linda scowled. "Everyone went out with him." She frowned. "When he and I got together, he was going out with Peaches. He was slow to dump her, and at one point, he was seeing us both. Finally, it was me and him and no one else. I thought, but I was wrong, because he and Gloria were having a thing. That's when you showed up. And somewhere in there was your mother. By the way, it's not cool to date your mom's leftovers." She made a *tsk, tsk* noise of disapproval.

"Arturo was a friend."

"Yeah? Why were you driving to his house the night he died?" Linda clutched the steering wheel as she swerved into the passing lane. She slammed the gas pedal toward the floor. The engine roared. Her face contorted. She raised a fist in the air. "Don't lie to me. He didn't have a problem telling me he'd hooked up with you, a fresh, pretty girl. No one knew about me, the thirtyish, mousy female. He loved to talk about his rich senior dates or the hot, young ones, but not about ours. He kept me a secret. And I did everything to please and make him happy. What did he do? He used me. "

"I'm sorry," Tommie whispered. "He lied to you." Sweat poured down her body.

"The paper printed a picture of you at his memorial and recognized you as the woman he was seeing. I was a nobody."

"That was a rumor the press printed." Nausea built in Tommie's stomach. *Don't get sick. Talk her down.* "I didn't sleep with him." She clutched the edges of her seat as Linda passed and nearly clipped a car. "Please stop. You're upset. Let's straighten this out and stay friends."

"We were never friends. I thought you'd confess about your relationship with Arturo if I was nice to you. That's why I shared all that stuff about my old boyfriends the day I gave you a ride. But you held out on me. Doesn't matter. I know what you did. I've been shadowing you. When you went to meet him at the coffee shop, I trailed you there. I saw the way he looked at you. I could tell he'd bumped you up to next on his list of women."

Tommie forced herself to speak. "You drove past me in the mornings?"

"I was trying to understand what he saw in you. You lived in a dump, but your mother's house was the worst."

"You followed me to my mom's?"

"I had time off from work. I realized you saw Arturo as a way out of that crummy waitress life."

"You put the clippings under my mattress?" What was wrong with Linda?

"A little light reading." Linda grinned, showing off all her teeth.

Dizziness began to shut down Tommie's brain. *Don't fade. Find out the truth.* "The phone calls? The note on my car? They were from you."

"Hey, I'm not claiming I did every one of those. You've probably ticked off hordes of folks, and you must admit my rhyme was great." She laughed.

Tommie's heart was pounding so fast she barely could catch her breath.

"I could have gotten rid of you sooner, but imagining you afraid and hiding in that dumpy place was too good to pass up. Until now. They're working on arresting Peaches for the Alvaro murders. She'll go to prison, and you'll disappear. People will believe you ran off like before. No one will look for you. I'll go on with my life here."

She could barely think. *Pay attention and fight.* Tommie lifted her chin. "My flat tire?"

"Cutting the rubber wasn't easy." Linda rolled her eyes. "Here's the story. I was supposed to meet Arturo the night he invited you to dinner, but he canceled on me. I'd had enough. I couldn't stand the humiliation of him sleeping around or listening to his lies. I had to confront him. That evening, I followed you. I'd gone high-tech and planted a tracker on your car. My idea was to walk in on him with you. When you sped off in the wrong direction, I decided to have it out with him."

"You . . . shot him. And Gloria." And now Linda would shoot her. Ripples of terror snaked over her spine.

Linda fell silent, her knuckles white on the wheel. "She was with him when I arrived. The truth hit me. They hadn't broken up. She was his quickie before you. I lost it."

"I understand." The words were difficult for Tommie to push out. "He taunted you with his women."

"That wasn't all he did. He robbed me of all my savings. I went for the get-quick-rich scheme he pitched. I couldn't pay my bills. The landlord sent me an eviction notice. Arturo didn't care. If I had reported him to the police, Thalia would have sided with him. She would have told the cops lies, fired me, and written horrible references about me. Never mind, all this gossip. Going the legal route wasn't worth the gamble."

Linda tightened her stranglehold on the steering wheel. "I had to get my vindication another way. I had imagined him begging and apologizing a million times. I wanted him to admit he was a cheat. He acted as though I was trash."

"He emotionally abused and used you. I can relate. It's happened to me."

"Not like Arturo. He took everything away, and I'd loved him." Tears leaked down her cheeks. "He was such a liar." She cut across a neighborhood of homes until she was at the intersection. Wabasso Bridge was straight ahead. Would she drive off it? Was that her latest scheme?

Linda stopped for a red light.

Jump out. Tommie eased her finger toward the seat-belt release.

"Touch the button, and you'll lose a hand. I have a gun holstered under my skirt. I won't miss when I pull the trigger."

A cold sweat washed over Tommie. She should have listened to Jace and stayed home. Now she's never see him again. Okay, she wasn't a little kid. T*hink. Get away.*

"I'll park on the Jungle Trail in the wildlife refuge. We'll take a stroll to the water to talk. You'll have a little accident with a wandering reptile." She sighed. "I'll try to save you, but I'm sure it will be too much for me. The gator will win and drag you away."

What? "I'm not going near the river with you." Tommie shuddered. The light clicked green. The car crawled forward in the line of traffic.

A chill slipped between her shoulder blades.

"Okay. I'm a fair person. You get a choice. Enjoy a walk in the infested swamp or stay on land, where I'll kill you, and a creepy, crawly creature will snack on your remains. Either way, your afternoon won't go too swimmingly. Ha."

They rode up the concrete bridge suspended above the Indian River. On the other side was the Jungle Trail. There, Linda intended to murder her.

CHAPTER THIRTY-ONE

Paying little attention to the stylish communities, Jace drove down the beach road. His instincts were twitching. Something was off about the whole Peaches-as-the-murderer scenario. She'd threatened Tommie at Gigi's house and had gotten caught with a 9 mm handgun. Obviously, she hadn't thought through her attack. The young woman didn't strike him as a planner.

The Alvaros' killer planned the assault. He or she, dressed in black, had arrived under cover of dark, used the secluded lanai entry, and escaped the police. That shooter had brought bullets.

Jace recalled how the hairdresser's high-pitched, sweet voice had dropped low and confidential when she'd spoken about Arturo at the memorial. The words had felt genuine. But she had assaulted Tommie.

Had Peaches hit a breaking point? Had she suffered one prior to the shootings of Arturo and Gloria? Suddenly, he became aware the vehicles were passing him. He pulled into a curbside parking spot and shut off his engine. He pulled out his phone from his pocket and scrolled through Peaches's social media pictures until he found a selfie of her with Arturo. Their arms were wrapped around each other. A wide smile tugged her lips upward. *Me and my bestie,* she'd tagged it.

As he studied the images, he spotted someone else. He enlarged the picture of the two in front of the counter at Thalia's salon. In the background was Linda Martel. She was seated in her tall receptionist chair behind and to the side of the couple. Her gaze was glued to them. Her eyes bulged with a loathing glare, and her mouth twisted into a sneer of contempt.

He doubted Linda knew her anger about the pair had been captured on camera. He glanced at the date—the day before the murders.

The old saying "if looks could kill" rushed to his mind. A warning clicked in Jace's head. He might have dismissed Linda's involvement in the homicides too quickly. He had to talk to Tommie. Set her straight and advise her to stay away from the suspect.

Jace moved down his messages. He discovered one from Tommie that he'd missed earlier. She'd gone with Linda to the inn. What? That wasn't good. He needed to find her and fill her in and fast.

* * *

Linda's car crept up Wabasso Bridge. "One-lane traffic," flashed an electronic sign.

"No wonder we're moving so slowly. An accident." Linda pointed to the scene. A car had smashed into the rear bumper of another auto. The collision forced the passing vehicles to funnel into a single queue on the byway. "Why can't the public learn to drive?" Linda mumbled. "That drive probably deserved to be hit."

Tommie debated how fast she could release her seat belt and

jump out while ducking a bullet. She barely could breathe, let alone run. She gazed below at the intracoastal blue water. They were sixty to seventy feet above the river. She'd never survive a dive of that height. She squeezed back tears.

They'd almost reached the top of the bridge when her phone buzzed. *Be strong.* She wiped a hand over her eyes and sat up straight. "It must be Jace."

"Ignore it." Linda's lips disappeared into an angry line.

"He'll think something's wrong if I don't speak to him. You have to turn around."

"Tell him we're having a girls-only day. Do it, or I'll shoot you and dump your body in the swamp."

Tommie's stomach turned inside out as she answered. She pushed his name out of her dry throat. "Jace. Linda and I are on a road trip. Remember when we went to see those gators I loved at the Jung—"

Linda tore the cell from her grip. "Hey, Jace, Tommie will catch up with you later. Bye." She tossed the phone over her shoulder into the back. "Enjoy your last ride, Miss Murphy."

Tommie's skin crawled. Her breathing came in pants. The backed-up traffic crept off the bridge onto Orchid Island. They were about two miles from the Jungle Trail.

Talk to her, the small functioning part of her brain ordered. "Let's go home. We'll straighten this out."

"Nope. People have lied and walked all over me for years. My father was the worst until Arturo. I did everything to make both of them happy. I liked to help everyone, but no one cared. Bet Arturo was sorry when I shot him." She laughed.

Her sick cackle caused goose bumps to rise on Tommie's arms. A fuzzy night slipped into her memory. She was fleeing from the two dead bodies. A figure in black leaped in front of her car. The shadowy form paused in the headlights and grew clearer. The mysterious person was the same size and shape as Linda. And she had a gun.

With her fear building, Tommie blinked and stared at the receptionist. If it hadn't been for the car's blinding lights and the police sirens, Linda would have fired at her that night. There wasn't a sliver of a chance for Tommie now. Linda would finish the job she'd left undone.

Think. The turn for the Jungle Trail was a heartbeat away.

"What's with that car?" Linda nodded toward the oncoming traffic and decreased her speed. "The driver is in my lane and is coming straight toward us. He's a maniac. Is he a cop? He's blowing his horn and flashing his lights."

Tommie spotted the sports utility speeding at least fifty in a thirty-mph zone while dodging others on the street. Passersby stopped or slowed, staring in shock and fear at the out-of-control driver. But she knew him. Jace. Hope spun in her chest.

Suddenly, Linda shot left onto a dirt roadway. The tires squealed. A sign hanging from a sawhorse warned the Jungle Trail was closed due to washouts. Linda sped around the barrier. Trees and foliage surrounded them. Puddles of water dotted the route. Rocks and pebbles flew up, clinking against the sedan.

Tommie gripped her seat belt. "Please stop. I didn't date Arturo. You misunderstood."

"Don't lie to me." Linda's gaze darted to the rearview mirror. "It's your PI. He's following me." She stomped on the gas and hit a deep hole. The car shook. They lurched back and forth in their belted seats. The motor whined.

Jace, catch up. Linda will feed me to the alligators. She muffled a cry. *I won't give up.* She was strong. *S*he could do it. Anger ripped through her. Her thumb hovered over the release.

Linda glanced over her shoulder. "He's still after us. Idiot." She zigged and zagged, hitting and missing ditches.

Tommie's stomach jolted this way and that. *Stop her. Now!*

She pressed the metal button. The alarm dinged a warning at the unfastened seat belt.

Freed, she dove into Linda. She grabbed the steering wheel and yanked it. The car skidded out of its lane. Linda shrieked. She jammed her elbow into Tommie's cheekbone. *Thwack.*

Stunned, Tommie's hold loosened. She fell back into the passenger seat.

Panicked, Linda jerked the wheel in the opposite direction with both hands. The auto spun out to the other side and plunged down a low embankment. Linda's screams filled the air.

Branches scraped the car. Scrubs, tall grass, and stones whipped and clunked against the vehicle. They traveled right toward a group of white pines. They were going to hit. Her heart bursting, Tommie threw her hands in front of her eyes. The hood of the car slammed into a tree trunk. She ricocheted against a rapidly deployed airbag, pinning her in the seat. Silence. Her ribs, chest, and cheeks throbbed like she'd been kicked and stomped. Breathing was painful. Dust floated in the air.

Linda stirred, moaning.

The airbags deflated. The pressure on Tommie lessened. She was alive. She tried to think through her smarting rasps of breath.

Linda unfastened her harness. She pushed her door wide and rubbed her eyes. She sat facing out, her legs over the side of the seat.

"Tommie?" Jace shouted.

She looked back. He stood on the bank, yards from her. She hit the unlock button.

Linda peered in his direction. Her hand skimmed along her skirt to the outline of a handgun.

"Gun!" Tommie yelled. She shoved on the handle as she hurled herself out of the car and tumbled facedown into a trench of mud and shallow water. She lifted her head and spied Linda still on the edge of her seat.

The receptionist pointed her gun at Jace through the open door and pulled the trigger. The shot echoed.

Cringing, Tommie crawled across the muck to the front tire. She crouched and spotted Linda, standing outside the car.

Linda fired again. Immediately, a return bullet zipped over her. She dashed behind her door for cover.

"Drop your weapon," Jace bellowed, using the protection of his vehicle on the edge of the slope.

"You first," Linda called. "Your girlfriend and I are going for a stroll. You can join us."

"Cooperate, and the police will go easy on you. Throw the firearm down toward me," he ordered. "Do it."

"Not a chance." She tightened her two-handed grip.

On Tommie's right were the woods. *Escape*. She could slip away, hide, and follow the edge to safety. She glanced back.

No. Jace needed her. She would help him. How? Tommie's gaze landed on a rock near her feet. Briefly, her mind darted to her childhood when she'd practiced getting the ball over the plate to show those boys. She grabbed the stone, aimed, and pitched it as Jace fired again.

With a *thud*, her missile hit one of Linda's wrists as a bullet whizzed by her. She let out a cry. Her gun fell to the grass. She bent forward in pain, pulling her hands together to her body. Whimpering, her jaw sagged downward.

"Jace." Tommie waved her arms in the air. "It's safe. Hurry."

He was there immediately. He kicked the handgun away from Linda.

"My wrist is broken," she cried. "You shot me."

"I fired a warning." He commanded her to lie on the sandy loam, hands behind her head.

"I can't," she bawled. "I need a doctor. I'm wounded."

"You'll be fine." Tommie rounded the sedan. "It was a stone, not a bullet, that struck you. I threw a perfect pitch. The cops will get you medical care."

Sniffling, Linda finally complied with Jace's last order, and Tommie joined him.

"Are you hurt?" he asked, keeping guard over the prone woman.

"A little bruised." Tommie rubbed her shoulder. "Just glad to be in one piece."

"Take my cell from my pocket. Call 911. When the ambulance arrives, you'll get checked out."

She clutched his phone. "Linda killed Arturo. And Gloria."

"She's done hurting anyone ever again, or she's a dead person." His jaw tightened.

"She wanted to feed me to the gators." Tommie fought the tears, but they streamed down her cheeks.

He sidestepped to her, and she pressed against the side of his warm, firm body. He wrapped his arm around her and held her for an instant.

Everything was all right now. Jace was here. "How did you find me?"

"I'm a PI. I downloaded a specialized stealth tracking feature on my phone. First, I went to the Google app, and I—"

"Never mind, I know. You have special detective tools."

"It helped that I was minutes away, and I caught the hint about the Jungle Trail. And Linda didn't shut off your phone."

"Add the fact that it was a slow day on the bridge." She wiped her forehead with the back of her wrist. "I got it."

"I got you," he whispered. He quickly scanned her features as though searching for proof she wasn't hurt.

"You always do." Her heart ached to stay next to him, soaking up his comfort and strength. Instead, she stood tall and tapped the emergency numbers.

CHAPTER THIRTY-TWO

Tommie arrived at the beach before Jace. As she considered the last few days, she kicked off her flip-flops and let her feet sink into the wet sand at the edge of the water. Linda Martel had been arrested for the murders of the Alvaro cousins. Authorities had detained her when she was unable to make bail.

The media blasted bits about the homicides every day. All the stations promised news of sex, betrayal, and murder. Tommie expected the story would grow old soon. But the sordid tale of the man who'd scammed the women who loved him, sold lots of papers, and attracted viewers.

Tommie and Jace had been named in articles as the brave citizens who had captured the person who gunned down Arturo and Gloria Alvaro. The two had worked to avoid the press. But the public couldn't get enough of the tragedy. Thankfully, no one had bugged her when she'd snuck away this morning.

She fastened her gaze on the end of the path. No signs of Jace yet. She tapped her fingertips on her thigh. He'd suggested the get-together. She'd picked the place and proposed they meet half an hour before she gave her apology to Lucas Davis.

What would Jace say to her? Nerves danced up her spine as she waited. Their business arrangement had been temporary and, like all men in her life, he'd move on. Today, he probably wanted to discuss her unpaid bill.

She turned and glimpsed him at the end of the dunes. He wore his khaki cargo shorts, a white shirt, and a jade backpack. She covered the prickle of uncertainty and happiness with a shout, "Hello!"

He raised a hand and crossed the shore at a fast-paced stride. His sandy-blond hair had grown a little longer, and he peered back at her with a calm she didn't possess. He set his pack next to her flip-flops. "How are you?"

A warmth slid through her as he spoke. "Never better. And look at those bare feet. You're a man of the beach."

"I do my best to live up to your standards." He grinned before sobering. "It's been a while since we talked in person."

"Too long. You missed a bit of news. My mom confronted the driver checking out her home. She found out he was planning to buy her rental. Too bad the landlord hadn't informed her he was going to sell. I collected my stuff at the inn. Gigi, Clara, and her niece went with me. Picasso is visiting my mother at her house. She claims he's protecting her. I guess her allergies are cured. And I had a robocall, a real one."

Okay, she was rambling. She pressed her lips together to force herself to slow down.

"You hang with a tough posse, my grandmother, her friend and niece."

His teasing words eased her nerves a fraction. "No one will dare to cross us." She clasped her hands in front of her to keep from fidgeting. "Linda seems like a person who lost her way."

"Her parents are here to support her. She's not alone."

An awkward moment of silence fell between them.

“Let’s walk,” he suggested. “You have twenty minutes until you talk to Lucas.”

“Works for me.” She sensed he was about to say goodbye. He must have wanted to make sure she was safe and well before officially ending their business contract. That was so Jace. Anything else between them existed only in her dreams.

She matched his pace as they strolled along the coastline. His arm brushed against hers, reminding her that those shared hours were ending. Soon they’d just run into each other on the street and pause for uncomfortable greetings. The kisses and lovemaking would fade to memories. And she’d pack her bags and drive away.

She raised her chin. She’d handle it. Determined, she pushed up her sunglasses on her nose. The daylight glittered and reflected off the blue ocean.

“Do you have a speech for Lucas, like the script you used with me?” He knit his brow and tossed her a look.

“Don’t worry. This apology is of utmost importance to me. I will follow your advice. I’ll give him the short version. Why do you think he finally invited me?”

“Maybe an opening came up on his schedule.”

“I suppose.” She shrugged. “An hour ago, he sent me a reminder and asked if I would be interested in volunteering for a new program he’s starting. I’d teach surfing to kids who can’t afford the sport. He expects my answer when we talk.”

“Sounds perfect for you.”

“I agree. My boss called to congratulate me and told me I had a job waiting for me. I’ll be good for now, moneywise. Lucas offered me one of his boards to use during the lessons. That was exciting. I’ll donate the longboard to the group when I return it to him for final repairs.” She wet her dry lips and continued talking. “Life changes fast. Every day, I’d wake up with a stomachache, afraid of what would happen. But now I feel . . . normal."

"A positive change." He slowed, and they paused by the water.

She raised her head and soaked in a slice of the world she loved. The warm sun, the squawking birds gliding through the air, and the gentle, briny breeze that left the taste of salt on the tip of her tongue. "How was working a homicide, Jackson? Good? Bad?"

"If nothing else, I can vouch that sharing blood doesn't guarantee a loving family. I appreciate my small, caring circle of relatives a lot more. Speaking of kin, Gigi cut out my photo from the paper. She glued it to the collage in my bedroom at her house and included your picture in her display. She told me Pop is dancing in heaven. He's thrilled we solved the Alvaro mystery."

"I'm honored to be on her wall of fame. Gigi is always thoughtful."

"That's not all. My grandmother emailed an article about the investigation to my mom and dad. Apparently, they're boasting about us and boring everyone near and far with the story."

"Cool. Your parents are super proud of you. Me too." She'd helped him with the case and shown him the improved Tommie. She twisted her fingers. "Speaking of parents, I pray my mother doesn't blow her job interview at the dollar store. That would be perfect for her. The bus stops at the curb, which means she can ride to work and expand her rental search."

Jace rubbed his chin. "I confess watching Yvette on the TV doing interviews about the homicides has been odd."

"Mom is enjoying her short moment of celebrity caused by the media." Tommie frowned. "She actually claimed me as her child. My biggest fear was I'd be exactly like her, but I've grasped the idea we're two different people. We have our own unique paths to follow, although they often cross."

"We all hit a few bumps on our route."

"I'm grateful I had you and Gigi to show me the way." What would she do without them? She pressed her mouth shut to stop from blubbering. A new thought struck her. "We never discovered who shot at Thalia's car window."

"Grey and his men will get to the bottom of it," Jace said. "We're officially done. Though it's unusual not to find him popping up wherever we go."

She fished out her phone. The time on the screen announced she had fifteen minutes before her meeting. "Waiting is nerve-racking." She stuffed her cell in her pocket, and they walked to her flip-flops by his backpack.

"I'll be here when you come out," he said, picking up the conversation.

He probably wanted to know if Lucas would forgive her. She ignored a jab of disappointment. "I have something for you." She pulled out a folded envelope from her pocket.

"What's this?"

"Open it." She handed it to him.

He ripped the flap and pulled out the contents. "You wrote me a check?" He stared at it.

"It's your pay and the correct amount, not the low number you quoted me. There's a little extra for the phone, dog food, and leash. I took care of the bill for the camera, but I ended up donating it to the inn for security."

"The Yellow Flamingo must have been grateful."

"We did some compromising. They've already improved their doors and locks."

"You're a clever woman."

"I learned from the best."

"Where did you get the money?" He ran his thumb over the dollar figure as though he could erase it.

"From the donations that poured into Thalia's GoFundMe tip

page. Everyone lobbied for me to get the reward. They agreed I was responsible for Linda Martel's arrest and indictment since she kidnapped me and that led to her capture."

"You're always a surprise, Thomasina. Now, I have one for you." He put away the payment and rummaged inside his pack to pull out a lunch-size paper bag. "Just a souvenir from my bureau drawer at Gigi's." He passed it to her.

What was this? She scooped out a faded blue ribbon with an orange smiley face on it. "I'm not sure what to say." She flipped it over in her hand. "Give me a hint."

"You're holding the first-place prize from the jack-o'-lantern contest, where I entered, unknown to me, your carved pumpkin."

"The one you turned into a pirate? Are you kidding? You kept the award? Sweet." A streak of happiness rushed through her.

"Of course, you deserve it, and we'll earn another. We're on schedule to enter the city Christmas decoration competition at our house this year."

"Thanks." She wiped at her eyes to hide the burning tears. What was wrong with her? She put away the gift and remembered. "Our house?" Was he confused? "You mean Gigi's? I won't be there much longer."

"I'm talking about you, me, and Picasso." His voice was strong with conviction. "Tommie Murphy, you always believe in me. When the odds were against us, you encouraged me with your fighting spirit and ideas. Your faith in me led me in the right direction."

She felt her mouth drop open.

He seized both her hands. "I keep remembering when you crashed into the tree in Linda's car," he whispered. "For a moment, I thought I'd lost you. Worst moment of my life. Afterward, I had to work out what to do with the truth of how I felt." He inhaled deeply.

His confession set free the tears she'd tried to ignore.

"I'm trying to tell you . . ." He locked his sea green eyes on her. "I love you. Truthfully, I've loved you for as long as I can remember, Thomasina, although I was slow to realize it." He flashed his tempting smile. "This may sound foolish, but will you be my girlfriend?"

She swiped at her damp cheeks and put her hand over her chest, where her heart was pounding. "I will. Who else would chase down a killer who had kidnapped me?"

"That was kind of insane, but how could I not go after you? You'd be the first in line to rescue me if I was in trouble."

She smiled and said the words she'd never planned to admit. "I love you, Jace. And I want to be with you."

He gave her a quick kiss. "You can move in tomorrow when we hold our rescheduled Thanksgiving meal. We'll make our announcement over the turkey. Gigi will be thrilled."

"I guess I can wait a day," she teased, leaning into him, wanting to hold on to each second.

"Then I'll bring you up to speed on our new investigation."

"What?" She straightened and scanned his expression for a clue.

"With all the publicity, I've had a ton of job offers. I'd appreciate your help if you're willing."

"Seriously? I can see the sign on the office door." She stepped back and stared above his head. "Ace Investigators Jackson and Murphy."

"Uh, we'll negotiate the name later."

Her pulse raced until a doubt clouded her mind. "We're not pushing forward too quickly, are we?"

"I've wasted a lot of time. I'm not taking a chance you'll slip away now."

"What will Gigi say about me moving in with you?"

"She'll say, 'Welcome home.'"

The meaning of his words sank in. Her search for a place to

belong was over. This was where she could be herself. The better Tommie belonged here. And with Jace she was her best. No more running or hiding. Tommie pulled in a deep breath before she could speak. "I woke up nervous about how the morning would go, but it's the most wonderful day I can remember."

"Mine too." Grinning, he grabbed her hands and tugged her against him.

She tilted her chin up. "Do you think we'll always be this happy?"

"We may have to work on it a lot. In fact, we should start now." And he kissed her.

ABOUT THE AUTHOR

Nora grew up in rural New England, where she currently lives with her family. For a few years, she spent time in Florida during the winter. She loves writing about both areas in her romantic suspense/mystery stories.

And if you read sweet romances, be sure to grab Nora's holiday book, *CHRISTMAS at the EASY BREEZY. It* takes place in the White Mountains of New Hampshire and is available now. The sequel will feature two minor characters you met at the Easy Breezy, along with some new ones to love. You can find Nora LeDuc on Amazon, Goodreads, Facebook, BookBub, Twitter, and her website: Noraleduc.com. Thank you for purchasing *LOVIN' YOU Crazy*. If you enjoyed the story, please let others know by leaving a review on Amazon.

Also by Nora Leduc

CHRISTMAS at the EASY BREEZY

BEACH KISSES & SUNSET WISHES (short story)

TRAIL OF SECRETS

MIDNIGHT GIRL

SWEET DREAMS

THE DEVIL WORE SNEAKERS

GONE BEFORE GOODBYE

TRUST ME

DEAD WOMEN TELL NO LIES

STAGING MURDER

PICK UP LINES FOR MURDER

MURDER BY HEART

MURDER CAME CALLING

UNDER A FOOL MOON

GIFTS FROM THE HEART

LOVE'S WICKED JEWEL

ALWAYS MY HERO

MISS MCNEAL'S PIRATE

www.ingramcontent.com/pod-product-compliance
Lightning Source LLC
LaVergne TN
LVHW050534160826
845677LV00011B/2028